True to Me

ALSO BY KAY BRATT

True to Me

A By the Sea Novel

KAY BRATT

Published by Lake Union Publishing, Seattle

www.apub.com

Amazon, the Amazon logo, and Lake Union Publishing are trademarks of Amazon.com, Inc., or its affiliates.

ISBN-13: 9781542008075
ISBN-10: 1542008077

Cover design by Shasti O'Leary Soudant

Printed in the United States of America

To Amanda
My Gypsy Girl

Chapter One

Quinn held the small box in her hands, so focused on the contents that even the busy Savannah traffic outside the condo couldn't penetrate her thoughts. The box felt weightless. Other than the tiny molecules painted on the side, it was plain and unassuming.

But it could be the link to her future.

Or her past.

At this point in her life, both were uncertain.

The only thing she knew for sure was that she needed to begin living again. Before she could do that, she needed to put her mother to rest. In her latest self-help book, she'd read that grief never ends, but it changes. That it's a passage, and not a place to stay. Quinn needed to pull herself out of the pit of sorrow she'd been living in before she drowned in it.

An hour earlier, she'd watched the final episode in the latest season of *Long-Lost Family*, a series that highlighted family reunions between people who'd never met, and she couldn't help but think of what results the small box could bring to her own life.

After checking the activation code, she scanned the terms and conditions, noting that whether she was pleased with the results or not, she couldn't sue. That meant even if they turned up a serial killer for a father, too bad, the company wasn't responsible. The consent form was especially entertaining, asking for her signature to better understand the human species.

Quinn could definitely use some assistance in that department.

She filled the small tube with her saliva and capped it. The motion felt strange. Sterile. Such a scientific method for an enormously emotional subject. Quickly, before she could change her mind again, she dropped it into the envelope and sealed it shut, then packed it back into the box. Tomorrow she'd drop it off on her way to work.

Her heart thumped in her chest, beginning the countdown. One second gone, two seconds, three. The waiting would feel endless. But hadn't she already waited her entire life? What was a few more weeks?

This was it. If all went well, it could mean the end to a lifetime of wondering and longing. *Weeks,* the advertisement said. In only weeks she would, or could—or maybe only possibly—have a match. A match didn't necessarily mean she would have what she needed dropped into her hands. Possibly not names, or even explanations. But it meant information. Information could lead to the truth, and the truth to her father.

Her stable, comfortable life had turned complicated. How does a woman come to grips with the fact that the mother she'd known and loved for thirty years had kept such a huge secret from her?

It was a slow progression from the onset of illness to her mother's death. Quinn had been there for her as much as any daughter possibly could. There had been time. More than enough time. So why had her mother waited until her very last moments to confess?

"Wesley Maguire isn't your father," she'd whispered, holding Quinn's hand to her face before telling Quinn her final wish. "Take me back to Maui."

In her shock, Quinn hadn't had time to process the proclamation, much less to ask if he wasn't her father, then who was? The confession was startling, and her mother's eyes had begged for forgiveness, even as the light in them faded away.

The weeks that followed were heavy with grief, and in the moments when Quinn could set her sadness aside briefly, she'd searched through every document she could find in her mother's apartment, sorting through the tangled yet mundane details of a life now gone.

While part of her struggled through the realization that she was truly alone in the world—or at least had no family to speak of—the other part of her felt the need to find some clue as to who her real father was. And why had her mother kept it a secret? To give herself the illusion she wasn't behaving obsessively or erratically, she told herself that she was simply putting her mother's affairs in order—ripping off the Band-Aid before she even had a chance to heal.

With an intensity that would make her fiancé, Ethan, proud, Quinn sorted through years of hospital bills and treatment summaries. Lists of medications and books filled with fantasies of alternative medicines.

Receipts. So many receipts. At the end, her mother had made sure to leave no bills behind for Quinn to have to deal with. No unpaid mortgage or car loans. No outstanding medical bills. All of it prepaid, even with a cushion in case she dragged on longer than the doctors predicted.

How strange that she would receive a credit on the cost of her mother's death. That was something she couldn't even begin to process.

After all the medical and business papers were dealt with and organized, she started on the boxes stashed under her mother's bed, sure that there she'd find a clue. Instead she found box after box of old pictures, school papers, and crafts. Her mother had kept everything. It took hours, but Quinn looked through stacks of photos of her life from kindergarten until college graduation, many of them of her and Maggie, her best friend from childhood.

She picked up one and smiled. In the shot the sun shone down on Maggie's hair, making it almost seem to be on fire, a red that flamed bright in her younger years before it began to lighten. The contrast between the two of them was evident—Quinn's golden brown, native Hawaiian skin a startling contrast to Maggie's pale, freckled face.

Putting the photo aside, she dug deeper through brittle corsages and ticket stubs from the many events they'd attended together. So many memories, but nothing from her mother's earlier past.

Quinn persisted.

She started on her mother's jewelry box next, separating out the costume pieces to see if there was anything of value. She found a diamond stud earring but couldn't find the match to it. Finally, she emptied the box and turned it over, and when she saw that one of the corners had come loose at the bottom, she pulled it and realized it was a false bottom.

Underneath was a single photograph.

In the picture, two young women dressed in graduation caps and gowns sat astride horses, their closeness evident in their body language and expressions. Even through the adolescent features, Quinn could tell one of them was definitely her mother. She turned the photo over and saw *Carmen Crowe and Me* scribbled on it with a date of a year before Quinn was born.

Who was Carmen Crowe?

Quinn wished she'd pushed her mother more to talk about the past. Over the years, as Quinn grew older and more curious, her mom had only told her that Maui was a beautiful and magical place, but her childhood had been ugly. The few times Quinn had tried to squeeze more out of her had caused her mother to retreat into silence. It was clear that her mom had loved Maui, but whatever it was that had kept her from returning there must've been traumatic. Quinn had hoped one day her mother would be ready to talk about it.

That day never came.

But if Quinn could find this hopefully living, breathing person from the photo, it could help her find out something about her mother.

Carmen was obviously someone important. Important enough that it was the only photo of her past she'd saved. So was she a best friend? Cousin?

As though her mother's death wasn't hard enough to get over, Quinn was also spiraling because of the quietly explosive way she'd left. She couldn't quite believe it or even process it. Not that Quinn had known her father at all, but it was still mind-boggling that she'd spent her life resenting the wrong man. All she knew was the man she'd thought was her father, Wesley Maguire, was someone her mother had been with for a short time many years ago. When they'd parted ways, Quinn was the only thing left of their relationship.

She'd been too young to remember him, but her mother had tried to reach out to him occasionally. As a young girl, Quinn had dreams that he'd show up at her door, ready to take her to the annual Daddy-Daughter Dance, holding a bouquet of flowers and apologizing for taking so long. He would be tall and good-looking, his eyes sparkling down at her with pride.

That never happened, but she'd still held out hope that he'd find her again in time to attend her high school graduation.

That didn't happen either.

By the time Quinn was in college, she'd given up thinking he'd magically appear to walk her down the aisle on her eventual wedding day. And now her mother's words echoed through her head at least a hundred times a day.

Wesley Maguire is not your father.

After the dust settled and the impact of that statement had finally worked its way through her brain, Quinn still couldn't hate her for it. The truth was, she would miss her mother so much. Already missed her. Her mom had been kind and loving, completely devoted to Quinn. Whatever she'd done or whatever secrets she'd kept, there was no doubt it was out of love. Now that her mother was gone and Quinn had no one but Ethan, she ached to know her father, or at least know who he was. She also realized that whatever she uncovered might be better left buried, but she was ready to learn the truth, good or bad.

And here she was, holding a small cardboard box that could be the key.

She stood and put the box on the table beside the door. Ethan was expecting her to call and give him a rundown of her day. He wouldn't understand if she tried to tell him that she'd barely been able to function, much less figure out dinner. That she'd faked her way through the day, accomplishing almost nothing on her list, her entire system on full alert because of what she was about to do.

Ethan assumed she was still off because of her mother's death. He also knew that Quinn couldn't think of much else other than fulfilling her mom's wishes by taking her ashes to Maui and putting her to rest. He'd bought tickets and insisted she book the hotel reservations, declaring they'd make a vacation out of it. After Quinn memorialized her mother, of course.

They were set to leave in a month.

"It will help lift you out of this mood, Quinn," he'd said.

While he went on and on about the adventures Maui had to offer, Quinn was quiet, thinking of the moment when she'd have to leave her mother behind on the island. Traveling there was not going to be the mood-lifter he thought it was. Not for her.

There were things he didn't know, like the mystery of who her father was. It didn't feel right to tell him yet—she wanted this to stay between her and her mother for the time being. Quinn had a strong suspicion that the information her mom had been so intent on keeping to herself had probably poisoned her body, inviting the cancer in and allowing it to eat away until nothing was left but the shell of the woman Quinn had nearly worshipped. But even as her mother made her final will and testament, she'd not been able to bring herself to disclose the details of a story that could set her daughter free. *Why?*

She took a deep breath and readied herself, then picked up the phone.

Her fingers stiffened stubbornly, as though they didn't want to obey, but eventually there was a ring. Ethan picked up quickly.

"Hi," Quinn said.

"What's up?" he answered, his voice already hurrying her along. He was always running behind. "You headed for the gym?"

"No, I'm not. Listen, I need to talk to you." She felt her stomach clenching.

"Can it wait? I have a meeting in ten."

"No, it can't. I need to tell you now." *While I've got the courage,* she almost added.

"Hold on," he said. "Let me shut the door."

She could hear him bumping around, not sure what he was doing, but when he returned, her resolve weakened. Then she thought of her mother. A woman who deserved more than her daughter doing a quick dump of her ashes and then living it up around the island.

"I'm going to Maui alone," she blurted out.

"What do you mean?" He sounded confused.

"Ethan, I appreciate that you want to go and support me, but I need to do this by myself. I'm not looking forward to saying goodbye to the last of my mother. I want this to be a quiet and reflective time. A time to honor her in my own way."

"And you don't want me with you?" he said, his tone turning petulant.

"It's not that I don't want you with me. This just isn't the time to try to enjoy a vacation." *And I am hoping to find my real father.* That was another detail she wasn't ready to tell him.

"Quinn, I know you are still in a bad place, but you aren't thinking straight. We'll talk about this when I get home this weekend."

"No, we won't, Ethan. I've already canceled your flight. I'm serious about this. I'm sorry if it hurts you, but we'll plan to go again together after I've done what I need to do."

He sighed, long and frustrated.

"Sounds like I don't have a choice," he said. "I need to run."

He broke the connection, and she was left holding the phone to her ear, grasping it so tightly it made her fingers ache. When she lowered it, she was shaking.

Quinn liked routine and avoided drama at all costs. She felt safest in the cocoon she'd built around herself. But all that was about to be undone. Starting with a nondescript white box and a plane ticket, there was a secret with her name on it that Quinn meant to unravel.

Chapter Two

Four weeks later, Quinn arrived in Maui and stood looking out the glass doors that led to a small balcony. Her hotel room was on the highest floor, and the sound of silence engulfed her, unsettling with its hushed roar of reprimand.

She opened the sliding door and stepped out onto the balcony, breaking the quiet of the cocoon-like room behind her. The warm Hawaiian breeze caressed her neck, and the sound of the waves breaking in the distance made her feel grounded again.

Goose bumps ran up her arms, and she could feel her mother present there. Quinn could sense her approval of the reasons she was there.

People moved back and forth on the ground, some rather quickly, pulling their luggage, and others slowly strolled the paths bordered with thick, tropical vegetation. Nowhere did she see someone walking alone, as she had been only an hour before, performing what felt like the longest walk into the resort lobby and up to the front desk.

"Aloha," a young woman had said, a brilliant white smile ready and waiting. "Welcome to Lahaina."

Ona, as her name tag read, was beautiful with her long dark hair and sun-kissed skin. The woman radiated hospitality, her eyes warm and engaging. The youthfulness of her unlined face made Quinn feel much older than her thirty-two years.

After nearly thirteen hours of travel, she knew she looked a sight. She let her hair drop around her face like a curtain as she fumbled in her purse for a copy of the reservation confirmation.

"You'll be in room five sixty-five," the clerk finally said, sliding the key card across the counter.

Huge hotel faux pas, announcing her room number out loud, but Quinn was too tired to point it out to the fresh-faced clerk. She took the card, thankful for a room in which to get out of her travel clothes and shower.

"Have a great stay, Ms. Maguire," the clerk said.

Maguire. Quinn felt like an imposter as she headed through the lobby to the elevators, following the small map that showed the sprawling resort and its many buildings. A minute later, she found refuge in a luxurious suite that looked out onto stunning scenery.

The sudden lump in her throat surprised her, but, then again, Maui was supposed to be a lovers' paradise, and watching the people below reminded her of her solo status. She instinctively thought to call her mother and regale her with a description of the beauty before her and the details of her trip over, but, just as suddenly, she remembered the reason she was there, and that she'd never have that daily phone call again.

She didn't turn to look at the vase on the bedside table where her mother's ashes sat waiting. Quinn still didn't know what she was going to do with them. That was one thing Ethan would be happy about— that the ashes were no longer in their home.

They hadn't had much conversation about the change in plans since that first phone call. He'd been away more than home in the few weeks leading up to her trip, and most of their communication had been through voice mail or text. The icing on the cake was when she'd emailed him the link to a house on Maui that she'd decided to buy.

"You've really lost it now. No one buys houses on a whim," he'd said, calling her immediately and begging her to tell him she wasn't serious.

"That's not what the Realtor said," Quinn argued. "Most of his properties are snatched up, sight unseen, within days after they're listed. It's a tight market on Maui, and I had to move fast. Now, when we go together, we'll have a place of our own."

She could practically hear him simmering with anger on the other end.

"Look, this is how I want to invest my money, Ethan. Maui is where my mother is from, and I've always dreamed of going there. We can set it up for short-term vacation rental, and it'll be a great source of income."

"Who's going to manage this *great source of income?*"

"A property manager," Quinn replied calmly. "I've already researched all of it and have a list of them to interview."

He took a long, audible breath and changed his tone to one of calm patience.

"You need to at least go see the house first, and if you still want it, attend the closing in person."

"It has to be done before I can get there, so they're doing a mail-away closing," she said. "They do it all the time."

"This is not the time to have a debate," he told her. "I'm trying to save you a lot of headaches."

"You're right, Ethan. It's not debatable. It's my money, and I'm doing it." They'd ended the phone call without even exchanging good-byes. Since then, they'd barely had a chance to talk. It made her sad that their communication had changed so vastly over the years. Once upon a time, they never would've spoken to each other that way.

Quinn felt sorry for Ethan, because part of her knew that she was behaving abnormally. However, she'd spent years being guided by first her mother, and then by Ethan. Even at work, she had a power-hungry district manager, and she rarely got to call her own shots. All her life she'd been the epitome of a responsible person, listening to, and taking guidance from, those around her, even when it meant putting her own wants aside. Using part of the money her mother had left her to buy a property where her mom had been born just felt right. It would ensure that Quinn would always have a place to come back to on the island where she'd laid her mother to rest.

If Ethan had been home more often since her mother's death, maybe she wouldn't be doing out-of-the-ordinary things and making rash decisions on her own. He sold software to high-tech companies, and the travel was brutal but mandatory. There was no denying the long absences had put a strain on their relationship.

She'd always let him do his thing. So now it was her turn, and she hoped he'd give her the same consideration. He'd be angry for a while, but eventually he'd see she'd made a sound decision—a profitable one, even—and he'd get over it.

Relationships were that way—you had to take the bad with the good. Ethan wasn't perfect, but he did love her. There were other perks in their relationship too. For one, he still looked like he'd stepped from the pages of a magazine. He'd learned how to put his appearance to good use too. His chiseled looks and gregarious personality had made him a lot of money. The bottom line was that when other men thought of the most successful men in their lives to emulate, Ethan was probably at the top of their lists. On the other hand, women were attracted to him like bees to honey. He could have his pick from just about anyone, and Quinn still couldn't believe he'd chosen her.

He wasn't always easy to live with, but she knew he was a catch. She'd been shocked when he showed interest in her over the many prettier girls he could've chosen in college. He was the best option she was ever going to have, and she'd told her mother just that after their first date.

But will he love you when the beauty fades? A question her mother had asked too many times, her disapproval of Ethan seeping out in quiet words during the difficult times when Quinn had run home to lick her wounds.

She and Ethan always worked things out, and her mother's question was one Quinn didn't want to explore but also one she'd never forgotten. Pushing her own doubts aside and biting her tongue on a regular basis had thus far been the key to their longevity. She didn't know a lot of couples who had made it as long, and, for their endurance, Quinn was proud. Ten years was no small feat and, as their friends teased them, was probably the longest engagement of anyone in their small or wide circle.

Quinn looked down at her ring, a symbol of their promise to be together forever, but one that had yet to be formalized. The ring no longer sparkled. The newness had worn off, and now it just felt like a familiar piece of her. Would it be different once they were married?

A rumble in her stomach reminded her that she hadn't eaten a real meal in nearly a day. She turned and went to the bed, sitting cross-legged on it before picking up the leather-bound hotel guide. She flipped to the "Room Service" section, then called in an order of garlic rice with a side of French fries and a cold (fully and guiltily caffeine- and sugar-loaded) Coke with ice.

Screw the protein, greens, or fruit she'd normally be ordering.

Sometimes having such a healthy partner was tough. Along with Ethan's good looks, he was exceptionally fit. He found time for his workout regimen no matter where he was. He'd worked hard to develop a six-pack that he could wash clothes on and biceps that made an admirable bulge under his perfectly ironed, tailored shirtsleeves. Secretly, Quinn thought he was terrified of middle age and what could happen to his body if he relaxed even for a minute.

She appreciated his commitment, but his diligence could also be irritating when it came to his watching what she put in *her* body.

They didn't fight about it, but she knew he wanted her to be slimmer than she was. It was in the way he raised his eyebrows if she ordered anything but the healthiest dish on a menu, or the way he'd once held up a pair of her slouchiest pants she'd left at the end of the bed and said he'd almost mistaken them for his own.

He knew they weren't his. He'd just wanted to make a point. Get her to work harder to lose the extra weight she'd put on that year. The pounds, that no matter how hard she worked out or how little she ate, refused to budge.

Or was she just being paranoid—too sensitive, even?

Why couldn't men understand that some women were simply wired for curves? That no magic pill or amount of exercise would transform them into the phantom willowy creature that society strove for, an elusive goal that drove many women to years of self-doubt and hatred?

On the other hand, it showed that he cared about her health, so how could she be resentful?

But today—she swore to herself—just today, she'd indulge in what she wanted instead of what she needed. She kicked off her shoes and lay back on the comfortable white pillows, releasing a long, pent-up breath of exhaustion.

She reached over and grabbed her laptop, opened it, and signed in to her Lineage account. The screen popped up, and there stood her very own ancestral tree, looking about as lonely and forlorn as a tree could look. The main box bore her name, but it was still connected to only empty boxes around it.

Her imagination conjured up dozens of nameless figures rushing to jump ship, snipping themselves from the branches as they slipped away, eager to avoid being discovered by her.

She slammed the screen shut. Her thoughts went immediately to Ethan. She could call him, but if he didn't answer, it would deflate her mood even more. And if he did answer, there wasn't much she could tell him at this point. She didn't want to argue with him about the house, and that only left her plans for her mother's memorial, of which she had none yet. His attitude about even that would probably make her sad. He'd never understand the loss her mother's death was to her and probably thought it was as simple as finding a beautiful lookout and scattering her ashes over a cliff and into the ocean.

Quinn felt a catch in her throat. She and her mother had been closer than most. Growing up, it was just the two of them, moving from place to place and scrimping to make ends meet. She had to give it to her mom—even without an education, she'd always found a way to provide a decent home in a semisafe neighborhood. Over the years she'd worked as a nanny or a housekeeper, and sometimes both at one time. Those positions paid the rent and put food on the table with enough money left over for Quinn to have the things she wanted.

Yes, her mother had rocked it as a single parent, and they were fine with it being just the two of them. Or at least that's what they both pretended. When Quinn thought about her birth father, wondering if he'd loved her at all, she never let those feelings out. In those first years, undocumented in a time of no cell phones or social media, absent of photos, had he ever held her? Rocked her to sleep? Whispered things a father would say to a soft, tiny girl?

When social networking took off, Quinn had spent hours trying to track him down. Searching his name and going through every hit to see if that Wesley Maguire had any connection to California or Hawaii. Or carried a resemblance to herself. But she'd always come up empty.

After college she tried not to obsess about what it was that pushed her mother into leaving her family and culture—discarding it like wet boots after a heavy rain. It was curious. Her mother had traded all she'd ever known for a man who would prove to be disloyal, and a life on the mainland, in a small town where everyone thought Hawaii was a foreign country or simply a scene on a postcard.

Why?

She didn't want to hurt her mother, so she held her questions inside, letting them burrow there and grow thorns.

Then the cancer came. Soon they were battling two long years of sickness that led to the confession, then death.

Her mother's passing had only opened the door to more questions. Like where did the inheritance money come from? The money was one of the biggest surprises of Quinn's life. She'd expected the estate attorney to tell her there was next to nothing left after paying the medical bills. Instead she'd been given a small fortune. She should've been really happy at such a windfall, but it was perplexing why her mother hadn't used some of the money over the years. While their lifestyle had been comfortable, it was modest, to say the least. Quinn wanted to find out more about the inheritance. *Needed* to find out more.

The note her mother left her was such an unusual action from a woman who had never wanted to talk of the past, but it pushed Quinn into endless hours of online research that led to nothing. She thought of the photo. She'd found a Carmen Crowe on Facebook—actually, about seventeen of them. But none of them from Hawaii or who matched the projected age. She knew it was most likely that Carmen had married and dropped the name Crowe.

Sending her DNA off was really a last resort. So far nothing had happened. No magical leaves appeared on her bare-limbed tree. No long-lost relatives popped up willing to embrace her. It was as though she and her mother had been dropped onto the earth without the cumbersome, yet sometimes needed, support of family. Something just didn't add up, and Quinn was determined more than ever to find out just what.

A knock at the door startled her. Her food had arrived, and that meant dinner, a bath, then a fall into what she knew would be a restless sleep. There were big things looming ahead of her, and if Quinn knew her subconscious, it would be a night of dreaming about them.

Chapter Three

Some women were born with natural beauty, the kind that allowed you to roll out of bed, run your fingers through your hair, and face the world without reservation.

As much as it saddened her, Quinn wasn't one of them. It would take her some time to get her face on and look appropriate for the public. She sat up, stretched her arms over her head, and tried to blink away the grogginess. Feeling heavy with fatigue from a restless night, she slid out of bed and crossed the room.

She opened the door to the balcony, and suddenly the quiet was gone, sucked out in an instant. In its place, birds chirping and the sound of the surf crashing against the beach filled the room, shifting the solitude into something bearable.

At the desk, she pulled out the chair and sat, then turned on her computer and opened Facebook.

She typed "Elizabeth Senna" into the "Search" field.

Hundreds of women sharing her mother's name showed up. She changed her search to "Elizabeth Ellen Senna Maui." It didn't do much to narrow the choices. Obviously, Senna was a popular family name.

Moving on to the ancestry website, she logged in and opened the messages box. She hoped for at least a distant connection to show up.

Nothing.

She looked at her watch, then closed the laptop and headed for the bathroom, still perplexed that in this age of technology and loss of privacy, she'd unearthed absolutely nothing helpful. Was the universe against her finding her heritage?

After a quick shower, Quinn dried her hair before coaxing it into a low-hanging twist. She expertly applied her makeup, her hands graceful and nimble, nearly moving without any thought.

One of the valuable lessons that Ethan had taught her was that one's appearance was the first tool that could be utilized to achieve success. When they met, it was easy to always look her best with minimal effort. But later, when she'd noticed the telltale signs of the end of her twenties—a few crow's-feet and a not-so-enviable difference in the elasticity of her skin, she contacted a makeup artist and took lessons until she learned to make herself completely presentable, even on barely a half hour's notice.

Now people told her all the time she didn't look like she was in her thirties, but she knew they were just being kind.

Quinn followed her usual regimen, the familiar routine soothing her nerves. She tried to ignore the way her eyes strayed to her neck and the looseness that was beginning there. Another ten years and she'd be looking into a neck lift, and that was a depressing thought.

Once her makeup was done, she dressed in her freshly ironed slacks and a billowy white shirt, slipped into some low heels, and strode out to her car.

She hit the road, excited yet anxious.

Driving out of Lahaina, she clutched the steering wheel and followed the curvy, scenic highway. The rented Jetta felt small and insignificant beneath her in contrast to the unending and breathtaking views she passed: majestic mountains on her left and the bluest blues of the rolling ocean to her right.

Hawaii truly was a paradise, and she felt a rush of guilt for leaving Ethan behind, for not allowing him to experience this with her.

The beauty around her couldn't be described in words, though she'd texted him when she stopped for a coffee at a local shop, letting him know she missed him and was thinking of him.

He didn't respond.

Her friend Gina had tried to call and then texted her during the night: Why did you skip spin class? You aren't answering your phone. I'm worried . . .

Oh, God forbid she miss spin class. Quinn rolled her eyes, but she did consider calling her or at least texting. In all honesty, though, they weren't that close. Gina was her friend only because her husband, Kevin, and Ethan had gone to school together. Sure, they did a lot of "couples things" together, and Ethan was always on her about going to spin class so she didn't disappoint Gina, but Quinn had never felt a genuine connection to her. She hadn't really had a close friendship since Maggie, her best friend.

With Maggie, Quinn could be herself and never have to worry about how she came across. And Maggie had the big family that Quinn had sometimes dreamed of having. When she spent time at Maggie's house, she felt like she was one of them.

Maggie was feisty yet playful—especially around her brothers. Quinn couldn't count how many practical jokes they'd played on them. Maggie had a knack for thinking up crazy but harmless ways to repay them for being too protective or just downright irritating.

In junior high, Quinn and Maggie had shared the view from the outside of the popular crowd. Then high school came, and Maggie blossomed, quickly transforming from the redheaded pixie she was to a beautiful young woman. Her long hair turned into a much deeper red, and she suddenly had legs that Quinn would die for. Her transformation from tomboy to beauty queen landed her in a different crowd, but Maggie was loyal. She made it known that Quinn was her best friend and that would never change. So Quinn was in, too, and treated with a certain respect, though she never quite felt welcomed by the popular girls.

She and Maggie had headed off in different directions after that, attending different colleges. Quinn had tried to keep in contact, but when Ethan came along, he monopolized her time—and thoughts—to the point that the guilt of letting their friendship wane finally propelled it into total obscurity.

And Maggie stopped making an effort too. But Quinn missed her. She missed having a friend she could be open with, confide in.

She looked at her phone peeking out from her bag.

Other than from Gina, her screen remained ominously empty of messages or missed calls. One would think that as the corporate director of sales and marketing for a high-end resort, Quinn would have made hundreds of contacts. And she had. Just none close enough to call friends—at least not ones she had contact with in real life, as opposed to just on social media. Her work required a lot of travel, but when she had time off, it was usually burned up planning her schedule, working out, and spending time with Ethan. There wasn't really time for anyone else.

She took a deep breath and blew it out slowly. It wasn't the time for indulging in a self-pity party. She winced when a Jeep went around to pass her, top down and music blaring. The driver was a thin reed of a girl, her long blonde hair whipping in the wind as her head bobbed to a beat that reverberated through the Jetta.

Carefree.

A few years ago, when it was time to buy a new-to-her car, Quinn wanted a Jeep, a longing that had started in high school but one she'd never realized. Ethan had researched all the industry reports and recommendations, and she had eventually settled on a Honda sedan, the car most known for dependability and longevity.

Now Quinn watched the Jeep ahead of her and felt envious for a brief second.

Once she turned off the main highway, the smaller road was bordered by magnificent banyan trees, an army of silent protectors with arms open wide, welcoming her toward something she could finally call her own.

A hidden gem, the Realtor had promised, pushing aside her concern that there were no interior photos available. Fully furnished and turnkey ready. The listing details sounded charming, and Quinn could probably recite it word for word. *Banyan Bungalow: A rare piece of old Hawaii on the island of Maui. A livable original 1926 Craftsman-style American bungalow.* The listing also described a one-bedroom apartment on the property that, with a little work, could be used as a vacation rental for additional income.

But how much work? The unknown of it perhaps put a damper on her excitement. However, the plumbing and the electrical in both dwellings were good, so at least the most expensive areas weren't going to be an issue. Anything cosmetic would be easy and could be fun to take care of.

Supposedly, the small house was situated only three hundred feet from the beach, facing westward to get the most beautiful sunset views. But the image she'd held in her mind for the last few months was from the photo that showed the walkway leading up to the cozy blue door and the majestic monkeypod tree that flanked the house. Over a hundred years old, her Realtor had said.

Of course, over a hundred years old could mean big problems.

There was so much against her buying the house, yet one day she woke up and looked in the mirror and knew she had to do something new. Something to make her feel alive, before she felt completely dead inside. It was the small part of her that hadn't yet been pushed completely down by life's punches. A tiny flicker of excitement that grew bigger and bigger with each subsequent email back and forth to Maui.

As she became more determined, Ethan grew more concerned. He advised her that she could wind up in over her head, making a decision out of grief. For once, Quinn decided to follow her gut rather than Ethan's advice. He would forgive her once she proved him wrong.

Hopefully, she was right.

The Realtor assured her it was a sound investment and told her if she wanted it, she would have to move fast. But she didn't know him from Adam, and, of course, he had a family to feed, so who knew how desperate he was to make a commission.

She turned onto South Kihei road and spotted a few chickens pecking in someone's yard, noting how skinny they looked.

As she went on, the style of houses began to show more variety. Mixed in with the smaller one-story homes were a few obviously newly constructed mini-mansions. Quinn hoped her home wouldn't be one of those sandwiched between two mammoths and made to look small and insignificant.

When a chicken ran out in front of her, Quinn slammed on the brakes. She realized she'd been holding her breath for at least a half mile.

She missed hitting the squawking creature, but her heart raced.

Relax. It will be fine.

The next few miles were a blur, her excitement making it nearly impossible to concentrate on her surroundings any longer. Finally, she made the turn down Halama Street—her street now—and watched the numbers on the mailboxes until she came to the one marked 7895. Slowly, she turned into the property, hearing the gravel crunch under her tires as she rounded the small, curving driveway.

She rolled to a stop and put the car out of gear, then shut off the ignition and leaned back, taking a deep breath.

Well, this is it.

Her first look at Banyan Bungalow was anticlimactic, but Quinn tried to reserve judgment as she climbed out.

She shut the car door and leaned against it, taking in the property. It was picturesque—sort of. Or maybe once was. Could possibly be again.

Someone had once put some time and thought into the landscaping. It was artfully done, though a bit overgrown. She was relieved that the monkeypod tree was there, casting a big shadow over the walkway, looking a little worse for wear.

She'd expected the house to appear empty and lonely, but it actually didn't look too bad. The owners had left behind a couple of rattan chairs that could be cleaned up and possibly repainted. A ragged doormat that read "Aloha" remained too.

For a moment she stood admiring the expansive porch with the hardy forest-green planks and the white trim that framed the floor-to-ceiling windows and porch. The steps leading to the door were painted red, now faded, but Quinn could imagine them fresh and welcoming again, especially with some brightly colored pots of flowers flanking them.

Between surfing Pinterest and all the home improvement shows she watched, she had a million ideas to improve the curb appeal. Once more, she wished Ethan was with her for the reveal, but he had high standards, and if it didn't appear perfect on first look, he'd have a hard time envisioning what it could be.

She walked up to the porch and climbed the steps. Her pulse quickened as she stopped to fish in her purse for the key that the Realtor had mailed her.

Before she could get her hands on it, the door opened.

"What do you want?" a teenage boy said, running a hand through his wavy brown hair. He leaned against the frame, holding his cell phone, a bored expression pasted on his face. Quinn could see a small girl sitting on a couch behind him, her arms wrapped around a matching dark-haired doll, her eyes glued to a cartoon on the television.

"I—I . . . ," Quinn stuttered, completely tongue-tied. She was expecting an empty house. The Realtor said it would be move-in ready. Just wait until she talked to him. She felt her temper flare, and a marquee of colorful words ran across her imagination.

She finally composed herself and straightened to her full height. "I want to know what *you* are doing here. This is my house."

He let out a harsh laugh. "*Your* house, huh? Well, that's righteous."

Before she could reply, a woman came hurrying out of a side room and to the door. "Pali, go on. I'll talk to her."

"Fine. You talk to the fancy *haole*. I've got plans, anyway." He rolled his eyes at her as he walked away, joining the young girl on the couch. He kicked up his feet on the coffee table—Quinn's coffee table, no less—and turned his attention back to his phone.

Quinn wasn't sure whether to be offended by being called a *haole* or not. She'd read it just meant "mainlander," but the way the boy had said it sounded much worse. But he was a kid. Obviously one with an attitude problem.

She turned her attention to the woman, who appeared beyond frazzled. But at least she was making an attempt to be polite. Quinn was beginning to feel dizzy with shock. Was she even at the right house? Could she have gotten the number confused? It sure looked like the photos, but maybe there was another house just like it on the same street.

It would've been so much simpler if that was the case. She dreaded what Ethan would have to say about her predicament. But he wasn't here, and for once it was up to her to fix things.

First, though, they needed to remain calm.

"Look," Quinn began, "I think there might be a misunderstanding. I'm Quinn Maguire, and I bought this house."

The woman held her hand up for Quinn to stop talking. They locked eyes as she wrung the dishcloth between her hands, a silent plea for mercy, Quinn would think later. It took her a few seconds to speak, and when she did, everything became more complicated.

She looked toward the living room first, then leaned in, speaking in a hushed voice. "I'm Maria. Please, let me apologize for my son. We're in a state of shock. We just got the news yesterday that we've been evicted. I guess you could say, since we didn't even know our home was being sold, I would appreciate you giving us some time to get out."

Quinn stared at the woman, absolutely speechless. Of all the possible things she'd thought could go wrong, the previous owners still living in her new home was not one of them.

Chapter Four

Only half an hour before, Quinn had been ready to accept all the challenges of becoming a homeowner. Now, however, she sat at the kitchen table and waited for Maria, the previous owner, to return and explain why she was still living in a house that didn't belong to her or how she didn't know it was being sold in the first place.

As Quinn waited, she looked around. The room was interesting. The seventies-style orange countertops definitely needed to go, and the floor tiles had seen better days too. She thought the cabinets themselves might be salvageable, with a good sanding and a new paint job. Maybe some different handles on them.

At least the original wainscoting was still in place. That was going to look nice freshened up. The kitchen had good bones and, with some changes, could be exactly how she envisioned.

Quinn felt silly, remembering that she wasn't here to have coffee with a friend and fantasize about new floors. Her dream house, unfortunately, had come with a family included.

She wondered if she had any sort of trial period where she could back out of the contract. Did house buying include such a clause? Sort of like the thirty-day trial on a new mattress, or the twenty-four-hour clause when you bought a new car? And wasn't this a criminal matter? Should she call the police? Tell them she'd bought a home and didn't know it included people, and she wanted them out? What kind of monster would that make her?

"Just let me get them settled so we can talk privately," Maria had said after leading Quinn into the kitchen, then disappearing into the family room.

To make things worse, Maria had a nice face. Probably about forty or so, she fit the mold of just a regular stressed-out mom. Quinn wished the woman wouldn't come off as so nice. That would've made it easier for Quinn to stand her ground.

She heard a discussion start. The teen boy didn't sound happy either. The girl piped in with a comment, and her mom shushed her, but she did it kindly, with a gentle voice.

Quinn couldn't count the times someone had asked her and Ethan if they had children or when they were going to have them. She never could understand how a stranger could look so innocent when asking such a personal question.

"We are childless by choice," she'd answer, though, truth be told, it was more Ethan's choice than hers. She never pointed out that they hadn't even crossed the first milestone of getting married. They'd been together so long they automatically looked the part.

Now, with the sound of the cartoon blaring and the boy giving his mom all the reasons she should let him use her car, Quinn let herself think about what motherhood would've been like. She wanted to believe she'd have been a good mom, but the truth was that taking care of herself and Ethan while juggling a high-paced career was exhausting, and she'd never really thought she'd be able to take on a child too. Even if she had wanted to, Ethan had made it clear in the first year they'd been together that he had no intention of ever procreating. He took it as a personal affront that so many children were being born in a world that was already overcrowded and facing an inevitable lack of resources one day. Yet, when she'd brought up adoption, he wasn't interested in that either.

Quinn's own childhood had been just fine, but if she were being honest, it had also been lonely at home. If—and it was a moot point now—she had gone the route of being a mother, she would've never had just one. Her imaginary child would have siblings, something that Quinn had always longed for.

The front door slammed, and other than the cartoon, the house was silent. At least the little girl wasn't trying to give her mother a nervous breakdown.

Maria returned, her face red and sweaty. She took the seat across from Quinn. "I'm so sorry. He's going through quite a bit right now. He's not usually like this."

He's going through quite a bit? Quinn had just spent a fortune on a house that someone else was living in! She stared at Maria, wondering how to phrase all that without sounding like a completely unfeeling robot. She decided to just cut to the chase—put it out there like pulling a Band-Aid off.

"Look," she began, keeping her tone neutral and as kind as possible, "I don't know what's going on in your personal life, and you have my sympathies, but I've got closing documents to prove that this is my property now. I'm sorry, but I'm confused as to why you haven't moved out yet."

"Have you ever been to Hawaii before?" Maria asked.

"Well, sort of. When I was a baby."

"I can tell. You're a bit shell-shocked. People come to Maui expecting to find nothing but paradise. If they ever run into the real Maui, far from the grounds of the fancy resorts, golf courses, and restaurants, they see where real people are struggling to lead real lives, and they are shocked. Because of people like you, the prices of homes and rent have risen astronomically. Believe me when I tell you that finding a new place to live isn't going to be easy. I can't afford the rent most are charging out there now."

Quinn stared at her, not knowing what to say. In a way, the woman was right. When she'd ever thought about Hawaii before, she'd only seen visions of beaches and palm trees. Mimosas and poolside umbrellas. She'd never considered the local families there struggling just to keep a roof over their heads.

"I'm sorry," she said, and meant it. "But the fact is I bought this house. There's obviously been some kind of misunderstanding. I don't mean to seem as though I don't care, though."

Maria nodded. "Thank you. And I'll admit—I'd be really upset if I were in your shoes too. Let me get the papers." She stood and went to a kitchen drawer, pulled out a sheaf of papers, and returned.

She set them in front of Quinn and pointed at one that had the word *notice* in big block letters across the top.

"This is what I found posted on our door yesterday," she said. "I haven't even had time to contact an attorney yet. I had no idea the bank was taking this house until a day ago, I swear to you."

She stared hard at Quinn.

"How could you not know?" Quinn said. "If the bank was involved, that must mean you weren't paying for it. They obviously sold it to a broker who put it out there publicly, where I found it."

"But we didn't owe anything on this house," Maria said. "It's been in my husband's family for more than sixty years, and when his parents died, it went to him. We've lived in it for more than twenty years. I called this morning and talked to my friend who works in the loan department. She looked it up and told me that Jaime put it up for collateral for a loan late last year. He didn't need my signature because this house was in his name long before we married, and we never added mine. She said the mailing address on file was a mailbox downtown. That's why I hadn't received any of the notices until they came and put these on the door."

"And where is your husband? Has he—um, passed too?" Quinn asked.

"No, as far as I know, he's very much alive. You didn't see him when you signed the papers?" Maria asked.

"It was a mail-away closing. They sent them to me, I signed, then sent them back. The Realtor said he does it that way all the time. You don't know where your husband is?"

Maria shrugged. "He left more than three months ago. No one knows where he is." Then she burst into tears, her shoulders shaking as she rested her face in her hands.

Public displays of emotion made Quinn feel helpless. She had no idea what to say, or do, to make it less awkward.

She reached over and patted the woman on the shoulder. "What kind of person does that?" she said, feeling genuinely furious at a man she'd never met.

Maria looked up and gave her a stern look, bringing her crying under control. "I don't know what has happened, but I know this: my Jaime is a good man. Or at least he *was* a good man. He was probably taken in by some harlot." She composed herself, straightening her shoulders, a proud expression coming over her face before it crumpled again and more tears came.

Quinn felt helpless. And torn. On one hand, she was really upset that the Realtor had not done his due diligence and made sure the property was empty. He told her he had done a walk-through and everything was fine! But she was human, too, and it sounded to her as though this woman—Maria of the many tears—was in a worse predicament than she was. Maria had nowhere to go, an absent husband, a mouthy teenager, and a young daughter to care for. At least Quinn could hop on a plane and go back to her organized and semisuccessful life. She had options.

But Maria . . . well, Quinn had yet to hear any options from her. And it sounded like another round of tears might be on the way. "Don't cry. We'll figure this out," Quinn said, thinking quite the opposite as she visualized money being thrown out of a car window. "Have you filed a missing person report?"

Maria used the end of the dish towel to blot her tears. She pushed her hair out of her eyes, forcing the curls together and then wrapping it all into a twist behind her head and tucking the end inside itself. It made her look even older.

"I tried. But they said since he took clothing and toiletries, it appears he left on his own free will, and adults have the right to do that. I just can't believe this is happening to us," she said. "This is the only home my children have ever known, and now we have to leave? And my father. He's too old for this."

Quinn's heart sank. "Your father? He lives here with you?"

Maria nodded. "Of course. Well, I mean, he's not here right now. He's at the beach. But he lives here, and my mother did, too, until she passed."

The surprise must've shown on Quinn's face, because Maria looked indignant

"Here in Hawaii, we don't send our elders away. Most families have multiple generations living in the same house. This won't just affect me. I have a lot of people depending on me. It's not going to be easy to just up and leave."

Quinn sighed. That part she couldn't help with. But she could be charitable. "How much time do you think you need?"

Maria looked around, taking in the kitchen area filled with things that made it a home. A spice rack hung on the wall, some bottles low on ingredients, proving that the display wasn't just for show. A pot was on the stove top, the burner glowing softly beneath it, tendrils of steam rising from the top.

On the windowsill a row of small pots held a variety of herbs, the names spelled out in bright pastel paints in a child's handwriting.

"I don't even know where we can go," Maria finally said, her eyes filling again. "I have no job. I have some family on the big island, but they had to evacuate to a smaller home after the volcano eruption and don't have room for us. And Pali has to stay in this school district. His place on the football team is his only chance at a scholarship." She lowered her voice to a whisper again. "My daughter, Alani, doesn't even know anything about this. Her best friend lives next door. They've grown up together, seeing one another every single day. It's going to kill them to be separated. I don't even know how to tell her. I said you were a friend of mine from the mainland."

Quinn felt dirtier than pond scum. She was probably the furthest thing from a friend right now, unless friends were known to swoop down and kick you out of your own home. "I know this is hard. But this was all done legally, Maria. It's not my fault your husband didn't tell you what he was doing."

Maria's eyes widened. "Legally? Wait, are you going to call the police?"

This was excruciating, and Quinn wished she could blink her eyes and disappear. But a lot of money was on the line. It wasn't as though she could just tell them, "Never mind, go ahead and keep the house," and she'd find something else. For a split second, she wished Ethan were here to step up and make everything fall into place.

"No, I'm not calling the police. I'll come back tomorrow, after you've had a chance to process this. I won't just kick you out today, but we need to agree on a move-out date. Maybe by the weekend? I can't stay in a hotel forever, and I have a lot of changes planned to the house. I need to start the remodeling while I'm here," Quinn said.

The girl walked in, her ponytail swishing from side to side. "You can stay in the guesthouse," she said, smiling at Quinn. She looked to her mother, her eyebrows up. "Mama, you said she was our guest. Pali should give up his room."

First Maria looked surprised; then she nodded. She turned to Quinn.

"Yes. You take the guesthouse, and I'll talk to my uncle in Oahu about *visiting* him," she said, emphasizing *visiting* to make it clear to Quinn not to say anything in front of the girl. "I can have Pali's things cleared out of there in an hour or so."

"Oh, no. I can't. I'm fine staying at the hotel," Quinn said. She sure didn't feel like it was her home yet, papers or not, and camping out on the property just didn't feel right.

"No—please," Maria insisted, "I'd feel less guilty if you took the guesthouse. It's just messy right now because my son has been staying out there. But I'll tidy it up and give you fresh linens. I can cook for you. I—I—"

"Maria, please." Quinn reached out and took her hands, stopping them from wringing a hole through the towel. She couldn't believe what she was about to say. "We need to have a solution by the weekend. I'll even help you pack. Then I can get a contractor out here on Monday."

Alani looked at her mother, confusion across her face.

"What is she talking about, Mama?"

Oops. Quinn stood. She'd had enough drama for one day. She felt completely wrung out herself, probably even rivaling the dishcloth.

Maria put her arms around Alani. "We need to talk, honey."

"I'm going next door," Alani said as she wiggled out of the embrace and went out the back door.

That was Quinn's cue. "I'm sorry. I'll see myself out," she said. "You might want to go ahead and start contacting movers for a quote. Can you give me your number?"

Maria nodded, but it didn't look convincing. She went to the counter and jotted her number down, then handed it over.

Quinn retreated through the living room, eyeing the wainscoting that needed painting, then the spectacular built-in china cabinets in the wall.

Through the dining room she caught a glimpse of the large bay window looking out into the rear of the property. The window went from floor to ceiling, flooding the room with sunlight. A quick glance at the hardwood floors showed their damage too. They needed refinishing.

Despite the rough edges, the Realtor hadn't lied, after all. The house was a hidden gem, and once she was finished with it, Quinn had every confidence it would be a showstopper. She wished she had time to check out all the rooms, but she needed to leave and give Maria privacy to talk to her kids. She would call her in the morning to talk specifics.

Not to mention, the emotional charge in the house was more than Quinn could bear. It was going to be a long way back to the hotel. For once, she hoped that Ethan didn't call her to check in that night. She needed more time to figure out just how much to tell him so that she could keep what he'd tell her back at a minimum.

Chapter Five

The next morning Quinn pulled the brim of her hat lower to block the sun from her eyes. She was tired, having spent the night fighting off stress-filled dreams starring an indignant Ethan. Now the waves crashed gently against the beach, a monotonous yet intoxicating sound. Still on East Coast time, she'd woken before dawn, but waited until the sun rose to come down and take a corner table at the outside restaurant.

She thought of the breakfast that Maria was probably getting prepped and ready to serve. Though she couldn't accept the offer, she also couldn't stop thinking about the cozy-looking guesthouse. Quinn spent her life running around hotels, and there weren't enough amenities in the world to make it feel comfortable on her time off. She just wanted to forget her real life for a while, and the familiar hotel environment wasn't making it easy.

She also felt uncomfortable being there solo, as though each couple or family who walked up wondered who she was and why she was alone. She ordered a bagel and side of fruit, then tossed it down and finished it off with a cup of orange juice before signing the bill and heading toward the beach. At the beach, she pulled a resort chair to a secluded spot on the sand.

Now her skin tingled from the sun, but the breeze caressed her, lulling her into laziness.

Her first thought that morning was to call the Realtor and give him a piece of her mind. If he'd really done the walk-through he'd lied about, he would've known Maria and her family were still there. Quinn had actually picked up the phone and begun dialing.

But remembering Maria's stricken face stopped her. The Realtor would most likely insist on involving the authorities.

She hit the "End" button on her phone.

Hopefully, they could get everything straightened out without causing the woman further trouble. Ethan would tell Quinn she was letting them walk all over her, but she just couldn't kick the woman when she was already down.

Now Quinn's phone lay abandoned in the room, thrown there in a fit of frustration. No messages or missed calls from Ethan. Quinn wasn't happy about it either. She would not dial his number again. It was his turn.

Nothing to report on the Lineage site either. She was beginning to dread opening her account and facing those glaring empty boxes. That morning, she'd closed her eyes and said a prayer, then looked.

The universe wasn't listening. No connections reported. And she still didn't have her new house. She was beginning to believe the entire journey was cursed.

Sleeping hadn't been easy either, especially when she knew that as soon as it was a decent hour, she would have to go back there again and face Maria—and her children—and basically take their house out from under them.

She felt a roll of nausea—her normal reaction to stress—and wiped at the perspiration beading across her forehead. If she wasn't so afraid, she'd go cool off in the water. She loved the ocean, but only from the safety of the beach. That sounded ridiculous even to her, considering she lived in a town that was a magnet for water people.

Shifting in her seat, she felt her chair begin to wobble to the side, just about to tip over and throw her into the sand. She struggled to balance her weight back into the middle; then suddenly all movement was stopped.

"Care to paddle out?" a hoarse voice asked.

She strained her eyes, using a hand to block the light. A man leaned over, his hand on the side of the chair to steady it. He pushed down, grounding the uneven side deeper into the sand, stabilizing it before letting go. She saw a board propped at his feet.

"Oh, thanks. Something happened with this chair. Not sure what."

"No problem. So, do you want to go out?"

"No, I don't think so," she said. "I don't surf."

"Wasn't asking you to surf. It's a paddleboard. You kneel and use your arms to get out to the waves; then ride them back without standing until you get the hang of it. I can show you."

She couldn't tell if his tone was mocking. Was he saying he didn't think she could surf? Was that some sort of insult based on her very nonmuscular body? Now her cheeks burned, and it wasn't from the sun. She resisted telling him she had spinning class twice a week and jogged—okay, maybe walked—just as frequently. No, she wasn't into lifting weights, so her fitness might not be as visible to the eye, but that didn't make her a complete sloth.

"But," he continued, "if you're up to surfing, we can do that too. I've got a few boards on my truck."

He must've sensed he needed to rephrase. But the truth was, she couldn't surf. Or paddleboard. Ethan was the athlete. She was the sideliner. He depended on her to be waiting for him, holding the gear or towel or whatever he needed. He was amused by her fear of the ocean but thus far hadn't pushed her to overcome it.

"Thanks, but no. I'm just resting today," she said. He was a big guy, but the sun at his back put his face in a shadow. From the sound of his voice, Quinn guessed him to be at least her age, if not older.

"Fine. Suit yourself," he said, then walked toward the water. He was ankle deep when he turned and came back. "Just so you know, I usually do my thing solo. I'm not sure why I stopped and asked you. Just thought you looked like you might need to have some fun, but—" He paused. "Oh, never mind."

She still couldn't see his face clearly, and she hoped he couldn't see hers under the wide brim of her hat, because she was sure it was flaming. Why hadn't he just gone on and left her alone? Now he'd made it awkward.

"Well, okay. Thanks for asking."

He nodded, then strode into the water, and when it was waist high, threw himself onto his board and paddled out.

Quinn watched him for a moment. He was far enough out now that she could look without fear of him catching her. From the distance, it was hard to tell much about him. She'd seen other surfers that morning wearing black wetsuits. Not him, though. It appeared that he sported only a pair of swim trunks. No shirt. His hair was dark. Cut short. His profile was strong—a defined nose and forehead, but the other features were still shadowed by the sun.

She could, however, barely make out some sort of tattoo snaking around one of his biceps. He moved gracefully, his form seeming to be one with the motion of the waves, as though confident they would carry him and not let him down. It must be an amazing feeling, but she wondered if he thought about sharks, or if being in their domain was thrilling enough to counteract the chances he took.

Ethan was that way—the kick of adrenaline was what made him tick. He'd bungee jumped off high bridges, skydived out of planes, and once on a dare had climbed out of a seventh-story window and Spider-Manned his way down to the ground. He always had to have a challenge, something to tame. Sometimes Quinn thought that was why he'd picked her. He saw through her facade of self-confidence to the girl who might shatter at any given moment.

Well, here she was in Maui, and things weren't going exactly as planned, but she hadn't shattered yet. More than that, she hadn't allowed him to step in and fix everything.

Somehow, she'd figure out what to do with Maria, and she'd not only get the house emptied of the unexpected family but would turn it into a place that would make Ethan shocked by what she could do on her own.

∼

A few hours later, Quinn approached the house warily, her car moving like a snail as she turned into the driveway. Once she'd left the peace of her beachside chair and traversed the pool area, now packed with families, then stepped into the elevator and rode up listening to another couple happily chatting about where they'd go for dinner, she felt those old insecurities slip back in.

She tried to call Ethan then, just to hear his voice, but was unsuccessful in reaching him. She wavered between wanting to be independent and worrying that he'd been right about the entire situation.

Her bravado faded quickly, and she'd waited until nearly noon, trying to work up the courage to arrive at the house to insist on a solution from Maria. A few cosmetic issues that a shipment of tiles and a coat of paint could fix was one thing, but never had she imagined she'd be dealing with people still living there. It didn't feel like she owned a new home yet, that was for sure. She wanted to blame the jet lag on her sudden reticence to get things done, but something told her it was her fear of failure.

Still, she'd already bought the house and couldn't just walk away from it or let someone else straighten matters out. So she got into her car and headed there, intent on making some sort of progress in the mess that was now her life.

As soon as she climbed out of the car, she heard a burst of yelling and then a door slam around the back of the house.

Pali was obviously awake. So much for the myth of teenagers sleeping late into the afternoon. Or maybe someone had dared to poke the sleeping dragon.

She was considering just turning around and leaving, coming back later when things were calm, but then the door opened, and Maria appeared.

"I know I'm in a tight place, but I won't take your charity," she said, then waved an envelope.

"Oh, hi, Maria. Good morning. Not sure what you're talking about, though."

Maria put a hand on her hip and narrowed her eyes, staring at Quinn for a moment. "You didn't leave me five hundred dollars last night?" she asked. "In this envelope behind the storm door?"

Quinn was taken aback. She wanted them out of her house, but she hadn't even considered paying them to leave. Now she felt stupid. She should've offered the money yesterday.

She shook her head. "Nope. Wasn't me."

Maria relaxed, the sternness leaving her face as confusion set in.

"Then I don't know who did. That means I can't give it back. Can't say I don't need it, though. The kitchen is practically bare of groceries, and if I don't get a new tire on my car, we'll all be walking. Pali needs new cleats for football, too, though he says he can make do with last year's pair."

Quinn stood at the bottom step, biting her lip. Five hundred dollars could also pay for a moving truck, but Maria obviously hadn't thought of that.

"Come in," Maria said, folding the envelope into her pocket before waving Quinn up the steps. "I'm making some brunch for Kupuna. Don't say anything to him about the money."

Quinn wasn't sure what a *kupuna* was, but she followed.

Maria led her through the living area to the kitchen. The coffee she was brewing smelled intoxicating. The girl was there, sitting at the table with an old man. They were studying a paper between the two of them, though Alani held the pencil.

He looked up, his face impassive, and it felt like he looked right through Quinn. If she could guess, she'd put him at around eighty years old. He wasn't a large man, though he appeared to be strong and wiry. His skin was dark and seasoned from the sun in a way that could only come from decades of embracing the outdoors. The many lines around his mouth and eyes were deep, but they made an interesting road map of years of wisdom and experience. What he had left of his hair stood up in silvery tufts, and as she looked, he ran his hand through them.

"This is my father. We call him Kupuna," said Maria.

The old man nodded, but Quinn felt silently chastised.

"Aloha," he finally said, before returning his attention to his granddaughter.

"Aloha," Quinn replied, feeling awkward, especially now that she knew what it meant and had a feeling that the old man was being gracious by using it.

She'd read an article on the plane ride over that described the misunderstanding of the word used for greeting. Most mainlanders were under the impression that *aloha* was the word used for both "hello" and "goodbye." But the article stated it was much more, that *aloha* meant "love," "peace," and "compassion." More than a word, a life of *aloha* meant the heart was overflowing, and when using it, one should be sincerely happy to see the person they said it to.

To be fair, Quinn's heart wasn't feeling overflowing in the least. As a matter of fact, it was jumping around like a frog in a fire, every fiber in her being anticipating the upcoming difficult conversation.

"Please, sit down. Would you like some breakfast?" Maria asked, pulling a chair out and beckoning for Quinn to take it. She gestured to a plate on the table that held mango and what could have been papaya, though Quinn wasn't sure.

"No, thank you. Just coffee would be good."

The bagel she'd had seemed like ages ago, but Quinn wasn't there for pleasantries. She also didn't want to have their talk with a child, and now the grandfather, there. But if she was patient, maybe she could get Maria off to herself once she'd finished cooking.

Maria quickly poured her a cup of coffee and brought it over along with a jar of sugar and a tiny pitcher of cream.

"Kona coffee, of course," she said, setting it all down before returning to the stove.

Quinn gratefully took the mug, doctored it, and took a sip. She nearly closed her eyes in ecstasy as she let her taste buds do a happy dance. Why was Hawaiian coffee so amazing?

While Maria cooked, Quinn watched Alani with her grandfather.

He was helping her with some sort of multiple-choice quiz. She read the questions aloud. He didn't give her any answers, choosing instead to gently guide her to find the solution herself. She talked herself through it while he barely glanced at the paper, instead using his calm presence to encourage her along.

"Did you swim today?" Alani looked up, addressing the question to Quinn.

Quinn could kiss her for breaking the awkward silence.

"No, but I did go to the beach. It was lovely. Do you like to swim?"

Alani nodded. "Pali's going to teach me how to surf."

The grandfather let out a small chuckle. "I think you'll probably conquer the board yourself before he gets a chance to be your instructor. He's too wrapped up in football right now."

"And girls," Alani said, grinning at her grandfather, which made him laugh again.

"No, Alani, he also doesn't have time for girls," Maria said.

Alani looked at Quinn and gave an emphatic nod coupled with raising her eyebrows. She obviously knew something her mother didn't, and Quinn smiled back at her, feeling her heartstrings pull at her soft innocence. Maybe somewhere deep down she understood that her father was gone, and her world was not as it should be, but her sunny outlook was still there, her eyes twinkling with mischief.

Maria pulled some plates from a cupboard, filled them, and delivered them to the girl and her grandfather. She went back and returned with three glasses and a pitcher of juice, setting them down.

"You've done a good job on your schoolwork," Kupuna said to Alani, then picked up his fork and began eating. Alani poured them juice, then followed suit, her gusto at digging in so fast a contradiction to her small stature.

It smelled good. The plates overflowed, the traditional breakfast of eggs, rice, and a slice of fried Spam making a colorful presentation. Quinn almost wished she had accepted the offer of food. Then she remembered why she was there, and her appetite retreated.

Maria fixed herself a plate and a cup of coffee and sat down across from Alani.

"Your brother will be in when his nose tells him there's food on the table," she said, winking. She turned to Quinn. "Don't pay attention if he moves through here like a thundercloud. He's not happy about losing the guesthouse, but he's packing up all the same. Should be out by noon."

"Oh no," Quinn said, already shaking her head. "We need to talk about that."

Her goal was to get them out of there. She wasn't moving into the guesthouse. Things had to be in order before Ethan came.

The grandfather put his fork down and wiped his mouth, staring a hole through Quinn. "Just what plans do you have for this house?" he asked.

Quinn felt the flush creeping up her neck. She didn't meet his eyes because she felt like a thief.

"First would be the kitchen," she finally said, looking the room over. "It needs new countertops, and the cabinets need painting."

"I've wanted new countertops for years," Maria said, talking around the huge bite of eggs she chewed. She sounded like she was trying to lighten the conversation as she peered up at her father.

"Then what?" he asked, ignoring Maria's comment.

His expression was so solemn. Quinn fidgeted. She wanted to tell him that she wasn't exactly sure, but she felt he knew that she already had a list compiled. Something told her he'd call her out if she even tried to slip a little white lie out there. As though he were some sort of shaman with special powers to see into her head, which of course she knew he wasn't.

"I'm sure the hardwood floors in here used to be beautiful. I'd like to restore them to their original glory," she said quietly, praying her answer wouldn't offend him or Maria. This was their house, after all, and they probably thought it was fine just as it was.

He nodded. "That sounds like a good start."

Quinn almost fell out of her chair. He was agreeing with her? Could it be that he would be the hero—the one who got Maria and the kids out and let Quinn have the home she'd just plunked down a lot of money for?

"You will stay in the guesthouse. While we are looking for a new home, I'll arrange for our—I mean, your—work to be done in the kitchen. I can get the island discount. It'll cost you triple if you organize it yourself. By the time it is done, we will be out." With that, he pushed his plate away and drained the last of his juice.

Quinn wasn't sure how to respond. His tone had made it clear that he'd accept no debate or arguing. Quinn had never known a grandfather, but if she had, she would've imagined one like Kupuna, a no-nonsense sort of fellow who could also turn to mush when helping a child with homework.

"How long do you think it will take?" she finally asked.

"It will take as long as it takes," he said, then stood and turned, shuffling out the back door.

It slammed in his wake, and Quinn jumped.

As long as it takes? What was that supposed to mean? Did the old man think that everyone was on island time? She had a life to get back to.

She looked at Maria, who had stopped eating and bore a stricken expression.

"I'm so sorry. He's accustomed to being the patriarch. It's the Hawaiian way, but I can talk to him," she said, but Maria's eyes implored her with a silent plea that Quinn could feel all the way to her bones.

This was one of those moments in life that defined the kind of person you were. Quinn could make it simple. She had every legal right to involve officials and could probably have the house empty by nightfall. She didn't even have to be present to watch them gather their things and leave.

But could she live with herself afterward?

Her thoughts scattered back and forth, from one angle and option to another so quickly she felt dizzy. Was this the universe's way of teaching her a lesson?

Before she could get any words out, the door opened, and there stood Maria's son, his expression defiant when he saw Quinn—his sudden enemy—sitting there.

"Your room is ready, Your Highness," he said, crossing his arms and glaring at her.

Alani sat upright and clapped her hands. "I love that! Can I be the princess?"

Her outburst broke the tension, and Maria laughed first. Alani looked from her mother to Quinn, confused. Her innocent expression was priceless and prompted a miracle.

Pali's scowl dissolved, and he laughed too.

Quinn felt instantly lighter. How bad could it be? It could even be an experience she'd never forget, if she could possibly allow herself to embrace the positive in the circumstance instead of focusing on the negative. Who knows, maybe she'd even learn something authentic about her mother's heritage.

Alani was still waiting for an answer.

Quinn gave her one. "I think you're already a princess, Alani. And guess what? Your mom can be the queen."

Maria met her gaze, gratitude beaming from her now-moist eyes. She clasped her hands to her heart. "Thank you," she whispered. "I promise this will work out."

Quinn hoped so. If it didn't, she'd have to prepare herself for the worst "I told you so" lecture yet.

Chapter Six

Quinn finished unpacking her suitcase, stacking her clothes on the love seat of the cottage until she could ask Maria for hangers. Her mother's ashes were placed on the nightstand, an attempt to make the house less lonely. It was weird that she was even there unpacking. But as usual, it was easier to give in than to say no.

She'd taken her time going back to the hotel and checking out, hoping she'd figure out a way to wiggle out of the arrangement without making things worse.

But nothing had come to her, and she finally had to return to Maria's home—no . . . *her own home*—and settle in. The small guest-house was just that—small. But it was enough for her. Only four hundred square feet, it made her think of the tiny house shows all over television, a new fad sweeping the mainland. It seemed that people everywhere were becoming tired of dragging along too much stuff—physically and emotionally—and opting for new lives free of clutter to live in teensy homes that were barely bigger than a toolshed.

She could see the draw, too, and had binged on the tiny house episodes, thinking how freeing it would be to walk away from her fancy too-modern condo and start somewhere new, just a suitcase of belongings in her possession. A simpler life.

Now she was getting to test it out, whether she wanted to or not. Coming from the mainland, she supposed what was a completely foreign concept of inviting a stranger into your home was just normal in a place where hospitality was the core of the culture.

For such a small space, everything she needed was provided. In addition to a tiny bedroom, the guesthouse—or cottage, which she felt described it better—boasted a living area, a kitchenette, and a bathroom. The whole interior was decorated simply, in a style that continued the island theme: strong bamboo furniture with flowery cushions that begged to be snuggled into with a good book.

Outside was a cozy porch, or *lanai*, as they called it in Hawaii, boxed in by tropical trees and plants, including a banana and a lime tree where she could sit with a cup of coffee and have privacy from the main house.

Pali had taken out most of his things, though Quinn was a bit surprised to find a small ashtray peeking out from under the couch. It held ashes that smelled curiously un-tobacco-like. In her opinion, he was a bit young to be experimenting with weed, but it wasn't any of her business.

Maria said she'd made up the bed with fresh linens, and for that Quinn was grateful. One thing she couldn't make herself do was sleep on sheets that had been broken in by a teenage boy.

"I've stocked the small refrigerator with some staples, and you'll find coffee in the cupboard. Kupuna made a call to his contractor friend, and I need to watch for him to arrive," Maria said, then retreated back toward the house.

"Call me when he gets here," Quinn called out, and Maria held a hand up in acknowledgment. It was Quinn's house, after all, and she would be paying the bills. She hoped that Kupuna didn't think he was calling the shots.

She went to the bathroom and carefully set out her toiletries, lining up her makeup on the counter in the order she used it, another trick she'd learned to make her mornings more efficient.

In the kitchen, she checked the pantry cupboard, noting which spices were available in case she wanted to cook a meal. She was tiring of restaurant food, but she had no intention of joining Maria's family at the table.

There needed to be some boundaries in place.

She was *not* their friend.

Then she saw that Maria had left a small vase of beautiful lavender orchids on the coffee table. Beside them was a note jotted on a yellow Post-it.

Welcome to Maui. Hope this new friendship will continue. See you at dinner. Love, Maria

Quinn sighed, then went back to unpacking. Finally, there was nothing left to do, and she sat down on the love seat, sinking into the worn but comfortable cushions. There wasn't a television, but a small stack of books on the side table caught her attention.

She picked up the one off the top.

Rogue Wave.

She flipped it over and read the book description. *An explosion sets off a series of massive waves that could obliterate all the islands of Hawaii.*

She put it back and rose, going to the lanai. Outside, she sat down at the table and leaned back, closing her eyes for a minute. She was weary. It had been a stressful morning, to say the least. Not every day did she move in with a family who just a short time before were complete strangers. Also, her time was running out. She'd asked for two weeks' vacation, but after that, she needed to return. To a job that was sucking the life out of her.

She had to admit, despite the awkwardness of the situation, leaving the hotel was somewhat of a relief. It wasn't as though she were enjoying any of the amenities like the pool or the restaurants. And she would technically be on her own property, though it still didn't feel that way. At least here she wouldn't feel so alone.

As though on cue, her phone rang.

Quinn jumped up and went back into the cottage. She pulled the phone from her pocket and looked at the screen before swiping. Her heart skipped, and she felt herself tensing.

"Hi," she said.

"What's going on, Quinn?" Ethan said.

No greeting and he had that tone. Not a happy one.

"Well, hold on. Let me sit." She was buying time; she knew that. She settled herself onto the love seat, leaning forward.

Big breath, then dive in.

There was a long pause.

"So, how is it?" he asked. "Is it all you'd hoped it would be?"

Quinn bit her lip. She could visualize him running his fingers through his hair, styling it to the left as he liked it to go, a subconscious reflex even when stressed.

"It's a beautiful home. But there are a few issues," she finally admitted.

"It's old, Quinn. It's going to be nothing but issues. I could've saved you—saved us—a lot of headache if you'd just listened. So what is it? Plumbing? Bad neighborhood? What are the problems?"

"No, the plumbing is fine, as far as I know. But unfortunately, there's a snag with the previous owners."

"A snag?" he said, his voice suspicious.

Quinn could feel her pulse escalate.

"Yes, a snag. They're sort of still here."

"Still there? Like in the area? What do you care?" Now he sounded impatient.

"I mean like still *here*—in the house. It's complicated, Ethan, but they haven't moved out yet." There, she'd said it.

He was silent so long that Quinn pulled the phone from her ear, looking at it to see if he'd hung up. He hadn't.

"Ethan?"

"I'm here," he said. "Listen, I don't even need to hear why they haven't moved out. But you can let them know they're on borrowed time, so they'd better be packing. I'll see if I can get a flight out tomorrow after my meeting."

Quinn felt a rush of panic. When Ethan slipped into business mode, he was like a bulldozer sweeping through, no thought of collateral damage.

"No, don't. I'm taking care of it," she said, nearly biting through her lip. "You don't have to come."

More silence.

She talked faster. "It's just a minor misunderstanding. They'll be moving out soon, but in the meantime, they're going to help me get some work started inside."

"Quinn," Ethan started, his voice low and pleading, "Listen to yourself. You always do this. All it takes is for some chump to hold up a sign begging for money, or a kid knocking on doors asking you to buy some two-dollar roll of wrapping paper for thirty bucks. You're no doubt getting taken advantage of. Again. These people are obviously squatters, and I'm sure Hawaii has a law against that."

Quinn felt a familiar feeling well up inside her. Something like frustration, but tinged with a helping of quiet resentment. She thought of Maria inviting her to sit at her table, to eat with her family.

"No, Ethan, they aren't squatters, and I'm not being taken advantage of. I've got this handled, and I'd appreciate it if you had some confidence in me," she said, cringing at how shaky her voice came out.

"Can you understand why I don't, Quinn? I told you not to buy that house, that it would only be a pain in the ass. Now I've got to deal with it. But I can tell you this much: once I get them out of there, we're going to flip it and get it off our hands."

Our? Quinn didn't remember him contributing any funds, and his name was definitely not on the papers. Now she was really irritated. But if she didn't play it right, he'd simply come over and do what he did best, and she'd be left looking like a heartless fool.

She thought of Maria standing there wringing that towel, and then saw Kupuna at the table, helping Alani with her homework.

Quinn was glad she hadn't left any paperwork related to the house behind. It was all in her carry-on, and the only other place she had details about it was on her laptop, and she had that too. So Ethan didn't have the address.

She breathed deeply, reminding herself to stay calm. He couldn't come stomping in and throw everyone out in a fit of rage.

"Ethan, I appreciate you wanting to help. I really do," she said. "But this time I'm going to have to say no."

"No what?"

"No to everything. Don't come right now. I'll call you in a few days," she said, then hung up the phone.

She was trembling. She'd never hung up on him before.

Her hand released the phone as though it had a mind of its own and thought it was holding a snake. Quinn stared at it, lying on the cushion, praying it wouldn't ring. Ethan was likely now sitting in shock more than three thousand miles away. Or possibly grinding his teeth, as he did when someone really ticked him off.

Now she had even more to make up to him. He was trying to help her, she knew that. But this time she needed to figure it out herself. She wasn't sure just why yet, but this felt too personal to let someone else handle.

"Quinn?"

She jumped, startled.

Alani was standing in the doorway.

"Yes?"

"Can you take me to the beach?" she asked, tilting her head to the side in an adorable way.

Quinn took a deep breath and relaxed her expression. "I'm sorry, Alani, but I can't. Why don't you ask Pali?"

"He's at practice," she said. "Mama is busy on the computer, and Kupuna is taking a nap. I'm supposed to stay quiet."

Quinn considered it. *Why not?* What else did she have to do but sit there and get more nervous at her sudden stand against the wrath of Ethan? Perhaps some salty air would take her mind off her now-regrettable act of bravery.

"Does your mom know you were going to ask me?" she said.

Alani nodded. "She said it might do you good to go."

Great. Now Maria was analyzing her. But she was right.

Quinn needed the fresh air on her face. Heck, she needed it to run through her body and cleanse the sour feeling the phone call had left behind.

"Okay, Alani. I need to change. Give me a few minutes, and I'll be out."

~

By the time Quinn changed into shorts and a T-shirt, Alani had returned with the girl next door. They waited outside the cottage, their appearances total contradictions to one another with their blonde and dark heads tilted together in a giggling conversation.

"This is Junie," Alani said, then led the way, the girl right on her heels.

Quinn followed, clutching her hat to keep it from blowing off in the strong trade winds. They followed a short trail that led straight from the cottage area to a wide span of beach. Quinn felt a thrill at how close her new home was to the water. At least that would make Ethan happy. If he could ever get past feeling like she'd betrayed him by buying it.

People were in the water, and Alani dropped her towel and ran out as fast as she could, taking on the waves like a daredevil. Her friend followed, falling in right beside her, the two splashing like tiny mermaids in the surf.

Their laughter was like a salve to the soul.

Quinn put her bag down and spread out her towel, then sat and searched the surf for Alani's pink suit and Junie's blue one. She found them both, then kept her eye on them, ferociously diligent to be sure neither of the girls disappeared beneath a wave.

If they did, however, she wasn't sure what she'd do. Scream? Wade in and search, as long as the water didn't go past her ankles? Obviously, Maria didn't know that Quinn would make a terrible lifeguard, or she wouldn't have trusted her to watch over the girls.

The girls played for at least half an hour before Alani turned toward Quinn. She held her arms up, waving.

"Come on out," she called, a smile in her voice. "The water is warm!"

Quinn shook her head. "You girls go ahead. I'm fine here," she yelled, loud enough for her voice to carry to Alani.

She wished she could go out there and be as carefree as Alani. She loved to look at the water, smell the salty spray, and imagine herself enjoying it like others did. She wondered what it would feel like to just drop her fear and embrace one of nature's biggest gifts.

Small steps, though. She'd stood up to Ethan that day, and that was one shark too many.

Slowly, she breathed out. Then in. Then out again, letting the fresh air fill her. Revive her spirit. It truly did feel peaceful, and she wondered how her mother had ever decided to leave. The powerful harmony of Maui felt like a sure fit for her mother's laid-back personality. Quinn was old enough now—or at least mature enough—to know that something bad must've happened for her mother to up and leave such a magical place. Maui was her mom's home, her birthplace. Could it really only be infatuation with a boy that had led her away?

Unless that was a lie too.

Quinn hadn't even thought of that. If her mother had lied about who her father was, maybe she'd lied about where she'd come from.

No. Something in Quinn's gut felt the pull of Maui so strongly that she felt she had to have blood ties there somewhere. If it turned out she didn't, she'd be devastated. She wasn't sure why, but the small island spoke to her, somewhere deep within.

Quinn wanted to claim it too.

Down the beach she saw a family gathered under a flimsy cabana tent. An old woman sat in a chair right in the middle of the gathering, children and a few adults on towels around her. Something about them made Quinn think they were locals. Dressed in worn beachwear, they fit into the scene naturally.

They were people who could very well be related to her mother. To her.

Every native Hawaiian she saw now made her wonder.

Quinn needed to make time for more research.

She returned her gaze to the girls. Alani and Junie were coming out of the water, their small legs lifting high to step over the waves as they clutched each other to keep from falling.

"Quinn?" said a voice from behind her.

Quinn turned to find Maria coming from the other direction. She had one hand on her hair, trying to keep it from flying into her eyes.

"Kupuna's friend is here. Do you want to come up and hear what he has to say about the kitchen counters?"

Quinn nodded, then stood and gathered her things. Alani had seen her mother, knowing their water time was being cut short. She and Junie ran up, and Alani threw her arms around her mother's waist.

"Ah, you're getting me wet, daughter," Maria said, laughing. "Let's go, girls. You need to get into some dry clothes."

Like a line of chicks behind a mother hen, Quinn and the girls followed Maria up the trail and to the house.

The sand was so soft and deep that it made walking difficult. Yet Maria was fast, nearly walking on top of the sand. *An expert,* Quinn thought, then remembered that the woman wasn't much older than she was. She just came across as older because of her sadness and responsibilities.

In the back lanai, the girls stopped at the outdoor shower.

"Rinse, then dry off before you come in the house," Maria said.

"You can do your feet first, Quinn," Alani said, moving over.

Quinn slipped off her sandals and rinsed her feet, glad that Alani had mentioned it. She would've walked straight into the back door and trailed sand on Maria's—well, on her own—kitchen floor and made herself look oblivious.

Instead, she tiptoed over to the door and set her shoes next to the pile of others left there, then stepped in.

Kupuna and a man were sitting at the table, the stranger's back to Quinn.

"Who you got on your crew now?" Kupuna asked him.

Maria cleared her throat. "Liam, let me introduce you to Quinn Maguire. She's the one who bought the house, and, of course, she'd like to be a part of the conversation."

Quinn approached, business face on and hand extended. She wasn't starting off another relationship too friendly like she'd accidentally done with Maria. She knew how to get things done in the corporate world, and she was going to use those skills to turn this into a once-and-done quick project so she could prove to Ethan she was capable. She had also watched enough home improvement shows to know that contractors were notorious for being irresponsible, childish bullies. She would have to assert herself right away.

The contractor pushed his chair back and stood, then turned to face her. Hawaiian for sure, but perhaps of Asian descent too. Whatever his heritage, it made for an interesting blend of features. He was a big man—tall and obviously strong—reminding Quinn of a large oak tree.

He nodded quietly, then took her hand. His was warm. "Very nice to meet you." A small smile began to spread over his face.

Something wasn't right. Quinn didn't get a bully vibe from him, but she did feel a sense of déjà vu.

"Again," he added, an amused glint in his eyes.

She studied his face, then noticed his arm and the tribal tattoo that snaked around his bicep.

"You're the surfer," she said, feeling strangely insecure.

"Sometimes," he said. "Today I'm a contractor."

"You two know each other?" Maria asked.

Kupuna was quiet as he rubbed at the table's scars under his fingers, listening intently.

"No," Quinn said quickly. "He was just on the resort beach at the same time as I was and asked if I wanted to paddleboard."

"Why were you out there?" Maria asked him. "You know you don't like to share the water with the tourists."

He shrugged. "I needed a change of scenery. Not sure why, I just felt drawn there on my way to Napili Beach. I go where the ocean pulls me."

Maria narrowed her eyes at him, her expression doubtful.

He ignored her silent reproach and turned his gaze to Quinn.

"I'd like to hear your ideas about the kitchen," he said to Quinn, finally breaking the awkward silence. He pulled a pad and pen from his shirt pocket, prepared to take notes.

Quinn relaxed. Maria took a chair next to her father, and the contractor—Liam—waited for her to respond. She felt relief. She wasn't going to have to argue to be able to plan her own kitchen. She started with the shabby Formica surface.

"Okay, I want new countertops for sure. Something not too modern, but definitely more updated than this," she said, running a hand along it.

"We can do that. Easy," Liam said. "I suppose you want granite?"

She raised her eyebrows at him. "You suppose?"

He nodded. "Most of the mainlanders who buy or build here want granite."

Quinn turned to Maria. "What do you think, Maria? I don't want to be like *most of the mainlanders.*"

Maria didn't reply. She looked thoughtful.

Realization flooded through Quinn. "Oh, Maria, I'm so sorry. How insensitive to ask your opinion when this is your house I'm remodeling for me."

Maria smiled. "No, it's fine. I'm happy to give my opinion. I love this house, and it deserves to be brought back to its former glory. To be honest, I've always wanted to use maple butcher block to match the cupboards. But soapstone is also nice."

"Both sound lovely, but I think I'll go with soapstone." Quinn turned her attention back to Liam. "I'm not sure about the cabinets. Do you think they can be cleaned up?"

He paused, studying the cabinet doors. The interiors were glass, but the paint around the panes was peeling. Even yellowed.

He opened one and peered inside.

"They're original," Maria said. "Most kitchens back then had these glass doors."

"I think I can clean them up and paint them white. Shine up that glass and they'll look great and can continue to be a part of this home's history," Liam said. "Where possible, I always try to refresh and preserve."

He looked at Quinn hopefully.

"That sounds perfect," she said. She was all for keeping the integrity of the house, if at all possible.

The girls burst into the back door and ran through, headed to Alani's room in a rush of flying hair and giggles. The interruption lightened the mood, and Liam seemed to relax.

"We could do wood paneling in here and paint it white too. That will give you more of a beach-cottage feel, which I'm sure you're looking for."

"As long as it's that shiplap stuff." She didn't mention she only knew about it from Chip and Joanna's makeover show.

"We can do that," Liam said. "Shiplap would look good too. And I hope you aren't planning on putting in new floors. These are original tongue-and-groove fir. They used to have a ruddy glow, and with some tender loving care, we can get them back to it."

"My thoughts exactly," Quinn said, feeling triumphant that they were all on the same page.

"I plan on helping with the floors," Kupuna said. "Pali and I will sand them, and you can finish them, Liam."

Right on cue, Pali arrived, slamming through the door. He took a chair next to Kupuna.

"I heard my name, Kupuna. What are you volunteering me for?" he asked.

Quinn noticed a huge difference in his tone with his grandfather in the room. Absent was the sarcasm—in its place, a welcome inflection of respect.

"We're going to help improve this kitchen," Kupuna said. He reached over until his hand was on Pali's arm; then he patted it affectionately.

Pali's eyes glittered at her, a simmering of resentment he was too dutiful to verbalize in his grandfather's presence. "Whatever you say, Kupuna," he said, slowly speaking the words.

"I'll make a note of that on the estimate," Liam said. "I won't have to hire a big crew, and that'll bring the cost down."

Quinn couldn't imagine the old man working on his knees, but she wouldn't insult him by saying so. After all, maybe he only meant to supervise Pali. She hoped the kid would do a good job.

"And we can help with the wood paneling," Maria said. "Quinn, can you paint?"

Pali laughed as though he found the idea ridiculous.

Quinn didn't appreciate it either. She could paint. But she wasn't going to be there indefinitely.

"Liam, how long do you think this will all take?" she asked, dodging Maria's question.

He scribbled on his pad for a moment, then looked up.

"It depends. I'm working another project, but I can squeeze in a few hours a day. The cabinets will take a week; the countertops can be done in a day or two. We can't start on the floors until those are done, but we can put up the shiplap and paint."

Quinn sighed. There was no way he'd finish before she had to leave.

"Can you give me an estimate on the cost?" she asked.

"Let me check some costs on the materials, and I'll get it to you tomorrow afternoon."

"Don't forget the family discount," Maria said.

Liam laughed, and Pali joined him.

"I thought you were only friends?" Quinn said, thinking she'd been had. She looked from Maria to Kupuna.

"We are friends. And family," Kupuna said. "In Hawaii, family comes first. We all help feed each other. He will be honest, and he will do the best job for the lowest price he can give and still make a profit."

Quinn didn't have an answer for that. As for family coming first, she could've pointed out that they were all sitting there together because Maria's husband, Jaime, had abandoned ship. But she couldn't bring herself to cause Maria any more pain. And it wasn't as though Quinn had much experience with family, other than her mother. She only hoped that she really was getting a good deal on the work and would end up with stellar results and not shoddy workmanship.

Liam flipped his notebook shut and pushed it back into his shirt pocket.

"Are you at least licensed?" Quinn asked, thinking that would be the very first question that Ethan would belt out.

All eyes were suddenly on her, and they weren't friendly.

Liam nodded. "Yes, I'm bonded and licensed. Now, if you're satisfied with that and don't require references or a criminal background screening, we can get this going. Tomorrow we'll look at the rest of the house and see if we need to address anything else," he said.

Getting references probably wouldn't be a bad thing, Quinn thought, but she held her tongue.

Maria clapped her hands together. "Great. Now it's time for lunch. Sit down, Liam, and let me fill your tank before you go. You too, Quinn," Maria said.

"I'm not arguing," Liam said. "But I'll need to eat and run. I got another job to bid on over in Kihei." He slid into the chair across from Kupuna. Gone was the businesslike persona, and in its place, he looked comfortable and at home. He turned his attention to the old man.

"Kupuna, do I have a story for you. You missed it Friday night at the poké shack."

Kupuna leaned back in his chair, ready to listen. Maria started a racket, pulling pots and pans from the cupboards. Across the house, the girls could be heard chattering, a movie on in the background.

Their normal felt so abnormal to Quinn. She was not a part of their puzzle.

"I'm not hungry," she said, ignoring the growl of protest from her stomach. "I have some work to do."

Maria looked as though she wanted to try to convince Quinn to stay but caught herself and held up a hand. She gave her a wave.

"Okay," she said. "If you change your mind, there'll be leftovers."

The others didn't even look at her as Quinn slipped out the door.

Chapter Seven

Quinn opened a can of tuna and paired it with saltines for her lunch. She pulled a bottle of water out of the fridge and went to the couch, settling herself in front of her laptop.

As she ate, she worked, spending an hour or so answering emails. When she felt caught up, she went to the bed and lay across it, groaning happily at the comfort that embraced her. Maria had taken off the brightly colored bedspread that Pali had used, and in its place was the softest, most feminine white comforter that Quinn had ever touched. It wasn't new—it had that homemade, used feel to it that was just right. Super lightweight too. Just right for the warm Maui air.

She wondered if Maria would sell it to her before she left.

At the foot of the bed was another new addition. Quinn reached for it and pulled the crocheted coverlet up and over her. It was a soft teal-green color, reminiscent of ocean water, or even beach glass.

Maria had great taste.

Quinn sighed, letting all her stress go. Lying down in the middle of the afternoon was completely out of character for her. Ethan always said people who napped were wasting their minutes, and those minutes added up to years over time.

Either the cottage was just too cozy or the stress must've been getting to her more than she even knew, because within two minutes everything faded out around her, and she fell into a deep sleep.

She woke nearly two hours later, feeling more refreshed than she could remember in a long time. She peeked out the door, curious as to what was going on. The main house was quiet, almost eerily so, and with that, she decided to take advantage of the moment.

Grabbing a blanket from the back of the love seat, she went out to the lanai.

She pushed the small table aside and shook the blanket out onto the wooden planks. She settled onto it, crossing her legs before closing her eyes for a moment.

It was rare that she got to practice yoga. Ethan thought it a bunch of useless mumbo jumbo and encouraged her to stick to the stationary bike or jogging, whatever could burn calories the fastest. It wasn't worth the ridicule to try to do it at home where he could walk in on her. And with her work schedule, there wasn't a lot of time to sneak it in elsewhere either.

She'd actually forgotten how calming it could be. Stretching her arms over her head, she wiggled her fingertips to the sky, exhaling as she reached higher and higher. She moved gently forward until she was on her hands and knees, then raised her middle until she was in downward dog.

"Why do I keep finding you in compromising positions?"

She dropped quickly, embarrassed to find Liam standing over her.

"I don't know. Why do I keep finding you standing over me?" she asked, irritated by his stealthy approach.

He didn't pick up on the hint to leave her alone. Obvious from the short laugh.

"What are you doing here? I thought you were coming back tomorrow?" She pulled at the tank top she wore, covering the square of cleavage there.

He sat down at the table. "No, I said I'd get you the estimate tomorrow. This is Tuesday. I always come on Tuesday afternoons and help Maria with dinner. I brought the pork."

"Oh. I guess I could've helped." She stood, wiping her hands together to rid them of invisible dust. Anything to keep from looking at him.

"She hasn't started yet, so she'll welcome that, I'm sure," he said. "There'll be about sixteen to twenty people coming."

Her head jerked up at that. "Sixteen to twenty?"

He nodded. "She does it every Tuesday. Friends and family, and whoever in the neighborhood is having a tough time knows they can stop by and feed their kids. Everyone brings a little something and together, it goes a long way."

Quinn sat down at the table. "That's really . . . admirable."

He shrugged. "It's not about that. It's just the way it's done here. My mother does the same thing on Sundays. Maria, Kupuna, and the kids usually come. They weren't there last week. I think that's because of what's going on here."

Her face flamed, but she wouldn't let him get away with making her feel guilty. She lifted her chin. "Look, I didn't know anything about Maria's troubles. I just bought a house that was for sale. I paid, and the contracts were signed, fair and square. Everything was legal."

He paused, scrutinizing her before continuing. "I'm not judging you, Quinn. I'm just telling you the facts."

Now she really did feel guilty. There was no judgment in his eyes. Only compassion for the family. "Sorry. I'm a bit defensive. This has put me in a bad position, but I still don't like seeing a woman as nice as Maria going through something like this."

"It's a sad situation," he said.

"Do you have any idea why her husband left?"

"I'd be the last one to try to understand what goes on between a husband and wife behind closed doors. And I'm not one for gossiping. They call that the 'coconut wireless' around here." He smiled lightly. "I leave that to others who are better at it than me."

"Oh, I wasn't asking for gossip," Quinn said. "I just wish there was some way I could help Maria."

"You're doing that now," he replied. "Most mainlanders would've kicked her out the day they got here to claim their property. You're giving her some time to figure out what to do. The whole family is talking it over, though resources are scarce for everyone."

They let the silence fall around them for a moment.

He looked up, his expression changing. "Oh, I also wanted to tell you that Maria showed me some old hurricane shutters in the attic. She said she'd forgotten about them. I think they'll look nice cleaned up."

Quinn felt a rush of excitement. Hurricane shutters would really help move the house more toward the beach-cottage look she was envisioning.

"I'd like that," she said.

"Good. Maria was hoping you'd say that. She's wanted them back up for years. It'll be easy. We just have to clean them, then sand them down and paint them a soft shade of white. With a little work, they'll be good to go."

"Thanks." Quinn could see the list getting longer and the money adding up. She hoped he wouldn't charge too much for adding the shutters on. She still had a healthy balance from the inheritance, but beyond what she'd allotted for remodeling issues, she considered the balance her nest egg, or her just-in-case money. Just in case of what, she wasn't sure yet.

"No problem," he said. "Want to talk story?"

"Talk story?"

He laughed. "Sorry, I forgot you're new here. Talking story just means we share something about ourselves. Our family. Our life."

She felt herself tense. That was an abrupt turn. Too abrupt, actually.

"It's complicated." She fidgeted with her toes against the leg of the table.

He shrugged. "I get it. You're guarding your privacy, and that's good. If you want to talk, though, I'm all ears." He pulled his ears forward like a monkey, and Quinn laughed.

He did have a way about him, she had to admit. He could go from tough guy to silly in a matter of seconds. She supposed sharing a little with him wouldn't hurt.

"I bought this house with money from my mother," she said.

He raised his eyebrows. "Now that's a good mom."

"The only problem is, I don't know where she got the money. She's native Hawaiian. She left here when she was pregnant with me, and we've always lived a simple life."

"So ask her?" he said.

"She passed away a few months ago. It was an inheritance."

His eyes turned sad. "I'm sorry."

Quinn nodded.

"What about a relative? Maybe someone recently left it to her, and she didn't have time to spend it before leaving it to you?" he asked.

"We never came back to visit, and I don't know any of my relatives." She closed her eyes for a second, frustrated at herself for revealing too much. He sure had a way about him.

He looked taken aback. "None of your relatives?"

"None," Quinn said, her voice so low it was almost a whisper. She opened her eyes and looked at him, smiling to hide her pain. "My mother cut off communication with her family when I was too young to remember. I'm pretty much an orphan. Unless there's some long-lost kin here waiting to embrace me with open arms, and believe me—that's a long shot. Especially seeing how I don't know how to find any of them."

Liam shook his head. "Wow. I can't imagine that. Here in Hawaii, *ohana* is everything. Not knowing your family must've been unbearable."

"It wasn't so bad," she lied.

His expression turned serious. "You know that coconut wireless I mentioned? Maui isn't very big. I'm sure I could ask around about your family. If you want me to, I mean."

Quinn weighed the possibility. Did she really want to know? She thought about the lineage company she'd sent her DNA off to. Was a part of her relieved that nothing had shown up? Life had been simple with only her mother to feel officially attached to. Later, when she and Ethan became official, it would get more complicated. How crazy would it get if she found a grandmother? Or cousins? Or, God forbid, unearthed her wayward father?

The thought made her feel a nervous flutter in her stomach.

"Thanks. I'll think about it," she said.

He started to say something else but was interrupted by Maria poking her head out the back door of the main house.

"You two planning to help out?" she called.

Liam tilted his head toward Quinn, a silent challenge.

"So . . . you want to learn how to feed a bunch of hungry Hawaiians?"

Quinn took a deep breath. It was ironic how much alone time she no longer had now that she'd bought a house. She gazed toward the cottage door. Her laptop was just on the other side, and she should probably do some more research. And call Ethan. She should contact her boss, too, to ask for another week. There were also nearly thirty more work emails she should answer.

She gazed back at him.

Everything else could wait.

"Fine. Let's get it over with," she said. After all, she'd wanted to learn more about her mother's culture, even if it did challenge her to put her introverted tendencies aside.

∽

Quinn leaned back, taking in the sight before her. It was dusk, and as the sun set gently over the water, she couldn't imagine a cozier scene. While the grounds on the resort were exquisitely designed and meticulously maintained, the atmosphere didn't hold a candle to what Quinn was feeling on this tourist-free sliver of beauty that Maria's family inhabited.

This was the Maui she'd wanted to see. To feel. Not the fancied-up resorts and golf courses that she worked in every day.

Preparing dinner and then sampling all the dishes was a test of endurance that Quinn almost failed. The food was simple, but delicious and plentiful. Her mother had introduced her to a few Hawaiian recipes growing up, but somehow she missed giving her the experience of tasting *laulau*. Quinn didn't understand why, because it was now officially her favorite food.

With Maria's supervision, she'd wrapped small portions of pork in layers of taro leaves, and then Liam had set them outside to cook in the underground hot-rock oven. When it was done, it created a deliciously smoky taste. The leaves had softened, and the meat was so juicy and tender that it melted in Quinn's mouth.

She went for seconds and wished for thirds.

There were also several different kinds of sushi and the mung bean noodles cooked in chicken broth that her mother had always loved. The table was overflowing with dishes people brought in, as everyone came with something, whether it was a simple fruit or a jug of homemade wine.

The biggest surprise was Maria's cookies. Quinn had never tasted anything like them. She was glad she'd gotten to have one, as they were the first thing to disappear once the people started arriving. Many of them got the cookies even before their main dishes, just to be sure they had one at the end of their meals. The cookies were small, buttery squares of shortbread—but unlike any shortbread Quinn had ever had. She'd asked what was in them, but Maria wouldn't tell.

"A secret recipe," Kupuna had muttered from where he sat at the table.

Maria laughed. "He's right. It's secret. My mother passed it to me. She worked in the cafeteria for one of the public schools here. Every day she baked the cookies and stacked them in five-gallon tins. They sold for a nickel, and the kids took them home wrapped in wax paper. People here on the island have been trying to re-create this recipe for thirty years."

"I bet I can figure it out," Pali said as he tried to peek over her shoulder.

She shooed him away. "One day your wife will get the recipe," she said, laughing at his antics. "It will be your inheritance. If you behave."

Quinn thought of her mother again, and the mysterious money.

While Maria was busy in the kitchen, Alani introduced Quinn around. The faces were so many that they blurred together. One small, elderly woman made quite an impact on Quinn, though. She introduced herself as Gracie Wang of the original Wang family, whose ancestor was washed onto the island of Honolulu from a shipwreck in the early 1800s. Her great-grandfather had jumped island and made his fortune in the Maui sugar plantations, then married a local woman. Auntie Wang, as she said she preferred to be called, was clearly proud of her heritage and made for an interesting character.

The entire affair was a flurry of activity, and everyone pitched in to put the kitchen and patio back together before most of them headed to the beach. Quinn followed and was amazed that in the blink of an eye, a circle of chairs and logs was set up, and someone had started a bonfire. As the adults found somewhere to sit, Alani and Junie and the other children ran around chasing the surf back and forth as their laughter rang out.

Quinn took a chair and used her feet to dig into the sand, letting it roll over her toes in a cocoon of warmth. Maria took the chair beside her.

Liam had disappeared briefly, but now he emerged from the path, leading Kupuna with one hand and holding a ukulele in the other.

There was something about the way he led the old man. Liam was gentle, guiding Kupuna around a few piles of brush, then to one of the best chairs, obviously left just for him. Kupuna settled in, staring off like he'd been prone to do.

Liam took a seat on a log and turned to the guy beside him to talk.

Then it hit her. And she felt immensely ignorant. In the glow of the firelight, she could feel her face burn with embarrassment at her oversight.

Kupuna was blind.

She should've figured it out earlier. So many times he'd stared off into space and had never made direct eye contact with her. She just hadn't put two and two together. Now she felt ashamed for being so nonchalant about meeting him. About talking to him. About how she'd treated him. That was what her brain was throwing at her faster than she could process. Just when she thought the situation about displacing a family couldn't get worse, it did.

Now she was throwing a blind man out of his house? She felt sick.

Maria settled back into her chair, then turned to Quinn. "Well, you ready to hear Liam make some music?"

"Why didn't you tell me?" Quinn whispered.

"Tell you what? That he plays? Just about everybody and their cousin plays around here. Liam just happens to be better at it than most."

"No, not that. Why didn't you tell me your father is blind?" Quinn asked.

Maria turned to look at her, though in the dimness it was hard to distinguish her expression. "I didn't think I needed to. Couldn't you determine that on your own?"

"No," Quinn said. But what she thought was of course she couldn't, because she was self-centered and focused only on getting what she wanted. She was a terrible human being, and every day she was there she was being reminded of it.

Maria put a hand out and squeezed her knee. It felt awkward, someone touching her with affection. "I think if I told Kupuna what you just said, it would just make his day. He never wants to be treated differently because of his loss of sight. And once he finds out he got past you for quite a while, you just might be his new favorite person."

Quinn didn't reply. Before she could think too deeply on Maria's words, Liam started to strum. Suddenly, his music lulled everyone into a quieter state. It was slow and sweet, and when he added his voice to it, it was pure magic. The soft sounds he was making were a direct contradiction to the raw, masculine figure that he cut. Quinn wondered who his significant other was, as it was a song clearly written out of love.

As the melody wafted through the night air, even the kids returned to the circle, perching on knees or finding another place to sit, drawn like moths to a flame. Quinn found herself falling into the moment, the tension she usually carried fading away until her body felt light and free.

"He had his heart broken once," Maria said, seemingly reading her mind. "It was a long time ago. That's how he is able to play so passionately."

When he slipped into a more melancholy tune, Quinn realized Liam was a man who knew sadness. Maria was right. No one could sing like that unless they'd known sorrow.

She was just about to ask Maria about it when, from the glow of the firelight, she saw a glint of a tear on her face.

Quinn leaned over close to her. "What's wrong?"

Maria shook her head. When the song was over, she turned to Quinn.

"There's a long story behind those words," she said. "And that was also Jaime's favorite song. Liam always played it for him. I miss him sitting here next to me, listening. We were supposed to grow old together, watching our children's children play on this very same beach."

Quinn didn't know what to say. How could a woman miss a husband who had wronged her so deeply? It was unimaginable. Abandoning a family without even leaving word of why?

"I'm sorry," she said, unable to think of anything better.

"I just worry about him," Maria whispered. "Our marriage was good. This doesn't make sense. But I pray to the gods every night that they will watch over him, wherever he is and whatever he is doing. That he will just make it through to the next morning. Then I begin the prayers again at daylight."

That was a serious case of commitment, Quinn thought. If Ethan dropped out of her life without a trace, she'd probably find a voodoo doll and stick pins in it every night, not say prayers of protection for him.

Liam started another song, the lyrics telling of a couple destined to be together but parted by a long distance. It seemed all of his songs were also stories.

But Quinn's mind was still on Maria. She realized that despite their different paths in life—one of them focusing on family and the other on career—they had a lot in common. Both of them were weighed down under a mystery that caused them worry and anguish. Maria didn't know what had happened to her husband and the marriage she thought was solid, and Quinn was clueless about where and whom she came from.

Would either of their mysteries be solved? Quinn didn't know the answer to that, but she did know that for the first time in a long time, she felt a kinship to someone other than her mother.

Then she had an epiphany.

What Maria needed most right now was to find out what had happened to her husband. Liam had to know something. Or his famous coconut wireless could find out. As he said, Maui wasn't that big, so how far could one man go?

Liam was the key to finding Jaime. And maybe her dad, too, if she ever decided she was ready to look. Quinn wouldn't take no for an answer. And when they found Jaime, he'd better be ready to be blasted, because Quinn wouldn't leave him alone until he found a way to make right all the things he'd done wrong. She'd make him face Maria and his responsibilities. It wasn't fair for Maria to struggle through such huge life changes alone.

If Maria had her husband to help them out, then Quinn also wouldn't feel so guilty about taking their home.

That settled it. She'd call her boss in the morning. He'd be shocked, but she was going to ask for a leave of absence. As for Ethan, he would just have to keep managing without her for a bit longer.

The song reached a crescendo, and a lump formed in Quinn's throat.

This time she reached out. Her hand found Maria's, and they clasped fingers, bonding as only two lonely women could do as, together, they listened to Liam's love song.

Chapter Eight

Quinn woke to a racket. A door slammed. Then a loud clatter. Door slam again. A minute or two later, another clatter.

Groggy from lack of sleep, she looked at the clock on the nightstand.

Six fifteen. Only a few days in Maui, and she was already easing into the laid-back lifestyle, reluctant to get up until she felt completely rested.

She groaned, then rolled out of bed and went to the window, peeking out from the side to remain hidden.

Liam was there, and just as she looked, he dropped another shutter onto a pile he'd built near the main house lanai. He hesitated, then turned to the window, his gaze curious.

Quinn jerked back, feeling exposed. How had he known she was there?

She backed away and went back to the bed, climbed in, and pulled the sheet up to her chin. She wasn't ready to face the morning.

Couldn't a girl ever sleep in?

Quinn was angry at herself, because after the beach scene broke up and they all cleaned up, she'd walked the trail back to the cottage alone. She felt restless inside, wanting something but not quite sure what it was.

When she'd finally gone to bed about midnight or so, it had only gotten worse, leaving her staring at the ceiling for hours until she finally fell asleep.

Then she'd dreamed of trying to find her way out of the world's largest cornfield maze. The frustration of not knowing which way to turn or how to find the exit made her feel as though she hadn't slept a wink.

But it was time to get moving. She had two goals to accomplish: discover her roots and get her house completed. That was it.

Oh, and find Jaime. If she could find a way to put Maria's fractured family back together again, it would bring her a sense of satisfaction and help ease the guilt of displacing them.

She had a lot to do.

Her phone lay on the nightstand, and she reached over and pressed the "Home" key. A few email notifications came up, but nothing from Ethan. He was punishing her, hoping she'd call and beg him to join her and fix her life.

Determined to get moving now, she tried again. Roll forward, feet on the floor, then a beeline for the shower. Ten minutes of scalding hot water and she started to feel human again.

She stepped out and rolled her hair in a towel before wrapping another around her body. Quickly, she applied her makeup, finishing it off with a soft pink lipstick. Her casual color, she liked to think of it.

When she leaned forward to see the end result, she wasn't impressed. The makeup didn't do a lot to cover the damage of a sleepless night. She should've brought her eye cream. In the anxiety storm leading to her trip, she'd forgotten a lot of necessities.

Well, it couldn't be helped. Moving on, she dried her hair, then twisted it up and secured it with a pearl-encrusted comb. She dressed in crisp white linen pants and a billowy sky-blue blouse. Only then did she allow herself to go to the small kitchen and make her first cup of coffee and grab a bagel from her tiny fridge. She toasted it, coated it with cream cheese, and took it and the coffee out to the lanai. Then she came back in for her laptop.

Returning to the lanai, she set the computer down and opened it, fingers crossed that overnight something magic had happened. She signed on, then took a bite and a drink as she waited for it to load up.

Around her, the birds chirped and a breeze brought her the scent of the lovely pink plumeria flowers that graced a tree just behind her. She loved the cozy porch. It was quickly becoming her favorite morning spot.

When her Lineage page popped up, she almost dropped her coffee. There were nine results in the "New Ancestor" section. Her heart thumped, and she reminded herself to stay calm, that it didn't necessarily mean anything. She needed matches from the same geographical area where she was looking—in her case, Maui. The thing about online genealogy searches was that it was like a team sport. It needed participants to strengthen and increase results. What if no one closely related to Quinn had ever dreamed of finding out more about their DNA? That could lead to a lot of dead ends.

She'd also read that some of the matches would turn out to be genealogists with extensive family trees, and not necessarily anyone close enough to have the information she sought.

Still, she quickly sent off a few inquiries through the Lineage database, asking those indicated as new ancestors if they knew or were related to any Sennas from Maui. When she finished, she leaned back, her hands shaking.

Liam chose that moment to burst out of the main house, some sort of power tool in his hands. He waved, and much to her chagrin, he crossed the area between them, arriving on her porch before she could get up and make a quick retreat.

Quinn closed her laptop.

"Do you wake up looking like that?" he asked, leaning over the railing and examining her from head to toe.

"What is that supposed to mean?" She kept her tone neutral. He wasn't going to goad her into bickering back and forth.

He shrugged, and his muscles rippled, distracting her from her train of thought.

"I just mean it's early. You look nice and all that, but are you going somewhere fancy already this morning? Don't you ever just let your hair down and leave your face clean?"

Now she was getting mad.

"My face *is* clean," she said, sending the words through gritted teeth.

"I just meant without makeup. I'll bet you look really good all natural, your skin free and your hair loose."

He was wrong about that, but he'd never see it.

"Well, anyway"—he stood and looked at the pile of shutters—"I thought you might want to help get those shutters ready while I work on pulling the cabinet doors off."

She didn't respond right away because, truthfully, the thought of doing the shutters herself really appealed to her, but not if he was going to be supervising her.

"Or . . . ," he said, stretching the word out, "I could just wait until Pali gets out of school and pay him to do all of them. But that'll add to the overall project costs, and I thought I'd save you a buck or two."

She thought of her goals and knew that Liam was probably going to be her best bet to get started in her search for Maria's husband. That meant that at some point, they were going to have to talk anyway.

"Fine," she said. "I can scrub and sand, if you show me how. But I don't know how to use power tools."

He smiled. "Anything will help my to-do list. But remember, we'll need to clean them good before we can even start to sand. Maria can show you where to get the bucket and a scrub brush."

"We? I thought you were going to work on the cabinet doors?"

"I am, but I'll need to come by every now and then and make sure you aren't taking any shortcuts," he said, winking at her. "Are you at least going to change clothes?" he asked, his eyes trailing down the legs of her white pants.

"Of course I am," she snapped. "But can I drink my coffee in peace first?"

He laughed. "Sassy. Good. I can handle sassy, as long as that means you'll have a lot of energy to get the job done."

~

Quinn stood, arched her back, and put her arms in the air to stretch. The shutters were clean, but it had taken just about as much elbow grease as she could muster. Maria had come out and offered to help, but when she mentioned that she was in the process of applying for jobs online, Quinn sent her back in. She needed a job more than Quinn needed help with the shutters.

Her body hurt, but it was a good kind of hurt. She felt useful.

Liam did make frequent stops to see how she was doing, but he was already coming out there to set up the cabinet doors. He planned to do some of the work there before taking them all to his shop to refinish them. When he began scrubbing them down not ten feet from Quinn, they worked quietly, separate but together.

Now she was done, but he still had a lot of windows to go. She should offer to help.

"Hey, you want to help me hit those last two?" He looked up and pointed at the end of the line. Apparently, everyone in Hawaii could read minds.

"Of course," she said. She was actually enjoying herself.

Before they could start, Maria called out that lunch was ready. They ate sandwiches with a delicious macaroni salad that Maria said was a local favorite. Kupuna joined them, and Quinn felt self-conscious, now unable to stop thinking about his sight. She wondered if his other senses were ultrasensitive. Could he hear her chewing? Breathing? And how did he get around the house so well?

"Kupuna, are you done?" Maria asked, then cleared his plate from the table.

"Mahalo," he thanked her, then stood. "I'm going to take a nap."

He went around the table and out the door, taking the hallway rather swiftly. It simply amazed Quinn. She had never seen the man use a cane, or even his hands, to feel for furniture or obstacles. However, she did notice that he avoided coming out to the lanai once he knew they'd stacked shutters and cupboard doors there.

"We've still got a lot of washing to do on those windows," Liam said. "Want to hit the beach for a quick swim first?"

Quinn wouldn't be swimming, but she did see an opportunity to talk to him about Jaime, so she nodded.

"I'll change and meet you out back," he said.

Quinn took her dish to the sink, but Maria shooed her away. "You've worked hard. Go enjoy yourself for a while."

Maria looked a bit depressed, and Quinn wondered if the job search had discouraged her, but she didn't want to open up a long conversation, so she let it lie and slipped out the back door. At the cottage, she checked her phone, hoping Ethan had called. But there were no missed calls, texts, or even a random email.

She heard the kitchen door slam and jumped up. Liam was ready, and she wasn't. Because it would look suspicious if she didn't dress the part, Quinn quickly changed into her black one-piece suit and tied a sarong around her waist, ensuring her hips were covered. With no time to spare, she slathered sunscreen on her face, neck, and arms, then tucked her feet into her sandals, grabbed a wide-brimmed hat and a towel, and stepped outside.

Liam led the way down the path to the beach. When they reached the sand, he dropped his towel and ran for the surf.

Quinn almost laughed. He was like a kid when it came to the ocean. It seemed to energize him and worked like the fountain of youth. Instantly, the serious contractor was gone, and in his place was an energetic, surf-loving young man.

She lay her towel down and sat, crossing her arms over her knees as she watched Liam dive under an oncoming wave, then burst up and out of the water once it passed.

It made her really nervous, and she could feel her muscles clenching.

He turned and waved, yelling at her to come in.

When she shook her head, he came striding out, water falling from him like a spray of bullets. A young mother and her two toddlers walked by, then entered the water a few feet from where Liam had emerged. The kids were fearless, their comfort around the water obvious in every move.

"What are you doing?" he asked, confused. He picked up his towel and wiped his face. "I thought we were going for a swim."

"I'm okay here, but I'd like to talk to you, if you'll give me a minute." She used her hand to shade her eyes as she looked up at him.

"Is it important?" he asked.

She nodded. "Yes. Very."

"Then you'll need to meet me in my office," he said, then turned and went back to the water.

He was such a frustrating excuse for a man, Quinn thought as she watched him go. Who could have a serious conversation in the ocean? With sharks and all kinds of other strange, indistinguishable fish fluttering around her in the darkness?

When he showed no signs of returning, she gave in. She'd go to the edge of the water, but she was not going past her ankles. She stood and slipped her shoes and then her sarong off, taking her time to build her courage.

She turned toward the ocean.

Please don't eat me alive.

She approached the shoreline. A small ripple reached out and tickled at her toes. When she looked at Liam, he was wearing a wide, satisfied smile that she would've liked to wipe off his face.

"There's nothing to be afraid of," he said, coming in closer and holding out a hand. "The sea is your friend. It doesn't want to hurt you. It wants to comfort you."

She waved his hand off. The surf came rushing in this time and slid over her ankles in a threatening tease before backing off again. "I'm not going all the way in. This is enough. Come closer so we can talk."

"Just a few more steps," he said, his voice cajoling. "At least to your knees. You can't really feel the rhythm of the water unless it's up to your knees."

That was nonsense, but Quinn didn't want to argue. She took another step, letting her feet disappear. Something touched her foot, and Quinn jumped, then felt silly. She could feel her pulse rushing through her, but she realized it wasn't logical to feel so alarmed by the water. She was born in Hawaii! The love of water should be running in her veins, just like it did in his.

It was frustrating, this knowing that she couldn't beat the fear, no matter how irrational she knew it was.

When she looked at him again, the ingratiating smile was gone.

He held his hand out again. "You can do it, Quinn," he said, his tone soft, comforting.

I am a strong woman, she told herself. Then she took a deep breath and another step. She cautiously took Liam's hand, and he led her out a few more feet until the water was at her knees. Her hands shook, and he clasped her fingers tighter.

Quinn tried to pinpoint the emotions racing through her.

It felt terrifying.

And amazing.

She looked into his eyes, and a giggle bubbled up in her throat. When it emerged, he joined her, his laughter mingling with hers. He wasn't making fun of her either. He was celebrating the milestone that he somehow instinctively knew she'd crossed.

She took another step with him leading her, the water waist high now. She marveled at the fact that she was in her thirties and had never been that deep in the ocean before. Her fear of the sea was a mystery to her. Her mother always told her that some people are born with different phobias, and that if she absolutely didn't feel that she could overcome it, then not to worry about it. The water could always be avoided.

But Quinn had worried anyway. She wanted to be strong. Independent. Phobias didn't fit into that description.

"It's nice, eh?" he said.

She nodded. Her breaths were coming fast and ragged, as though she'd just run a mile. The current was stronger than she'd imagined, and she struggled to keep her footing. Another tickle against her ankle caught her attention, and she looked down, seeing a hand-size yellow-and-black fish inches from her.

"I can see a fish," she said, surprised that the water wasn't as dark as her imagination had predicted.

"It's a yellow tang," Liam said. He was staring down too.

She almost screamed, but it wouldn't do to make those around her think there was a shark or something, when it was probably as harmless as an oversize goldfish.

Another wave came crashing toward them, and Quinn felt the sand shift beneath her feet. The waist-high water was quickly chest high, then chin high. She could no longer touch bottom, and she let go of his hands and began to tread water, trying to turn herself toward the beach.

"It's okay, Quinn," he called, his voice getting lost in the wind. He reached for her, but the force of the current pushed her farther away. "Just let the wave carry you."

I will not panic.

Another wave came—this time a big one—and then Quinn was completely underwater and flailing. The wave toppled her until she didn't know which way was up. She screamed, her lungs filling with the salty water that was strangling her.

Her eyes were wide open, and the salt stung. As she thrashed, trying to steady herself, a shadow came sliding in from her peripheral view.

It wasn't Liam.

It was the biggest sea turtle that Quinn had ever seen. It was actually the only sea turtle she'd ever seen in real life, and at first she was terrified. But she realized she wasn't thrashing anymore. The turtle had maneuvered itself just so until it was eye to eye with her, less than a foot away.

Its gaze had calmed her instantly, even as she knew she was nearly out of air.

As she looked into the turtle's eyes, she was taken aback at the intelligence within. She realized the feeling that came over her was a sense of familiarity that was absolutely impossible. Somehow, she knew this creature, and it knew her.

Keeping its eyes locked on hers, it began to move upward, as though showing her the right direction.

Quinn felt the burn again, breaking the magic of the moment and reminding her that she was still lost underwater, her lungs straining under the pressure. Using her arms and feet, she kicked up, and her head broke the surface. She coughed, sputtering water and mucus everywhere. Her eyes burned from the salt, but she still couldn't rub them. She treaded water as fast as she could.

When she could catch a breath, she turned, looking for the turtle, then for Liam. She wasn't a swimmer, but she knew enough to kick her feet and keep her hands going. It was enough to keep her from going under again.

The turtle was gone, and Quinn felt a sense of loss, but Liam saw her and began a mad stroke to cross the distance to her.

He reached her in seconds, grabbing her and holding her up higher out of the water, then pushing her toward the shore. "It's a riptide. Swim that way!" He pointed in a parallel line to the shore.

She dog-paddled, keeping her limbs moving, though now they burned like fire in the cool water. She was exhausted, but Liam stayed next to her, giving her a nudge when she slowed. It was shocking how far out the wave had taken her.

Her breath slowed when the water retreated down to her chest and she could feel the sand under her feet again. She swallowed, proud that she hadn't completely lost it, though without the guidance of the turtle, she felt sure she would be dead.

She continued to move her arms back and forth, wary that the water would deepen again without notice.

"You're fine now," Liam said as he guided her toward the beach.

But she couldn't stop thinking of the strange encounter under the water.

Liam looked stricken as they waded out onto the beach, then fell to the sand to rest. "I'm so sorry, Quinn. I don't know how I lost you like that."

She smiled gently, forgiving him instantly. He probably thought she was angry, but the truth was she felt triumphant. She'd conquered a fear, and more than that, she'd felt something shift inside her. The ocean—and the turtle—had made her feel welcome, both sending warmth down to her very soul, as though telling her they were glad she'd finally come home.

Chapter Nine

They sat side by side on their towels, and Quinn felt a new appreciation for the warmth on her face, as well as for the solid ground beneath her. She wrapped her arms around her legs, resting her chin on her knees as she gazed out at the clear blue water. Now the waves appeared graceful and hospitable, instead of dark and sinister.

She searched for any sign of the turtle, but it had disappeared just as quietly as it had appeared. She decided that, for now, she would keep the experience to herself. It felt too special, and too raw, to share it with anyone yet. All she knew was that if it hadn't come and calmed her and shown her the way up, the outcome of the incident would've been a lot different. Most likely, right now Liam would be comforting a raving-mad lunatic, if she had even survived.

She thought of her mother, who would've been astonished. Ethan would also be surprised, and she couldn't wait to tell him what she'd done. Minus the part about Liam's help, of course.

Liam buried his feet in the sand and sighed loudly.

"Too much excitement for one day," he said.

"I suppose you thought I was going to get all hysterical out there on you," she said, laughing slightly. She was glad he couldn't see how she'd acted under the water before the turtle had come.

He shook his head. "Nope. I sure didn't. You're stronger than you give yourself credit for. I knew you could do it." He reached over and poked her on the arm, smiling. "I didn't mean to lose you out there. I just needed to convince you to give it a try."

"I would've done it eventually," she lied, knowing that it could've been another thirty years before she got the courage to venture past her ankles.

Truthfully, she felt grateful to him. But that could wait.

"Why were you afraid?" he asked.

She shrugged. "I don't really know. I've been frightened of the ocean as far back as I can remember. My mother told me that she took me to Folly Beach when I was five, and I ran when I saw the ocean and refused to come out of the hotel room for two days. It happened again the next time we went, so after that we stopped vacationing near water. A silly fear that I just never outgrew, I guess."

She hoped her voice didn't convey that it was anything but silly to her, despite her words.

He looked pained by her confession. "I think I came out of the womb knowing how to swim and craving the water. It's only out there that I feel completely free, unencumbered by the problems and stresses of this world. The sea doesn't care about any of it, and that nonchalance reminds me that we are only here for a short time and to embrace the gifts of nature while we can."

He was right, of course. Quinn hoped that her newfound courage remained with her and wasn't fleeting. Of course, it would be nice to forget about everything, but right now she couldn't. Real life awaited just beyond the warmth of the sand between her toes.

"Listen, Liam. I need your help," she said.

"I was already going to offer my help," he replied. "Remember the elderly woman you met Tuesday night? Mrs. Wang? She's somewhat of a family tree hobbyist, and I think she could give you some pointers on the best way to trace your family."

"Oh," Quinn said. She had been thinking of the woman just that day when she'd analyzed her DNA report again. Surprisingly, Quinn's ethnicity report showed she was 41 percent East Asian. A mind-blowing discovery, to say the least. Though she wasn't exactly sure what it meant. "That's something to consider. But what I wanted your help with is finding Jaime."

He looked taken aback before he let out a long whoosh of air, grimacing enough to tell her what he thought about that idea.

"Before you say no, just listen," Quinn said. "Maria misses him. And she said he's a good man. What if he didn't want to leave? Maybe something could be done to reunite them. They have a lot of years invested to just throw it away, without even an explanation. She at least deserves that, don't you think?"

He looked at her, his expression sad.

"It's not that I don't want to help. I'd do anything to bring them back together. Not only for Maria but for the kids. Alani cries all the time missing him, and Pali won't talk about him, but I can see it's eating him alive. He needs his dad. But treading into a man's business—especially since he's my cousin—that's just not what we do here."

"I thought the people of Hawaii were all 'Ohana, family first'?"

"We are. If our family wants to remain family. But if they take themselves out of the circle, then we wait for them to come back. On their own."

"Then I'll do it," she said. "Just tell me what kind of car he drives."

She planned to sneak out a family photo and copy it; then she'd go around Maui and look for his car, show his picture, and just poke around to see if she could find any leads.

"Oh, no, I'm not letting you get yourself into trouble," he said. "If you insist on sticking your nose where it doesn't belong, I'd better be there to make sure it doesn't get cut off. I'll give you one afternoon to search, but only if you promise not to go back out and do it alone."

Quinn smiled into her arms. She'd take that. They could find out a lot in an afternoon if they were smart about it.

He stood and held a hand down to help her up.

"We might as well do it before we get back to the windows. Tomorrow I've got a full day of working on those cabinets. Before I start, I'm going to show you how to use a sander so you can knock out those shutters. Any woman who can conquer her fear of the ocean in one swoop can surely learn how to handle a tiny power tool."

"I just need a quick shower," Quinn said. She didn't mention she'd have to slap some makeup on and make herself presentable.

"I'll give you fifteen minutes. Let's go."

Quinn took his hand, and in one swift pull he had her on her feet and then was heading back to the house.

She stood there for a minute. Something inside her felt different— more free, since she'd made a truce with the sea. Another thing: she couldn't wait to get her hands on that sander. Darn right she could handle a power tool.

At least, she hoped she could.

Quinn had never moved so fast to get ready in her life. She cut her shower down to less than four minutes and used the other eleven minutes to dress and put her face on. She'd surprised herself at how efficient she could be when she really needed to.

Now she sat prim and proper in a summery cotton dress and sandals, gazing out the window as Liam drove her to Old Lahaina Town.

They'd decided to stop and talk with Gracie Wang before doing anything else. As Liam pointed out, she might even have some insight about where Maria's husband was hiding out, or at least she could guide them in which way to search. Liam assured Quinn that Auntie Wang knew quite a bit about what went on in Maui, even if she didn't always share it with others.

On the way, they searched a few places for Jaime's car. They went to the lumberyard and drove up and down the rows of cars. Jaime had worked there for more than two decades, and it only made sense to search there first.

Liam said he drove an aqua Toyota Camry, but it wasn't there. They continued to Auntie Wang's neighborhood, keeping their eyes on the road and parking lots for the Toyota until they arrived in Old Town and pulled up into Auntie Wang's driveway.

Liam put the car in park, and they got out.

The house itself was unique. A small, two-story clapboard home with an inviting porch. There were Chinese symbols carved into the middle of her shutters, and a series of chimes hung across the front, their soft tinkles from the wind creating a peaceful sound.

Liam knocked and stood aside, shoulder to shoulder with Quinn. She felt hesitant, still unsure about unloading her biggest secrets onto a stranger. And what if the woman held information that was useful? Was Quinn really ready to hear something that might change her life forever?

She wasn't sure, and that made her heart pound all the harder.

Auntie Wang pulled open the door and smiled, clasping her hands to her chest. "Liam, how nice of you to visit," she exclaimed.

Liam leaned in and kissed her wrinkled cheek, making her blush like a schoolgirl before she turned her attention to Quinn, examining her from head to toe. "Well, hello. I remember you."

"Auntie Wang, we've come calling to ask your advice on an important matter," Liam said. He reached out and took the old woman's hands in his, where they disappeared into the cave of his huge grasp.

Auntie Wang straightened to her full height, her expression turning to one of pride.

"Well, come in, dear. I'll be happy to help if I can." She stood to the side and allowed them to pass.

Now they sat waiting in the front room—the parlor, as the woman called it—while Auntie Wang bumped around in the kitchen preparing tea.

Auntie Wang had answered the door looking very eclectic in a loose, billowy, Chinese-patterned shirt over a flamboyantly Hawaiian sarong. She obviously worked hard to embrace her culture—all of it—and Quinn thought she was nothing less than adorable.

"She's very old school," Liam whispered as she'd retreated, raising his eyebrows at Quinn.

"No kidding," Quinn whispered back.

"We'll loosen her up by talking about your search before we mention Jaime," he said.

Quinn's armpits were beginning to feel swampy.

As they waited, Liam filled her in on the history of the house, warning her that Auntie Wang was very proud and protective of the property. It sat very close to the historical Front Street, and Liam told her it had been in Auntie Wang's family for several generations. It was located very close to the protected Wo Hing Museum and Cookhouse, a landmark of Maui built in 1912 as a social meeting hall for the Chinese who came to Maui on trading or whaling ships, and then later for those brought over to work on the sugarcane plantations and the mills. The building included an upstairs temple for religious ceremonies, but all the social events were held on the bottom level.

Auntie Wang shuffled in as Liam was describing the museum.

"Did you see it?" she asked, setting down a long mahogany board, similar to a cutting board but with a drawer. She pulled open the drawer, lit a tiny candle, and set it inside the board.

"I did," Quinn said. "We drove by it, but I hope to take a peek inside soon."

"Liam should also show you the Chinese Cookhouse," Auntie Wang said, smiling pointedly at Liam, then Quinn.

"What is that?" Quinn asked.

"It's a small wooden shack out back of the museum. Back in the day, it was a community kitchen where my people cooked in huge woks and steamers over wood fires, and many families gathered to eat."

Quinn nodded. "That's so interesting."

"In the Chinese culture as well as the Hawaiian, the kitchen is the center of life," she said, then hurried away again, only to return with an array of dishes and a kettle of water.

They watched Auntie Wang handle the skillful filling and emptying of pots, cups, and bowls. It was especially interesting when she poured the first steeping over some tiny clay animals that she'd set on her tea board.

"She feeds the animals for good luck," Liam said quietly. "See how dark her animals are? That means she's a very experienced tea taster."

Auntie Wang smiled quietly as she listened to his explanation.

Finally, she set a tiny cup in front of Quinn, then one in front of Liam.

"Sip slowly," she said. "Tea is not a simple beverage. It is an experience, meant to be appreciated. The small cups are a reminder that truly original tea leaves are scarce, and the tea they make should be highly prized."

Quinn took a tiny sip of the steaming concoction and let it swirl around her mouth. It tasted light and flowery.

"This is Dragon Pearl Jasmine tea from the Fujian province. If I haven't lost my touch, it should taste mildly sweet and a bit floral," Auntie Wang said.

"It's perfect," Liam said, nodding his appreciation.

"Very good," Quinn added. That was the truth. Never a big fan of hot tea, she was pleasantly surprised that she liked it.

"So, Liam, tell me what brings you by," Auntie Wang finally said.

He gestured at Quinn. "I'm going to let Quinn start."

Quinn smiled gently at Auntie Wang. "Liam told me that you dabble in genealogy, and I just happen to be looking for any family related to my mother. Or my father. I've never known any of my relatives other than my mother."

Auntie Wang frowned; her lips puckered as though she'd gotten a bad tea leaf stuck in her teeth. She leaned in, all her attention on Quinn.

"That's a shame. *Ohana* means 'family,' and they are the ones we live with, laugh with, and love with. To be without your family must be terrible. Tell me more."

Quinn took a deep breath. She hadn't truly admitted it yet, but since her mother had passed away, the loneliness of having no family had been eating her alive. The old woman was right, and it felt almost physically painful to admit it and let her secrets out.

"Yes, it's hard. But that's why I'm here. My mother is from Maui, or at least that's what she always told me. She met my father here, and then they ran away to the mainland, but she said he left us shortly after I was born. I've only had a name and never a face to remember. Now that she has passed, I've discovered that the name I had wasn't actually that of my father. I have no idea who my real father is. That's a big part of why I'm here, to see what I can find out."

"What about your mother's family? Are they still here?" Auntie Wang asked.

"I don't know who they are," Quinn said. "My mother was estranged from them, but she never said why."

"There must be a story there, dear," Auntie Wang said. "It would take a lot to divide a young woman from those who love her."

Quinn shrugged. "Once I hit my teenage years, I assumed it was because she'd gotten pregnant and they had a problem with it, causing her to leave. I never pushed her for an explanation."

Auntie Wang nodded, her expression kind and understanding.

"Would you like to share your mother's family name?" she asked.

"It's Senna," Quinn said. "Elizabeth Senna."

"Hmm," Auntie Wang said. "I know of a few Sennas. I could ask around."

"I've searched online but haven't found anyone related to her. So I don't even know if the name she used was real." It felt frightening at first, talking about her life, but, gradually, the fear began to transform into relief. She was finally getting the words out.

"You have a birth certificate, right?" Auntie Wang asked.

"I do."

"Have you ever applied for a passport?" Liam asked.

"No, why?"

He grimaced. "I hate to tell you, but if you can't find any of your mother's family here, for all we know, your birth certificate could be counterfeit. The only time they are examined closely is if you apply for a passport."

"And your father's name is on the certificate?" Auntie Wang asked.

"It says Wesley Maguire. But I know now that's not true," Quinn said.

"I can't say I've heard of many Maguires on Maui," Auntie Wang said.

Liam nodded in agreement.

"I know," Quinn replied. "I've searched Wesley Maguires, but none of them could've been him. In Maui or anywhere."

Auntie Wang shook her head. "Don't read too much into that. Many people who would be in your father's generation and older still aren't online," she said. "I am, but only because I've found it to be such an amazing platform to connect with family and learn more about our history."

"You're right about that," Quinn said. "My mother refused to let me set her up on anything that she'd have to give out any information or post pictures that included her. She said the world was too nosy."

"I know you've probably already considered this," Auntie Wang said, "but do you think your mother could've been running from something?"

Her words grieved Quinn, but after all she'd learned in the last weeks, she knew it was a possibility. Yet it was hard to believe someone as kind and doting as her mother could've done something so bad that she'd go to such lengths to run from it and never look back.

Auntie Wang reached over and took Quinn's hand, rubbing the top of it with her thumb. "Dear, I'm sorry, but there are two definite possibilities: she was either hiding from someone, or hiding from something. If it's the first one, she could've been a victim of some sort, but if it's the second, then, well . . . are you sure you want to open a possible can of worms? Are you ready for any conclusion, even if it isn't a happy one?"

Quinn nodded. "I have to know."

"Then we should start digging," Auntie Wang said.

"Oh. Quinn also sent her DNA into one of those lineage websites," Liam said.

That got Auntie Wang's attention. "And have you gotten any results back yet?"

"Not really," Quinn said. "So far the only surprise has been that my ethnicity includes East Asian and Scandinavian. Along with Polynesian descent, of course."

That pleased the old woman too. Quinn could tell by the way her eyes danced with the news.

"Well, you should know that many, and maybe even most, native Hawaiians are mixed with Chinese, Japanese, and other Asian cultures too. It's only logical, as Hawaii started out with mostly immigrants from those countries."

Quinn shrugged. "It doesn't really matter to me. I was surprised, though. My mother always said my father was fair, and that was where my European features come from."

Auntie Wang raised her eyebrows, studying Quinn's face. "European features? Hmm . . . Sometimes we see what we want to see, or what we expect to see. And then many of us only see ourselves as someone told us we should be."

Quinn didn't understand. She looked at Liam. "Does that mean that I don't look . . . ?"

He shook his head. "Let's not even go into what you—or we—think you look like. We need evidence to send us in the right direction, not suppositions."

"Very smart, Liam," Auntie Wang said, flashing him a proud smile. "I see your parents have raised a very wise son."

He laughed. "You do realize that I'm easing into middle age, right, Auntie Wang? I think I might've grown up some since the day you caught me swiping Old Man Johnson's pineapples at the farmers market. And much of my wisdom comes from you. How many times have you set me on the straight and narrow?"

She laughed. "You aren't the only one I've had to crack the whip on. Don't forget what your brother—"

"I do have one other name," Quinn interrupted, remembering the photo from the jewelry box. "I found a picture of what looks like my mom from probably just before she got pregnant with me, posing with another girl. On the back, she wrote *Carmen Crowe*."

Auntie Wang lost the smile. "Now that is interesting."

"You know someone by that name?" Liam asked.

"I'm not sure I know who Carmen is," Auntie Wang said, "but anyone who has been on Maui for very long knows the name Crowe. There are stories tied to that name."

Her reply sounded ominous. Quinn wasn't even sure she wanted to know, but she also didn't want to not know.

"Can you tell me more?"

"Oh, I can tell you quite a bit," Auntie Wang said, then stood and gestured toward a red velvet sofa and chair on the far wall. "But we'd better go sit somewhere more comfortable for this. It might take a while."

Chapter Ten

Auntie Wang took center stage in what Quinn assumed was some sort of Asian emperor's chair, holding court over them as she wove her tale. The painting behind her was a contradiction to the chair, its vivid colors and majestic Maui scene as Hawaiian as it could get.

As Auntie Wang spoke, Quinn scrutinized her face, marveling at how the woman could look Chinese and Hawaiian at the same time. Her skin was nearly flawless, and her eyes were expertly outlined and of the most unique shape. Her nose was small but beautifully sculpted. Yes, the woman was a classic beauty, and Quinn decided she was a masterful storyteller too.

"I don't know if this Carmen Crowe is of the Maui Crowes, but if she is, then she's connected to a colorful family," Auntie Wang began. "Back when I was a kid, the Crowes were known around here as one of the richest families on the island. But they weren't always that way. Theirs was a true rags-to-riches story, having sold most of the property they owned to a developer for one of those fancy resorts up in West Maui. But before the deal went through, there was a lot of fighting about it."

"Fighting between who?" Quinn asked.

Auntie Wang held a hand up. "I'll get there, but first I have to start at the beginning. You need to know what it was like to grow up in Maui long ago, before we were turned into a tourism landmark and all the foreigners flocked here."

Quinn listened intently. She'd always wanted to know what her mother's childhood was like, but that was a subject that had been closed to her.

"Before you were born," Auntie Wang continued, "and even before your mother was born, the island was quiet. Barely any traffic. And was not even on the map of popular places to visit. Did you know that Maui was the first capital of the Kingdom of Hawaii?"

"I did," Liam said, raising his hand.

"Of course you did. I wasn't talking to you." She gently chastised him, but Quinn knew it was a ruse. It was obvious she and Liam were crazy about each other.

"It used to be a whaling port, didn't it?" Quinn asked.

Auntie Wang nodded. "Up in Lahaina, yes. Even today the whales come back every year, but now that it's a well-known attraction and the tourists flock to the shores, there are fewer sightings. Back when the whales were plentiful, sugarcane grew wild and abundant here, and the entire island was fueled by the work on plantations. The big businesses that came after the sugar overthrew the Hawaiian kingdom and stole land for their crops and water for their fields, pushing many families away because they were unable to do what they'd done for generations."

She looked pained for a moment. "My own ancestors were a big part of that, I'm sad to say. But people will always seize a way to build a better life for their families."

"No shame in that, Auntie Wang," Liam said.

She continued, "Things changed, but Hawaiian life was still good. While Oahu was becoming a metropolitan kind of place, and the big island was attracting hordes of outsiders, Maui continued to be the secret, quiet oasis of the Hawaiian people. Back then, entire villages raised children, not just a set of parents. When I was growing up, I was welcomed into the homes of all my neighbors—Filipinos, Japanese,

Koreans, and all others. I have a palate even now for every type of food, matching any sort of culture that ever came here. My parents never worried for me, and many evenings I sat at the feet of a Kupuna—one of the neighborhood elders—while he entertained all of us children with stories and legends. It was a magical childhood, full of dreams about night marchers on the beaches, mermaids in the river pools, and gods of the sea."

She paused, her eyes closed as she remembered.

"Many people were thankful for the sudden riches our sugar brought. But some farmers competed with the sugar plantations. They grew taro. The big companies came in and started buying up land and securing water rights. Bitterness came to the island. Farmers who found themselves without the water or irrigation they needed began to earn their way as fishermen. Up in the mountains, there were sprawling cattle ranches. Some of them—those owned by families who haven't sold out—are still there today and worked by the cowboys."

"That was my dream when I was young," Liam said.

Quinn could easily imagine him as a rough-and-tumble cowboy.

"By the time I became an adult—and that was a long time ago," Auntie Wang said, "Maui began to lose its grip as the leader in the sugar industry. A new tariff was introduced, and the sugar prices were artificially elevated, causing many food producers and beverage makers to go out of the United States for their sugar. Some say the demise was because of all the fighting over water rights. Others claim the end came from the farmers' refusal to learn new, modern techniques and by cutting corners. My own father admitted that even before he got it, his soil was on the way to ruination, with barely any nutrient base. He said all over the island, the plantation owners refused to fallow. They were greedy, trying to process as much sugar as fast as they could. They didn't rotate crops, and all they wanted to do was burn, till, plant, then do it all over again, stripping the land of its true value."

"The left hand wants to blame the right hand, but in the end, all the people suffer," Liam said.

Auntie Wang nodded.

"Many lost their livelihoods, but soon the first businessman came to Maui and saw it through the eyes of a foreigner. He bought up some out-of-business plantations and developed our first high-class resort. Soon, other landowners were selling, all vying to become millionaires by way of the land they'd inherited."

"So the Crowes were some that sold out?" Quinn asked.

"Not completely. The Crowes owned one of the biggest ranches on the island. Located on the road to Hana, their land sprawled across more than five thousand lush acres through valleys and pineapple fields, nestled at the base of unspoiled mountains. The land was theirs since the beginning and was sacred to the family. A big spender came through and made the family an offer on all of it."

"And they sold it?" Quinn asked, feeling sad for a family she didn't even know.

"It's not that simple," Auntie Wang said. "Not everyone was on board. Obviously, the elders were against it. They remained traditional, defining themselves by their relationships to each other, their ancestors, but especially their land."

"I know this to be true," Liam said.

"Yes, you do." Auntie Wang exchanged a knowing look with him. "Anyway, the offer caused a huge rift. Fathers against sons, mothers against daughters, aunts and uncles waging protests. The elder Crowes wanted to keep the land and continue to farm what they could and keep cattle on the rest. But the younger generation, save for a few dedicated members, wanted the instant riches. The feud had the entire island in an uproar, spreading news of how insensitively the Crowes were treating one another—family turning against family—all over the love of money."

The story was engrossing, and Quinn soon found herself hanging on every word.

"I heard some stories about this but didn't know it was that bad," Liam said.

"That bad and worse," Auntie Wang said. "When some of the Crowes threatened to set everything on fire if they sold the land, the family finally hired an attorney from Oahu to mediate between them: Charles Rocha."

"I recognize that name," Liam said. "Don't the Rochas own that bed-and-breakfast on the road to Hana? The one that's still closed for business?"

"Yes, the Hana House. They bought it last year, among a few other businesses here on Maui that were floundering. But back then, they'd never been to Maui. That all changed when the Crowes asked Rocha to help them work through what was best for the family legacy," Auntie Wang said.

"I can understand hiring someone," Quinn said. "Sometimes it takes an outsider to mediate and bring everyone together."

Auntie Wang nodded. "At first, the town settled down, thinking the Crowes were going to behave now. But soon, a deal was made, and a large parcel of the land was sold to the investor, with the bulk of the profits supposed to come back into making the remaining land better. The family decided to stop fighting for water rights to grow crops and instead turn the ranch into a place of peace and beauty that would attract their own piece of the tourist trade. They could continue to raise cattle, and there would be enough money left from the sale of the biggest parcel to go into the pockets of each segment of the family."

"Then everyone was happy?" Quinn said, confused.

"Sure, if it had happened that way," Auntie Wang said. "Instead, the attorney they trusted so much to act on their behalf helped work out the deal, and the Crowes signed. The land was sold, and money came through, but it didn't trickle down to them as they'd thought it would.

The attorney found a loophole and was able to pocket the majority of the profits."

Quinn's eyes widened. "How could he get away with that?"

"Because the Crowes signed it away without reading the fine print. They sued, but the contract they signed was ironclad. When all was said and done, they lost the biggest part of their land to a fancy developer and barely got enough money to keep their own ranch going. The family continued to fall apart until it became divided, everyone choosing a side."

"So they lost the ranch too?" Quinn asked.

"No, it's still there. Only about a thousand acres or less now, but the family who remained committed to it and worked their fingers to the bone, growing their herds of cattle as well as opening the ranch experience up to the tourists, who by then were swarming to Maui. It's been a long, hard experience for them, and one filled with sorrow at the loss of so much of their ancestors' land, but they've survived."

"And the attorney? He got away with it?"

"Of course he did, but he's long dead by now. Before he died, he built a place up in Haiku, and as far as I know, his family is still there. His deeds didn't go unpunished, though. While his family only got richer from his crookedness, they've also been cursed with bad luck. He fathered a lot of children, and a couple of them took over his law practice. Others kept cattle. A few of them turned to drugs. I remember a few more rumors of more bad dealings and the lawsuits that followed. Once the Rocha ranch was mysteriously set afire, and they lost all of their livestock. The house was rebuilt, but the family never recovered."

"That's tragic," Quinn said.

"It is, and that's not even all of what has befallen them. What pains me is the burden for the generations who came after. Most of them have tried to live honestly. It's not their fault, but the deeds of the grandfather were a blemish on their family name forever, and the latest generation has had its share of bad luck too. A few tragedies, even."

"But they're still rich," Liam said. "I know of that ranch."

"They've accumulated even more riches, yes," Auntie Wang said. "But what good is money when you are always recovering from tragedy?"

Quinn shook her head. "But the Rochas took everything from the Crowes, so wouldn't that be justice?"

"It depends on if you believe in vengeance or forgiveness, I suppose," Auntie Wang said. "From what I've heard, most of the Crowes around today have dropped the vendetta against the Rochas. They are a peaceful family, and the old wounds have healed with the new generations. Like most Hawaiians, they've learned to be thankful for what they have left."

Quinn's face warmed at the silent reprimand. "What a terrible story. And to think, my mother was involved personally. That blows my mind."

"We don't know that for sure," Auntie Wang said. "The Carmen Crowe in that photo could be from another family altogether, though I don't know of any other Crowes that came to Maui who weren't related."

"Sounds to me like she was definitely one of them," Liam said. "If we could find this Carmen Crowe, she would be able to give us information about your mother's family."

Quinn's head was spinning. How would her mother come to be close to someone with such a reputation of sorrow? Though it really wasn't that far-fetched. Her mother had always been drawn to those in need.

Quinn felt there was even more to the story. Perhaps more tragedy but also details that the public didn't know. Like her mother, she'd always cheered for the underdog, and though her heart broke for the Crowe family, she also felt for the Rochas who came later and probably wished they were not born under the shadow of Charles Rocha's black deeds.

Liam stood. "Auntie Wang, we've been here a long time now, and we should go. You've got other commitments, I'm sure."

She smiled as she stood and yawned. "You're right. I have a committee meeting at the museum this afternoon, but first up is a short nap. Quinn, I will do some poking around about this Carmen Crowe character."

"Thank you so much, Auntie Wang," Quinn said. "And I'll let you know if the Lineage registry finds anything concrete."

Auntie Wang reached out and touched her hand. "I wanted to talk to you about that. I've been there, and I know how it feels to see a possible connection, then later find out it's nothing. It's devastating."

She was right.

"Yes, I'm sure it would be," Quinn said. "But it's something I need to do."

"It needs to be done, I agree," Auntie Wang said. "But why don't you turn it over to me and let me follow up on each lead? It will save you a fair amount of heartache, and when I find something that is a real connection, we can follow it together. There are more ways to look for your family too. If you have your birth certificate and your mother's, I'd like to see them."

Quinn considered her proposal. It sounded enticing. With all the emotions she was juggling at the moment, it might be nice to have a mediator to sort through everything.

"That would give you more time to help with the house before you leave," Liam said, raising an eyebrow at her.

Quinn looked from him to the old woman. Liam had a point, and she couldn't help but think about how good it felt to actually help with the remodeling of her own new home.

"And you should show her more of Maui," Auntie Wang said. "She needs to see where her family is from."

"I think we can squeeze in some sightseeing, if I juggle a few things around," Liam said.

"Okay," Quinn conceded. They were right. She was managing too much, and a little assistance could help her see things more clearly.

Keep an emotional distance from it all. Auntie Wang was perfect for the job. And she did want to see more of Maui on this trip. "Give me your email address, and I'll send you the link and my password. And the copies of the birth certificates. But you promise you'll keep me updated if anything at all comes up?"

"Cross my heart," Auntie Wang said. "And Liam knows my information. He can forward it to you." She beamed back at Quinn, filled with a new energy as she practically glided across the floor to lead them to the door.

Chapter Eleven

Quinn was up early. After a quick shower, she pulled on a simple T-shirt and shorts and pulled her hair back into a twist. After adding some earrings, she quickly went through her makeup routine; then she checked her phone.

Ethan had left her a message:

Thinking about getting a dog. What are your thoughts?

A dog? Quinn shook her head. She'd wanted to add a dog to their life for as long as she could remember, and he'd always said it wasn't the right time. *Now* he chooses to dangle the dog offer? While she was five thousand miles away?

He was obviously feeling his loss of control over her and thought the possibility of getting a dog would reel her back in.

She laid the phone aside and picked up her laptop, then signed in, opened her email, and waited for the new messages to filter in. She and Ethan had bigger issues to get through before adding more complications to their life. In a way it was sweet that he knew what would lift her up, but, on the other hand, it was irritating that he'd use it right now. She didn't respond.

As soon as her in-box refreshed, mixed in with a half dozen work emails, she saw a message from Auntie Wang. It was time-stamped after midnight, which was really only a few hours after Quinn had emailed her the link and password to the ancestry site.

Could she have found something that fast?

Her heart beat out of her chest, but she clicked on the message:

> Quinn, I have good news and bad news for you. First, your birth certificate is indeed a fake and doesn't come up under any Maui hospital birth records. Don't fret, we can still look up your mother and go from there. All we need to find is a relative of hers and that will get us started. Second news is better. You missed some steps on the genealogy site. I went through them, and you have a close match, but it's from an anonymous user. I sent them a message. No need to reply to this message, I'll let you know when/if I hear back. —Auntie Wang

Wait. Quinn scanned the message again.

Her birth certificate was fake? What did that mean? She was adopted? She was born somewhere else?

She felt dizzy for a moment. Why had her mother disclosed one truth that would lead to so many more questions? Quinn wished her mom would've had the courage to come clean much earlier, when there was still time to explore what else she was hiding.

And an anonymous match? Quinn didn't even know you could participate anonymously. Why would someone go to the trouble to register and then not want their information known?

Once again, something told her that if she could find Carmen, she could find answers. She opened Facebook and tried again to search for Carmen Crowe, this time without adding Maui. Carmen could've moved to the mainland too. Or another island.

Way too many Carmen Crowes popped up. Trying to find someone who looked like the same Carmen from a decades-old photo was daunting.

She might've married, too, dropping the name Crowe.

It was impossible to narrow it down.

Quinn felt like a failure as an investigator.

She closed her laptop, suddenly glad that she'd given the search over to Auntie Wang. Let the eager woman chase the bread crumbs for a day or so, and then just maybe they'd find something less depressing.

It would be good to keep busy today.

She slid out the door.

"Quinn," Maria called, her head poking just out her back door. "Come join us for breakfast. Please."

Quinn wasn't that hungry now, but Maria wasn't likely to take no for an answer, so she quickly crossed the small yard.

After a quick meal and some laughter that had turned sour when Alani asked her to attend Pali's upcoming football game and he groaned with disappointment, Quinn retreated outside, her feelings hurt. She didn't know why she should care, but she did. She reminded herself that the boy was missing his father and, on top of that, had just found out that they were losing their home.

Out the back door, the shutters were laid out and the sander plugged in, waiting. After her visit with Auntie Wang the day before, they had all worked together to finish scrubbing them, loosening and removing years of grime. With all of them working together, laughing and talking story, it hadn't even felt like work. Quinn had felt sorry when it was done, and they all retreated inside to get ready for bed. Liam was the last to leave after taking his time to inspect every shutter multiple times, insisting that Quinn keep him company.

When he couldn't find any more spots to complain about, he had said his goodbyes, and Quinn waved, then slipped into the guesthouse and went to bed.

~

But the morning was beautiful, and she decided to enjoy the quiet for a bit after breakfast, settling into the chair on her small porch.

Liam chose that moment to come from around the side of the house, a bundle of extension cords in his hands and a huge smile across his face.

"*Aloha kakahiaka,*" he called out. "That means good morning, in case you aren't up on your local Hawaiian phrases."

He winked.

The wink threw her, and she forgot what she was going to say. "Are you always so cheerful?" she finally asked, crossing her arms.

"Pretty much," he said. "Are you always so grumpy?"

"I'm not grumpy. It's just early." Maybe she was grumpy, but she wasn't admitting to anything.

He paused, his smile disappearing for a second before he recovered and put it back in place. "Fair enough. Let's get to work," he said. "I don't want to get behind on this project."

"Agreed," Quinn said, thinking of Ethan and his threats to come over and straighten everything out.

"But"—he looked back at her after picking up the sander—"Auntie Wang called me this morning and insisted I show you some of the island. She said you're like a lost water nymph with no idea which way to go."

He laughed quietly.

Quinn crossed her arms even tighter. "I'm not lost. And I'm definitely no water nymph."

"Now, don't go getting all flustered up. She means well, and, really, don't you want to see some of Maui while you're here?"

"I've seen some. I drove all over Lahaina the other afternoon, and I walked up and down Front Street."

He rolled his eyes.

"Tourist stuff. What about the Road to Hana? Did you drive that?"

She shook her head. "The girl at the rental car place said that was the one destination I couldn't take the car, and I'm not about to join a tour group."

He came and stood in front of her.

Quinn really did want to see more of the real Maui, but something about being so close to Liam in his vehicle—she wasn't even sure what kind—it just made her hesitate.

"That settles it," he said. "If we get done sanding today, tomorrow morning, bright and early, we hit the Road to Hana. The countertops are delayed again, so I've got my painting crew coming. They can handle it. I told Pali he was in charge, and that made him happy."

She started to ask for a rain check, and he put his hand up.

"Do you want to call Auntie Wang and tell her you refuse to see her island?"

She sighed. Going up against him didn't faze her, but the thought of arguing with the persuasive woman was a bit frightening. And she did want to see some of Maui. She'd promised herself before she got there that she was going to be brave and do things. So far that was a major fail.

Except for the water.

She'd gotten into the ocean and had survived. There was that.

And she'd had a magical moment with a sea turtle. How many people could claim that?

"Fine," she said. "But I don't want to stay gone long. I'm waiting on Auntie Wang to follow up on something. If she emails me again, I want to be close."

He raised his eyebrows. "Sounds important. Want to tell me more?"

"Not yet," Quinn said. "I don't want to jinx it. I don't even want to think about it right now."

"Then follow me. I have just the something that will keep your thoughts at bay. You are about to find out why men love power tools so much."

~

By evening, they were done with the shutters, and Quinn was freshly showered and sitting on her bed, staring at her computer screen. She'd begged off from dinner. She needed some space. Things were beginning to feel too comfortable. She reminded herself that she was still the one who was going to be putting the family out, though it seemed figuring it all out kept eluding them each day.

The clock read six thirty. That meant it was after midnight on the East Coast. Still, she needed to talk to Ethan. She wanted to feel that connection again. To remember that she had another life that needed her back.

She picked up the phone and scrolled to his name, hesitating for a moment before hitting the "Call" button. She leaned back on the pillows, telling herself to relax, this was the man she loved.

One ring, then two.

She didn't even know what she was going to say to him.

Did he miss her at all? Would he be mad at her for waking him?

Third ring.

If he didn't pick up now, it would go to voice mail, and she'd hang up.

It clicked.

"Hello," said a soft voice on the other line.

Quinn sat straight up in bed, pulled the phone from her ear, and double-checked it was Ethan's face looking at her from the screen.

It was.

But it wasn't his voice.

"Um . . . sorry, I thought I was calling Ethan . . . ," she said tentatively.

Silence on the other end. One second. Then two.

"Quinn?" the voice asked.

"Gina?" Confusion flooded her. "What are you doing there? Where's Kevin? Is Ethan okay?"

Gina hesitated. "He's fine. He's right here. Sleeping. I saw your name and it's—well, it's late. I thought it might be an emergency, so I picked up."

"It's only dinnertime here," Quinn said. But wait, Ethan was sleeping? Gina saw her name? She tried to understand through the fog that filled her thoughts.

"But—but, I don't—what are *you* doing there, Gina?"

From the other end of the phone, Quinn heard a long sigh. It sounded resigned.

"Quinn. I—I'm sorry," Gina whispered. She sounded as though she was pleading.

It hit Quinn like a brick wall.

It was after midnight, and one of her closest friends was lying in the same bed as Quinn's fiancé. It didn't take a rocket scientist to put it together.

And what about Kevin? For God's sake, he was Ethan's best friend. Not even thinking of herself, Quinn's heart squeezed for him. This was going to kill him. Kevin was a good guy. And totally in love with Gina. Everyone knew it. Ethan knew it! And what about Ethan? Did he not love her either?

Quinn felt sick to her stomach. Her head swam, stars gathering just out of reach. She wanted to scream at Gina. To insist she wake up Ethan.

"Say something, Quinn," Gina said.

Quinn resisted throwing her phone at the wall. What the hell did Gina expect her to say? Should she ask her what she thought of Ethan's physical prowess now? Or beg for details of how and why this had happened? Convince her to leave and never darken their door again?

There was a lot Quinn could say. Could demand.

Instead, she clicked the "End" button, cutting the connection that traveled between her and Gina instantly. But it didn't cut the pain. She dropped the phone and fell over to the side, bringing her legs up to her chest and wrapping her arms around them, her body going into a fetal position as she fought to protect herself from the onslaught of thoughts and the sudden nausea.

But she couldn't.

She thought of Gina, the image of her backside in spin class always coming first, since that's what Quinn saw the most of as her so-called friend competed to be the fastest and most enduring in the room. Quinn was usually sweating like mad by the end of the session, while Gina stepped off the bike still looking like she'd just arrived.

It was disgusting.

Yes, Gina was fit. Sculpted. Probably every man's dream.

And Ethan. Always the competitor. The risk-taker. He loved nothing more than a dangerous challenge. Always thinking rules didn't apply to him.

But she'd thought that commitments did.

She uncurled herself and lay back on the pillow, staring at the ceiling. One silent tear fought its way out of her eye and rolled off the side of her face, dropping into her ear and creating a tickling sensation. She brushed it out with her fist, surprised that she could still feel anything through the numbness that was traveling through every nerve cell in her body.

This time he'd gone too far.

Quinn wouldn't be waiting on the sidelines to cheer him on. From now on, he could hold his own damn towel.

Chapter Twelve

The next morning, Quinn found herself pressing her feet against the invisible brake on her side of Liam's truck when he got too close to the car ahead of them. They'd been driving only about half an hour, and already Quinn was feeling a bit carsick from all the weaving and bumping down the narrow roads.

She also felt sad. Defeated. Confused.

But she tried to push thoughts of Ethan and Gina out of her mind. She needed to process it slowly. He'd tried to call her all through the night. Texted her a couple dozen times. Quinn hadn't even read the texts. Not yet.

She wanted him to suffer. Make him beg her to respond.

While she resisted, she also wished a case of the most vicious food poisoning on him—wait, no, it needed to be smallpox. Or maybe something that would disfigure the face he was so fond of looking at in the mirror. Really hit him where it hurts.

But then she also wanted to know why.

Why? Why? Why?

Was she not enough? Did he do it to punish her for leaving him behind? Had this been going on before she left, even? She thought about how different Gina was from her. Sexier. Loud. Vivacious.

Basically everything she wasn't.

It made her feel worse.

Breathe, she told herself. *Just breathe.*

Inhaling deeply, she let the air fill her lungs, expanding in her chest and surrounding her broken heart.

To top it off, she was still reeling from the news that her birth certificate was fake. What did that mean? It was all so confusing.

But she needed to hide what she was feeling today. She didn't want Liam to be suspicious and start asking questions. It wouldn't take much for her to break down completely.

They'd left Paia Town—and some of the best coffee she'd ever had at Paia Bay Coffee—at least half an hour before, and Liam said the next stop on their list was going to be Twin Falls.

"So Paia is where all the surfers hang out?" Quinn said, still thinking about the town behind them and especially the colorful fencing she'd seen made up of surfboards of all sizes and shapes.

"That's it. Funky town, where all the surfers, artists, and hippies flock together. There's also a dash of incognito celebrities roaming around if you look close enough."

Just from the short look she'd gotten, Quinn had loved the laid-back vibe and small-town feel of Paia. There she saw more of what she considered normal people—not those floating around in fancy resort wear, playing the part of the pampered and elite. Ethan would've hated the atmosphere, as one of the things he loved most while on vacation was being catered to. She decided that she'd come back to Paia really soon and just spend a day exploring all the interesting shops and boutiques.

And people watching. She wanted to see more of the locals there, their expressions tolerant as they tried to live their daily lives among the constant crowds of the curious and sometimes demanding tourists. Their waitress had intrigued her, her long, thick hair streaked with blonde but also peppered with gray. Her skin was weathered, as it should be, the area around her eyes dotted with lines that looked well earned. She was friendly and inviting and, when asked, said that she'd come to Maui as a teenager and never left. When she said that it was nearly thirty years ago, Quinn thought that the island life must surely be some sort of fountain of youth.

"We could've gotten a breakfast sandwich up here for about three bucks," Liam said, pointing at a small store they were passing. The sign said Kuau Mart, and the parking lot had a few cars. Unlike the shops in Paia, it didn't look overly crowded.

"That would've been fine with me. Why didn't we?"

He laughed. "Auntie Wang would have my hide, that's why. She said to give you a proper experience, not a meat, egg, and cheese on a large croissant from the local mart. Though, I'll admit, they are legendary for their breakfast sandwiches."

Quinn sighed. "A croissant and a cheap coffee would've been just fine. You said you weren't going to treat me like a tourist."

He glanced at her before putting his eyes back on the road. "Be careful what you ask for."

They came up on a curve, and Liam pulled to the side, allowing the large truck on their tail to go around.

"Hana people," he said. "They might live in paradise, but they still have to go back and forth to work, and nothing ruins their day more than getting held up by sightseeing folks. The polite thing to do is pull over and let them by."

The truck blew its horn as it went by, and Liam held up a hand in the familiar Hawaiian gesture she'd seen him do earlier to another driver.

The horn scared her, and she jumped. Just inches from where the truck was, she could see a steep drop-off. Another foot and they could've been rolling down the cliff to their deaths. She concentrated on keeping her expression neutral, trying not to show how nervous she was, but her stomach clenched under the damp shirt she wore.

"What's the hand signal mean?" she asked, deflecting the thought of death.

"What? A *shaka?*" He did it again, shaking it at her. "It means hang loose, or to just chill. Was started because of the surfing culture here, but now everyone uses it."

Quinn pushed the hair back from her eyes. Liam didn't use air-conditioning as they rode. Apparently none of the locals did. They liked the clean Hawaiian air flowing through their windows, cleansing the soul, he claimed. Air-conditioning was poison, he said, laughing when she pushed back the sweaty strands of hair that the wind had blown out of her twist.

In town it had felt brutally humid and hot, especially considering it was only just before nine, but now it was cooling down the higher they climbed. She took a sip from the bottle of water he'd pulled from behind the seats. It wasn't cold, but just the moisture against her tongue brought relief.

"We'll help finish up the painting tomorrow," Liam said, breaking the lull in conversation. "I'll have to demote Pali, but he'll live."

"I can be up early to help too. I just hope he won't be angry that I'm here."

"If he is, he won't show it. He knows if he disrespects you in front of me or Kupuna, he won't be able to sit down for a week," Liam said.

Quinn felt her face flush. She hated the thought of someone not liking her. Years of being a people pleaser were too ingrained for her to just shake it off.

"I wish he didn't hate me so much." The night before she'd gone into the house to talk to Maria. Just inside the door, Pali was arranging a stack of boxes marked GOODWILL. Maria had taken Quinn's advice to first clean out all the years of clutter before beginning to pack what was left. Quinn was relieved she had finally begun the process and was making good progress. Liam had even taken a truckload of better household items to be dispersed around the family, including their shabby green couch and armchair, which Kupuna said weren't worth keeping.

"It's not you," Liam said, looking sideways at her. "It's the situation you represent. Don't take it personal. But on the brighter side, now do you feel like you can handle most power tools?"

She blushed. His question made her remember the lesson he'd given her, his arms around her, and his hands on hers as they glided across the wood in smooth, caressing movements. It had felt too close for comfort. Almost sensual. But she hadn't had the will to break away.

"I'm sure I could figure them out," she lied. "One by one."

He nodded emphatically. "No doubt. You handled that sander like a pro. I'd put you on my crew any day."

The shutters, once cleaned and sanded, had looked pretty rough, but Liam had assured her that with a fresh coat of paint, they'd look like new.

"But I don't want them to look like new," she'd said.

"Oh," he'd mocked her in a pitifully orchestrated girly voice, "you want them *shabby chic*?"

She'd thrown her head back and laughed loudly. Just hearing feminine words coming out of his masculine face had almost brought her to hysterical tears. She couldn't believe he even knew the term, but he was right. That was exactly what she wanted.

The moment had broken the weird vibe that their closeness over the sander had brought about, and she smiled, remembering it. It took some practice, but by the end of the afternoon, the sander beneath her hands moved slowly and smoothly, with languid strokes that felt almost forbidden.

Liam was something else. He could be tough as nails when he was working, soft and sweet when performing, and then amusing as could be when he wanted. Yes, she had to give it to him, he was quite the chameleon.

Like today. Magically, instead of the intense construction guy or the fearless surfer, she was looking at a gracious tour guide behind the wheel. He was full of surprises.

"Just a few more miles," he said when they rounded another hairpin curve. "Oh, Quinn, I forgot to tell you that I saw the car on the way over to Maria's this morning."

"What car?"

"Jaime's car," he said. "It's for sale at a car lot up town. I went in and asked about the man who sold it to them, and I was right, it was Jaime's."

"So he sold his car," she said. "What does that tell us?" For a moment, Quinn thought of *Dateline* and how so many people ended up being found murdered after their car was discovered abandoned or sold.

"Nothing, if that was the case, but he didn't sell it. He traded it."

"Traded?" she asked.

He nodded. "He traded it for a van and five hundred dollars. A Volkswagen, to be exact. And that tells me he probably got the van to live in. We see a lot of that around here. Go to any beach after dark, and you'll find a van or two, the occupants camping out in it. But at least that means he hasn't left Maui. If he planned to jump islands or go to the mainland, he wouldn't need a van."

Quinn thought of the $500 that someone had left Maria. So maybe Jaime hadn't abandoned them completely, after all.

"Did he give you a description of the van?" she asked.

"He didn't. Once I got excited, he clammed up. Said it wasn't any of my business. But on my way out, I stopped and asked the guy washing cars, and he said the only van sold in the last few months was a 1970 canary-yellow Volkswagen."

"So we just have to look at every yellow VW van we see then," Quinn said, already thinking of how they could map out the island and check it, section by section.

"I'm still not so sure that's a good idea. Obviously, he doesn't want to be found." Liam shot her a doubting look.

"I don't care," Quinn said. "He can tell that to my face after I tell him how badly he broke Maria's heart. And those kids. They need their dad."

Liam shook his head. "I'm just warning you. That's not the way things are done around here, but if you're going to be out there digging around, I'll help you. Or at least be there to shove off anyone who tries to take advantage."

"I'm sure I'll be fine," Quinn said. But she hoped that Liam really would come. So far, most of the homeless people she'd seen around the island looked harmless, but there had been a few she wouldn't want to come upon alone. Having Liam with her could mean the difference between a crummy experience and a tragic one.

Liam slowed down and then turned in and parked near a small building.

"Twin Falls Farm Stand," he said, shutting off the car and turning to her.

"More food?" Quinn asked. "I don't think I can."

"You will later. And this is how we repay the owners of the land that Twin Falls sits on. They make the best smoothies and have all sorts of local treats and tropical fruits. Even souvenirs. The upkeep of the trails and parking lot and all this traffic takes a toll. I wish more of the tourists would support their efforts."

He led her over to the colorful stand. While he paid for a few loaves of what he called the "famous Maui banana bread," she lingered at the eclectic collection of souvenirs, picking through until she found some unique wooden bookmarks. She didn't know whom she'd give them to, but she wanted to do her part too. She quickly went to the cashier and paid, then waited over on the side for Liam to finish.

When he joined her, he handed her a small package filled with long, brown candies of some sort.

"Coconut candy," he said. "Pali loves it. Maybe you can use it as a peace offering."

"Great idea," Quinn said, tucking the package into her bag. She was willing to try anything. She didn't need to win him over, exactly. But it would be nice not to think she was sleeping so close to an enemy.

After Liam returned to put the bread in the car, he led her to the beginning of the trail to the falls. She could already hear the rush of water in the distance.

"Be careful," he said, taking her hand.

Tingles shot up her fingers and then all the way to her brain at the sudden warmth he radiated through her. She thought of Ethan and wondered how long it had been since he'd tried to hold her hand.

That was unfair, she realized.

She also hadn't tried to hold his. Somehow over the years, the habit had just faded away.

A few minutes later they made their way through a majestic bamboo jungle, the stalks reaching high for the sky like some sort of fortress to protect the fragile nature within. Within, it felt surreal and quiet. Quinn was sorry when they left it behind.

"Now you're going to get those nice shoes wet," Liam said, guiding her over a small stream.

"I don't mind," Quinn said, but she cringed when she thought of what she'd paid for the popular canvas sneakers. She should've brought hiking shoes.

The wide varieties of exotic plants and tropical trees were beautiful, but, just as she was thinking of how exhausted and hot she was getting, the trail opened up and they were there.

It was a magnificent scene. The roar of the falls decimated any silence that might have thought about gathering there. Quinn could also hear birds and other sounds of nature as she and Liam approached the water.

Even the water was like a painting. The cool greens and blues swirled together, creating a lovely and cool-looking portrait of peacefulness.

A young couple was wading around, a small boy on the father's shoulders. Quinn smiled at what a perfect picture they made. A family enjoying some of God's most simple but remarkable gifts of beauty. On the bank another couple lounged on a large towel, eating fruit.

"Want to cool off in the river?" Liam asked.

She nodded, and they went to the edge of the water. He pointed at a large rock, and she leaned against it and took off her shoes. She was glad she hadn't worn socks, and she set the sneakers aside. After taking her bag and tucking it beside the rock, Liam removed his shoes and joined her.

He took her arm protectively and helped her into the water.

She gasped, her eyes wide with shock.

"Cold, eh?" he said, laughing.

"I wasn't expecting that," Quinn choked out. "But it feels nice."

After a minute or two, they climbed out and sat side by side on the bank.

"Wow, did you know you have a small birthmark behind your ear that is shaped just like a turtle?" he said.

Quinn reached up, self-consciously covering the small brown mark. "Yeah, I know."

"Don't tell me you don't like it," Liam said.

She shrugged. "What's to like?"

"It looks just like a sea turtle!" he said, his voice incredulous. "We call them *honu*. In Hawaiian culture the sea turtle is considered a guardian spirit. It can change shape at will, just like the Hawaiian god of the sea, Kanaloa. You're lucky to have been given such a significant mark."

"Well, I never appreciated it. When I was a just a girl, my mom would pull my hair back for school, and sometimes the other kids would make fun of it. I tried to hide it through junior high."

"That's really sad that they would try to put down such an exceptional gift," Liam said.

"My mom tried to help me get over it. She also told me turtles are special in the Hawaiian culture. We had a jar—or we still do somewhere. She called it our spirit jar, and we would write our wishes down and put them in there. My mom always said the spiritual powers of the turtle and the sea would make our dreams reality."

She wondered where the jar was now. She hadn't seen it in ages and would love to read through the notes and see what both she and her mother had written down so many years ago.

Liam was quiet, staring off into the distance as though he were somewhere else.

Quinn wasn't usually comfortable with intruding on someone's thoughts, but she decided to take a chance. She really wanted to know.

"What are you thinking of?" she asked.

He blinked, joining her again. "Of my childhood. This used to all be wild and unkempt. Such a secret place. Back then you had to jump a fence to get here. There were cows everywhere, and it was fun to play around them as we threw rotten guavas at each other. By the time we'd get to the water, we'd be covered in mud and smelly fruit and would race to the highest rock to be the first to jump in."

Quinn smiled. She couldn't even imagine a magical childhood immersed in such a tropical paradise and enjoying it with siblings. Her heart always longed for that kind of connection when she heard stories like his.

"Aww, shut your mouth!"

They both turned toward the insult that had broken the special moment.

A group of teenagers had come up and were talking to a woman who appeared to have just gotten off an ATV. She was pointing at the top of the falls and looked to be giving them a lecture.

"I asked you not to do that today. It's not safe due to the rains we had this week," she said.

"Who the hell made you queen for a day? You can't tell me what to do," the teen said.

Liam stood, and as he approached the small group, Quinn could see the sudden stiffness in his shoulders.

"Is there a problem here?" he asked, using a low, calm tone of voice that Quinn had yet to hear from him.

The three boys and the woman turned to him. The teen who was the main talker lifted his chin stubbornly and pointed at the woman.

"This crazy old bat is trying to tell us where we can and can't go," he said. "She doesn't own this place."

"It's too dangerous for rock jumping today," she retorted.

Quinn stood but stayed where she was. They didn't need to make the scene any bigger than it was. Already the dad carrying his toddler was getting out of the water, worry on his face as he joined his wife on the bank. The other couple was watching quietly.

"Lady, this is a public place," the teen said. "And you can kiss my—"

"Don't say it," Liam interrupted, taking another step, putting himself between the woman and the teenagers.

The atmosphere went from serene to electric.

When he spoke again, it was almost too quiet to hear, but Quinn strained.

"First of all, this isn't a public place. It's private land, and the owners are gracious enough to share it with the public. And second, but most of all, this isn't some *old lady*, as you put it. Her name is Auntie Ute, and she's been giving of her time and energy here for longer than you've been alive. What she tells you is for your own good. But you'd better believe that if you are foolish enough to ignore her warnings, she'll be the first one to administer first aid and keep you stable until the paramedics arrive. She's saved many stupid people like you over the years."

The woman, Ute, crossed her arms over her tie-dyed shirt and smiled proudly. "I remember you," she said to Liam.

Quinn noticed her accent sounded very European.

He nodded. "Yes, ma'am. It's been a while."

She gave him a sly grin. "I believe I gave you and your brothers a lecture or two when you were a wee bit wet behind the ears too."

He smiled slightly. "I believe so. But I don't think we ever disrespected you like this numbskull just did. Our upbringing was better than that."

The boy sneered, looking from Liam to the woman. "What is this? A family reunion?"

His friends snorted with laughter.

Liam turned back to the boy, his body rigid, reminding Quinn of a snake ready to strike. He nodded to the trail. "Would you like to take a walk off the path with me for a second? I believe we need a private conversation."

Suddenly the teen looked more like a child than the man he was trying to be only seconds before.

"Listen, dude . . . ," he began, his voice wavering.

Liam held a hand up to stop him from talking. "Don't call me dude. I tried to be nice about it, but now before you go a step farther around here, you'll apologize to Auntie Ute for being a mouthy little punk. Or if you'd rather, you and I will take my secret trail, where you might soon find yourself taking a long walk off the next short cliff."

It took another few seconds, but the boy spat out an apology.

"Now, if you can't behave yourself like the guest you are on this sacred ground, you and your buddies can leave," Liam said.

Quinn didn't think it sounded like a suggestion, and obviously neither did the boy, because he took off for the trail. His not-so-brave friends followed.

Ute laughed when one of them tripped over a rock and pounded the one in front of him in the back to catch his fall.

"I could handle that sort all day," she said to Liam, her tone tough as nails.

"I know you could, but you shouldn't have to," he replied.

She patted him on the back before moving toward her ATV.

"I always thought you'd turn into a good one," she called out, then started the four-wheeler and headed out on another trail that Quinn hadn't even noticed was there.

They watched her go. She made a colorful and amusing picture, her hair rumpled in the wind and her tanned hands expertly gripping the handlebars.

Liam turned to her.

"I think we've seen enough of Twin Falls. You agree?"

Quinn nodded, ready to move on. As they headed for the trail back to the truck, she couldn't get the vision of Liam standing up for the woman out of her head.

Chapter Thirteen

The rest of the afternoon flew by as Liam played tour guide to her curiosity. After they left the falls, they stopped and walked through a small part of the Garden of Eden. He said it included a meticulously maintained thirty acres of botanical beauties but took her the short route to where he showed her postcard-perfect panoramic views of the Pacific. He offered to take her to see the Puohokamoa Falls within it, but it had started to drizzle, so they ran back to the car.

"You've just seen where the opening scene of *Jurassic Park* was filmed," he said when they climbed back into the car.

"I haven't seen the movie, but now it's on my list."

At her proclamation, he gaped at her as though she'd grown horns.

"You have to see it. And the sequels." His tone invited no arguing, and she laughed. She wasn't much into nail-biting movies, but if it made him happy, she'd watch it. Especially now that she had a point of reference.

Back in the truck, they traversed more blind curves before cruising through Hana Town, a place so small and subtle that it was gone before she knew they were there. They had their windows all the way down when, from the tall grass beside the road, a huge owl flew up.

Quinn gasped at the size of it, then was captivated as the creature seemed to keep pace with the truck, flying right beside them so closely that she could see every detail of its wide span of wings and its sharp beak.

It was a moment she would tuck away as a favorite from Maui.

They moved on to Black Sand Beach, and Liam showed her the cave, where he snapped a few photos of her in the shadows before leading her back to the truck.

"You're getting a blur of a tour, but we can always come back to linger if you find a favorite place," he told her.

"That would be nice," she said, knowing that her time was running out, and she doubted she'd have much more opportunity to linger anywhere. Or would she? Maybe she really didn't need to rush home now.

In the truck she settled back, uncomfortably aware of all that had changed since the night before.

"I'm trying to get us to Ohe'o Gulch before the crowds get too thick," he said, speeding up.

"I haven't heard of that."

"That's the old name. You probably know it by Seven Sacred Pools. It's in the Haleakalā National Park and one of the most popular sites of East Maui. I used to cliff-jump there when I was a kid. Before it got famous and the crowds came."

"I can't wait to see it," she said. It was nice imagining him as a happy child, living the laid-back life that she'd always thought Hawaiians must live.

She checked her phone again but still couldn't get a signal. She told herself she was not looking to see if Ethan had sent her any more messages, but she could only lie to herself for so long.

"You okay over there?" Liam asked her when a sigh escaped her as she put her phone away for the tenth time. He glanced over at her for a second, his brow furrowed. "You sure are quiet."

"Yeah," she said. "Just wondering if Auntie Wang has heard anything."

And if my lying, cheating boyfriend has anything else to say, she thought as she tried to muster up a smile. She couldn't do it and gave up.

"No cell phone reception up here," he said.

"What do people who live up here do for communication?"

He shrugged. "They can get landlines in their homes for the most part, but on the roads it's spotty, and Wi-Fi isn't a given up here. Many don't have the internet and don't care."

"I can't imagine living in such a remote area," Quinn said.

Suddenly a pickup truck behind them laid on the horn and came careening around them, and Liam pulled to the side.

Just when Quinn thought he was going to cuss at Liam for going so slow, the driver threw up the island hand signal.

"That was scary," she said, breathing out slowly.

"You think so? He knows by my truck that I'm a local. If we had been in your rental car, he might not have been so friendly."

If that was friendly, Quinn hated to see the opposite.

Liam looked over at her. "Most of the Hana people have been here for generations. Some of them feel a bit irritated at tourists now and then. Invading their paradise, you know?"

She could understand that. It had to be hard for the families who really had ties to the island. So many strangers traipsing around their lands that were once private.

"How do you feel about the tourism here?" she asked.

He looked over and chuckled. "I don't mind, except for the ones who come over and do stupid things."

"Like?"

"Littering our beaches. Touching our wild *honu*—turtles, I mean—or getting too close to them to take a photo. Those kinds of things. Some tourists are hell-bent to go against the Hawaiian value of living *pono.*"

"Living *pono?*" she asked. He said the most interesting things. Tidbits she couldn't find in a travel book. Quinn could listen to him talk for hours and never get bored.

"That means making a constant conscious decision to do the right thing. In terms of self, others, and, for Hawaiians, most importantly the environment. The land and the sea are everything. Without them, we are nothing. We must all strive to live *pono*, or soon there will be nothing left."

He sounded somber.

"That's a beautiful way to think about living your life," Quinn said, matching his reverent tone. On the mainland it didn't seem important to many people to be reverent about the land. She'd always tried to do the right thing herself but didn't know there was an official name for it. That it was considered a way of life. And one from her mother's heritage at that.

Finally, they pulled into the national park, and Liam paid, then parked. It wasn't too crowded, and they made quick time on the trail to the pools.

"What the—" He stopped at a metal gate blocking off access to the trail that led down to the pools.

A sign posted said they were closed because of recent landslides.

"It's okay," Quinn said, seeing the disappointment on Liam's face as his shoulders slumped in defeat.

He looked around. "No, it's not. I grew up swimming in those pools and jumping off those exact rocks. They aren't locking me out."

"But those boys you lectured . . . ," Quinn said, trailing off.

"Those boys were young and stupid. They haven't lived long enough to respect the cliffs and water. I know what I'm doing."

Before Quinn could argue, he jumped the fence, then turned around and held his arms out. "Come on."

She shook her head. "Isn't this federal land? I don't want to go to jail for trespassing."

He beckoned her closer. "Quinn. Just climb, and I'll catch you on this side. No one's going to jail. Anyway, I know all the workers here if we did get caught."

She hesitated. She was a rule follower. Always had been. But his face. He looked so hopeful. All day he'd wanted to show her this one special place more than any other.

First a deep breath, then she climbed the fence and threw a leg over.

He caught her around her waist and set her gently down on the other side, as though she weighed less than a feather—a real boost for her bruised ego of always feeling like she needed to lose a good fifteen.

Quickly she followed behind him, glancing every now and then up at the trail to see if any federal agents were running after them. She felt like such a criminal, but honestly it also gave her a little thrill.

Down at the pool Liam found a bush with dainty pink flowers and plucked one off, then threw it in the water. He watched it carefully before stripping off his shirt and diving in, surprising her with his sudden disappearance.

She sat down by the water and watched him reappear.

He shook the water off his head and wiped his face, then grinned up at her.

"Want to come in?"

"Not today. But what's with the flower?" she asked.

"It's an offering. Hawaiian legend says before swimming in these pools, you should make an offering to the resident *mo'o*. Those are the old lizards. If the flower disappears, you don't have permission, and it's a warning to stay away. If it floats, it's safe."

With another look at the flower, he waded to the far side and began climbing the rocks. As Quinn watched, he reached one of the highest points, and then, as she held her breath, he dived off, making barely a ripple as he hit the water.

He was a different sort of athlete from Ethan. Smooth. Quiet. Humble.

With Liam, it didn't feel like he was showing off. It just felt natural to see him do the things he'd been doing his whole life, while respecting the environment around him as a living thing.

She was glad he'd rushed the road to Hana to get her to the pools before too many people arrived. It was the most enchanting place she'd ever been. As he climbed and dove again, then swam out, she gazed at the water, her arms hugging her legs close to her chest.

There were times in Quinn's life when she'd felt sad. Probably never more so than the day her mother had given up her battle. But for the most part, she tried to keep a positive outlook. Ethan didn't like for her to come off as melancholy or pouting. For him she always tried to hold that part of herself inside. Hidden.

She was in such deep thought that Liam had climbed out of the water and was beside her before she realized it.

"I know you're unhappy today," he said. "I don't know why, and I don't need to know. But I'm here if you want to talk."

She felt tears sting the back of her throat. She swallowed, pushing the lump down. His soft words shattered her facade, and she didn't like it. Or wasn't used to it. Never in her life had she talked to a man about her emotions. It felt alien to her.

"Thank you," she finally mustered. She wouldn't disrespect him by denying his acknowledgment.

When she said nothing else, he stood and held a hand down.

"Would you like to see a magical place before we go?" he asked.

They locked eyes, and then she took his hand. "Yes, I'd like that. I think I could use a little magic today."

Chapter Fourteen

Liam had promised her magic, and he made good on it. Quinn followed him carefully as he led her up the Pipiwai Trail, impressed by how he held back wayward branches or took her hand to help her over the difficult spots.

She wasn't much of a hiker, and the sign that stated it was nearly two miles up and two miles down worried her. But soon she was glad she'd put the anxiety aside and decided to live in the moment.

The jungle was in itself a wonderfully beautiful place, the many lush shades of green and scattered exotic flowers a beautiful backdrop to some of the prettiest scenery Quinn had ever seen. She especially enjoyed the tiny bridges here and there with the babbling creeks underneath. The sounds of the wind, water, birds, and unseen insects made an enchanting orchestra as they climbed past rocks and some smaller falls.

On the way up they passed a famous old banyan tree, and it was remarkable to see, but the peace she felt as they entered the bamboo forest was indescribable. They stood there for a time, taking in the nature around them. Quinn appreciated that Liam didn't try to talk, picking up on her need to be quiet and contemplative. Soon she realized there was another reason for his quietness. His face lit up with a victorious smile when the wind ran through the bamboo trees, creating a soft and melodious song as the bamboo stalks swayed gently up against each other.

Quinn stood so still to listen more intently that a dragonfly flew around her and settled on her shoulder for a few seconds before lifting off again.

The bamboo forest was definitely a place of wonder. Almost religiously so. She was filled with gratitude to Liam for bringing her there. He might think it silly if she spoke what she was feeling, but he had no idea how much her soul had needed that moment of peace.

Her mood lifted, and they continued up the trail, laughing as she tripped on the wooden planks placed strategically in the wetter areas of the path.

"If I can get you out on a board, we'll strengthen your sense of balance on the water," he teased, just as his voice was drowned out by the enormity of the last waterfall they approached.

She was feeling overheated and wiped the sweat from her brow. But she trudged on. She knew they were getting close to the main falls when the bamboo began to thin and the trees started coming back.

"Waimoku Falls," Liam yelled. "*Water that recognizes no friend.* Four hundred feet high, straight drop to the bottom. On her strongest days she can amputate a limb if you get in her way."

Terrifying but also stunning. Those were the most descriptive words that Quinn could think of, though she said nothing as she looked. She knew her words would get lost in the sound of the rushing water.

He moved closer to her.

The mist and the wind created from the falling water instantly cooled her, and it was so refreshing.

"We used to swim and play under it. But too many tourists come now. Too much of a liability."

He sounded sad, and it made Quinn feel terrible for the native people of Maui whose lives had been changed so much by the tourism industry swooping down and taking over.

"I'm sorry," she said.

He shrugged. "See those boulders?" He pointed to a gathering of huge rocks, each the size of a golf cart near the pools. Then he pointed up. "That's where those came from. Even a small rock falling can kill you from that far up. So I understand why they've had to do it. But many don't heed the warnings or the threat of a fine. Some pay the price with their lives. It's much more dangerous than the Seven Pools."

Quinn thought about his helping her over the fence to lead her to the pools earlier. He hadn't held the same reserve back there. Reflecting on risk and taking in dangerous places made her think about Ethan. All her troubles came flooding back, instantly filling her with dread.

She couldn't just gallivant all over Maui and ignore everything that was going on. The man she had been planning on spending the rest of her life with had betrayed her. The house she bought was inhabited by a family who had deep roots there. And her search for her birth father had thus far netted absolutely nothing.

"Hey, what's wrong?" Liam said. "You look like all the wind just got sucked out of your sails."

She didn't want to look him in the face. She was sure that her eyes were filling with tears. Probably tears of self-pity. And that disgusted her. She needed to get her life under control. Or at least the parts of it where it was possible to do that.

Figuring out what to do about Ethan would have to wait. She couldn't deal with him from thousands of miles away, and honestly, she didn't even want to. Not today. And maybe not even tomorrow.

"Quinn?" Liam said.

"I'm fine," she said. "Nothing's wrong. I'd better be getting back to the house, though. I'd like to see what Auntie Wang found out, and we need to go over the task list for the house again. Maybe you can give me a more firm date of completion. I really need to make some plans."

～

The drive home was quiet. Quinn had no words to make small talk, and Liam obviously felt the same. The vibe was off, and they both knew it. And it was her fault. A few times she wished he'd just talk. He could appease her curiosity about his family situation and why he was single. She'd never ask. That'd be too much.

But she'd love to know.

Not to mention if he filled the truck with his own story, it would help her forget hers. But that didn't happen, and by the time they were pulling into Maria's driveway an hour later, Quinn was in a state of despair about how wrecked her life was. How was she going to forgive Ethan for what he'd done? And what if this thing with Gina wasn't a fling? What if he loved her?

She needed to get home before it was too late. Before all she'd worked so hard for was completely gone.

In the next second, she told herself she was a complete fool.

She didn't know what she wanted. Or what to do.

Liam turned off the ignition, but his hands went straight back to the wheel.

"I hope I was an acceptable tour guide." He said it slowly and solemnly.

She was gathering up her backpack and her empty water bottle, but she paused.

"Of course you were. I've had the best day. Really, it was so nice of you to take me to see everything," she said, feeling as though her silence had hurt his feelings. "It was amazing."

He nodded, but he didn't look convinced.

His expression was heartbreaking. Like a disappointed little boy. But one with a strong jawline and handsome profile.

She stumbled over her words now.

"I—I'm sorry, Liam. I didn't mean to slip into a mood. It's just that I have a lot going on. Stuff that has nothing to do with the stress of the house. It's just a—it's a lot."

He looked at her.

"I thought after our long day together, we were becoming friends. But maybe you need more time."

"More time for what?"

This time a sigh accompanied his reply. "To trust me."

With that, he climbed out of the truck and came around and opened her door. Quinn stepped out, feeling awkward. She wanted to tell Liam that she did trust him. *She* was the confusing one.

Before she could say anything else, the front door opened and Maria was there, waving at them to hurry.

"Quinn, haven't you checked your phone?" she said. "We've been trying to call you!"

Her phone. Quinn had turned it on silent in case Ethan started sending her messages again, and she hadn't even thought to check it on the way home. Now she pulled it out and touched the screen.

Six missed calls from Auntie Wang and three from Maria.

Her stomach dropped.

Such urgency could mean only one thing. There must've been a reply from the anonymous match. She bade them both goodbye and headed for the privacy of the cottage to call the woman back, taking deep breaths as she went in an attempt to still the sudden flapping of butterflies in her stomach.

This could mean everything.

Chapter Fifteen

A week in Maui had flown by, but finally something was happening. Quinn pressed the "End" button and put her phone down. She couldn't believe it, but she had a meeting set up with the anonymous match. Auntie Wang said he wanted to talk to her in person before giving her any information. They set it for Thursday, which meant in three days she'd know something. Finally.

He wanted to meet at a restaurant in Napili called the Sea House and told Auntie Wang to have Quinn sit on the patio and order a strawberry daiquiri with two umbrellas so that he'd know it was her.

It was all so melodramatic.

She stood and went to the window. She could see across the lanai and into the house. Maria, Kupuna, and Alani were having dinner. Liam had gone home, claiming he was tired and had some work calls to make. Quinn had declined the invitation to eat and made a beeline for the privacy of the cottage to call Auntie Wang back.

Now things were getting real.

They still didn't know what sort of connection the man was, other than it was close. Close could mean an uncle. A brother. Or—her breath caught as she whispered the words to the empty room—*"a father."*

Quinn knew she should be feeling elated, but she wasn't.

All she felt was terror.

A part of her wished that Liam had stayed, but the other part, the side that knew herself so well, knew she wouldn't have told him. It was too personal, and she couldn't deny that he wasn't completely in the friend zone after the day they'd spent together. Sharing something so important with him would move him closer into territory that wasn't fair to Ethan when—or if—she decided she wanted to work it out.

The messages he'd left on her phone made her feel crazy—he said he loved her and he'd slipped, but it meant nothing. That he was lonely and vulnerable because he felt she didn't want him with her. That she was his everything. Quinn found herself believing it one minute, then feeling angry again the next. Would she ever be able to forgive and forget? Did she even want to try? And how many times had he *slipped* in the past that she was too naive to know about?

She felt such a keen sense of loss and longing for her mother that she was dizzy. If her mother were here, Quinn would be calling her. Telling her the news or asking what she should do.

But then, if her mother were here, Quinn wouldn't have had a reason to take the test or seek out the truth about who her father was. She wouldn't know that the man she'd always thought was her deadbeat dad actually wasn't.

Quinn remembered what Auntie Wang had said about the birth certificate.

It was so frustrating. Her mother had started all this, and now, when Quinn needed her the most, Quinn had to navigate it alone. A catch in her chest alerted her to how lonely she felt.

She went to the bed, and after pulling off her dusty clothes from her day out with Liam, she climbed in, too overwhelmed and weak to even think about showering. For once, she wasn't even going to go through taking off her makeup and the regimen that normally followed.

What was a film of sweat and dirt when she was soon going to meet someone related to her by blood?

In three days.

It would be only the second relative she had ever known. If he even was a relative. How much could a wad of spit really tell you about your family line or connect you with a relative half a world away? Was it really as accurate as people said? Could it be a mistake? What would she say to him? What would he think about her? And maybe he was a weirdo. A freak. A murderer who had hacked her account and was drawing her in as prey.

She turned over, clutching the pillow to her chest. Now she was getting melodramatic. But being alone with so many torrential thoughts was making her crazy. She needed to talk to someone.

A friend.

Liam was out of the question. The next thought that came to her was a surprise out of left field.

Maggie Dalton.

She hadn't talked to her former best friend in quite a few years, she thought as she cringed, remembering that she hadn't even contacted Maggie when her mother died. That would hurt her. Maggie had always said Quinn's mom was like a second mother to her.

In the trauma of the long illness and then her mom's death, Quinn wasn't in her right mind. She'd mentioned Maggie to Ethan, but he'd encouraged her to just focus on the arrangements, telling her that she didn't need a distraction. That Maggie would want to make a long visit out of it, and Quinn wasn't in a state to entertain. At the time, she'd felt he was right.

It wasn't fair to Maggie, though. Quinn knew her best friend would've been comforting. Not demanding.

Quinn sat up and swung her legs over the bed. She picked up her phone and found Maggie's number.

When she pressed it, she prayed that Maggie was still as forgiving as she'd been back in the day. Every spat they'd ever had was short-lived; Maggie's personality was one that didn't hold grudges.

It rang only once, and then a voice came on telling Quinn the number had been disconnected.

Damn. She needed to talk to someone. And if it couldn't be her mother, then she wanted it to be Maggie.

Maggie had always known what to say. What to do. While Quinn tended to slink into the corners around others, Maggie was the exact opposite and was never afraid to be outspoken or take a stand for them both. Maggie was their mouthpiece, if Quinn really wanted to be honest with herself.

She went to her laptop and brought it to the bed. She pulled up Maggie's email address and wrote a quick message telling her to please call as soon as possible, that the last number she had was disconnected.

The whoosh from hitting "Send" was followed up immediately by a chime that signified a new email. It was the message to Maggie, rejected as undeliverable.

What was going on? Maggie had changed her phone number and her email address?

Now that was strange.

Quinn stood and went to her bag. She dug through a side pocket until she found her address book, then returned to her cross-legged position, the laptop beside her.

The address book had been through many years and was barely staying together. Quinn was never without it. You never knew when your phone might get stolen, or you might lose it and have no way to contact anyone. You might even lose your laptop at the same time. Then what would you do?

Her address book was her next lifeline.

But because Quinn didn't have any family other than her mom, and barely any friends from the past, her book was mostly full of professional contacts, with just a few acquaintances scattered in. And passwords. Many, many passwords.

Quinn flipped through the pages.

There was Lea from the hotel in Houston. They'd gone for drinks once. And Rosalind, their social media manager for the hotel. Quinn had thought they were friends for a while, until she kept seeing girls' night out pics on Instagram and realized she was never invited.

She kept going past a few more pages as she looked for a name that might sound comforting to her.

None did, until she got to the *D*s.

Dalton.

Grace Dalton, to be exact. Maggie's mom.

She figured it was as good a time to call as any. It rang once. Then twice.

"Hello?"

It was Grace. Quinn would recognize her voice no matter how many years went by.

"Hi, Mrs. Dalton. It's Quinn," she said.

There was a pause.

"Quinn? Quinn Maguire?"

Well, how many Quinns did the woman know?

She always was a bit foggy. In an endearing way.

"Yes, it's me. Quinn Maguire. How are you?"

"Oh, honey, I'm fine. Other than the arthritis in my hips that is keeping me down. I don't venture too far from home now. How are you?"

"I'm—well, I'm okay. Listen, I'm trying to get ahold of Maggie, but the number I have has been disconnected. And I tried email, but that didn't work either." Quinn tried to keep the desperation out of her voice. Now that she was talking to Grace, the memories were flooding in, and she wanted to talk to Maggie more than anything she'd wanted in a long time.

Grace hesitated again before replying.

"Quinn, I can't give you her number," she said, her voice sad.

Quinn felt stunned for a moment. Maybe Maggie knew about her mother dying and was angry at her?

"Oh, well . . . okay, I guess," she replied. She wasn't sure how to ask why without inspiring the woman to say something that might put Quinn in an even worse emotional place than she currently was. "Can you tell her I called?"

"Of course," Grace said. "It's not you, Quinn. It's, well . . . it's everyone. She doesn't want anyone to have her information."

Now that was weird. What was going on with Maggie?

"Is something wrong, Grace?" Quinn couldn't not ask. And in her worry, she forgot to address her respectfully.

"I'll tell her you called. If she wants to tell you more, she can contact you herself. Is this the number you can be reached at?"

"It is," Quinn said, nodding her head, forgetting the woman couldn't see her. But she really needed Maggie. "Um, Mrs. Dalton?"

"Yes?"

Quinn swallowed the lump in her throat. "Can you tell Maggie I really need to talk to her? It's sort of important. Or, if I promise not to share it, you could give me—well, you know . . ." She stopped just short of begging the woman for Maggie's number.

"No, I can't," Grace said. "I'll tell her you called. But, Quinn, it's time to feed the chickens, so I need to go."

The phone went dead.

Quinn sat there, still holding it to her ear.

Finally, she put it down and leaned back, crashing into the pillows again.

She'd have to face everything by herself.

Suddenly she only wanted to shut everything out and sleep.

Chapter Sixteen

Quinn was navigating a long hospital corridor, a folder with her name on it stuffed under her arm. The folder held her identifying information, including the name of her father. She'd dodged the mysterious faces pursuing her and had just pulled the folder out from under her arm and was opening it to peek when the fire alarm began to shriek, and medical personnel from every room, nook, and cranny came storming at her.

She awoke sweating, her heart racing.

It wasn't a fire alarm.

It was her phone.

Ethan?

For a second, she felt a happy rush that he was calling her. Then as she struggled to reach the phone, she remembered what he had done.

She picked up the phone and squinted at the screen.

Unknown number.

Usually she wouldn't answer unknown numbers, but this time, something told her she should do it.

"Hello?"

"Quinn? Is that you?"

Quinn sat up in bed and switched the lamp on. "Maggie! It's me! I can't believe you called me back." She felt a rush of emotion just hearing her best friend's voice, so familiar she'd recognize it anywhere.

"Of course. Mama said it sounded urgent. And you do sound weird."

"I was asleep. I'm in Maui, six hours behind you. It's two in the morning here."

Maggie laughed. "Oops. Well, you did say to call you. What are you doing in Maui? Vacation?"

Quinn wondered how to tell Maggie everything she needed to say. Especially after she'd pretty much dumped her.

"My mom died," she blurted out, getting the worst of it over with.

"I know," Maggie said, her voice softening. "Mama saw it somewhere. That's all she does is sit on the computer. I'm sorry I didn't call you, but I didn't know until after the service."

"No, I'm sorry," Quinn said. "And it wasn't much of a service. You know my mom. She kept to herself. Not really anyone in her life except me. And her clients. But even those she kept separate from her personal business. They sent flowers."

"I've missed you," Maggie said.

Three little words that held a lot of forgiveness. Before Quinn could answer, she was crying. Finally, she had someone who cared about her and who could listen. Give her advice. Soothe her and tell her that it would all work out.

Quinn couldn't hold back the sniffles.

"What is it?" Maggie said. "Is Ethan okay?"

"Yes. I mean, well . . . no," she said, bringing her tears under control. "Oh, Maggie. My life is such a disaster. And I've got scary things in front of me. I'm a grown woman, and now that my mom is gone, I'm supposed to be adulting, but it's just too damn hard."

"Yeah, tell me about it," Maggie said. "I've got some stuff going on that will blow your mind. There's a reason you can't reach me unless you do it through Mama. My troubles might give yours a run for the money."

"Hold on," Quinn said. "I'm getting up. I need to make a cup of tea, because it sounds like this is going to be a long conversation."

As she headed toward the kitchenette, Quinn felt that the weight she'd carried to bed was getting lighter by the second.

~

At half past five, Quinn finally hung up the phone and climbed into bed. She and Maggie had talked nonstop, catching up on the last few years as they ping-ponged information back and forth.

Maggie had a stalker. She called him the Ghost.

And not some high school crush pining after her. This was serious stuff.

It floored Quinn and filled her with guilt that Maggie had been dealing with such a horrible experience on her own, skipping from town to town and job to job as she stayed just steps ahead of the psychopath, with almost no help from law enforcement due to the fact that the weirdo hadn't yet made physical contact. That was, until he broke into her home and was caught on camera.

Quinn was feeling goose bumps while Maggie told her story and only breathed normally when Maggie reported he was finally in jail.

"I can't get into all the details right now," Maggie whispered. "Charlie, my son, is here, and I don't want him to overhear."

When she said *son*, Quinn was speechless.

Maggie had a son!

Quinn instantly felt like an aunt—albeit a slack one. As Maggie bragged on and on, she made Charlie sound like an amazing kid, but imagining Maggie as a mom was difficult. She was always the free spirit, the one who Quinn thought would travel the world unencumbered as she tackled each experience on her bucket list.

But as life tends to go, that's not how things played out.

It was all hard to even accept. Maggie had been dealing with some bad stuff without a best friend by her side. Quinn wanted to be there for her now.

She needed Maggie too.

Quinn told her about her mother's earth-shattering deathbed declaration, the inheritance, Ethan's cheating, and the mysterious possible relative.

First, Maggie erupted when she heard what Ethan had done. She admitted that the last time she'd come around, Ethan had acted kind of creepy toward her too—a real sucker punch to Quinn, considering that during that same visit he was telling her that she needed to put some space between herself and Maggie, that her friend was a bad influence.

Quinn wasn't ready to completely throw Ethan under the bus, but she was glad to hear Maggie tell her over and over how Quinn could do better for herself, something Quinn was starting to wonder about now too.

They talked more about Thursday's meeting, and Quinn admitted that she was nervous but didn't feel comfortable asking Maria or Liam to accompany her.

Maggie being Maggie—usually a relentless fireball—quizzed Quinn on just who Liam was, but Quinn refused to take the bait. She didn't really know what to think about Liam herself. He was a friend, though the word didn't feel sufficient. So she moved the conversation back to her anxiety about the upcoming meeting and the many what-ifs involved.

"It could be my father," she told Maggie. "This time my *real* father."

A small part of her felt like a child, wishing that she would finally have a father figure in her life, a dependable man who cared about the daughter he'd sired. And what if all these years, he hadn't even known about her? Maybe that was the reason her mother made up the Maguire name. She wanted to keep Quinn from her real dad. That could also explain her mother's reluctance to have any connection to family.

As the minutes ticked by, they discussed every possibility. Then, Quinn almost started crying again when Maggie insisted she was going to leave her son with her mom and come to Maui. She wanted to be by Quinn's side when she met the mysterious possible relative.

They ended the call reluctantly, both wanting to hold on to their renewed connection for as long as they could. It just felt so right to be talking again.

Quinn laid the phone on the nightstand, then snuggled under the comforter, a small smile creeping across her face.

Maggie was coming.

Already that made everything seem a whole lot better.

She would not have to sort out her life alone. With that knowledge, she felt peace wash over her, and she finally allowed herself to drift into a calm, peaceful slumber.

Chapter Seventeen

Over the next day, Quinn kept to herself, spending the mornings answering work emails and pushing already-delayed meetings even further out. Some of her coworkers were getting impatient with her, but they were just going to have to wait. There was too much happening now for her to leave Maui. She'd submitted her request for a leave of absence. She hated to drain her banked vacation hours, but she could think of nothing more important that would come up.

Her request had caused a chain reaction, and Quinn's boss had sent an email asking for a call. That sent a shiver of fear through Quinn, but she wasn't even going to answer that one yet.

She simply wasn't ready to face her job again, and she sure as Hades wasn't ready to face Ethan, especially not when she was getting ready to finally meet another biological relative for the first time.

Even the thought made her heart skip around in a crazy way. One thing at a time, though.

First, Maggie.

Being the spur-of-the-moment fireball she was, Maggie had arranged for her mother to keep her son, then booked a flight that would have her in Maui less than eighteen hours after their call, insisting she needed a day to acclimate before the big meeting.

Quinn couldn't be more grateful. Having Maggie there would help keep her from taking a call from Ethan before she was ready.

By midmorning Quinn was dressed and anxious to head to the airport early. One bad accident on the road could leave her sitting in traffic for hours, and there was no way she as going to leave Maggie waiting for her.

Her phone rang, and it was Auntie Wang.

"Quinn, I just want to check in with you and tell you I've found a Carmen Crowe on the island."

Quinn sat down on the bed, feeling suddenly breathless. "Do you think it's the right one?"

"I don't know. She's around the same age, though. I'm meeting with her this afternoon. She wasn't really interested, but I talked her into it."

"Does she know what you want?"

"No," said Auntie Wang. "I told her I wanted to talk to her about being on the board for a new organization that promotes Hawaiian history. I appealed to her pride in being asked. I'll ask her about your mother face-to-face so I can gauge her reaction."

"Jeez, Auntie Wang. When she finds out you're lying, she's going to be really upset."

Auntie Wang giggled. "Nope. Because I'm not lying. I decided first thing this morning that I *am* going to put together a small organization to go into the schools and do historical presentations. This new generation thinks the only culture we come from is a long line of surfers. It might take an outside group to tempt their curiosity. Of course, I need Miss Carmen Crowe's input before making a decision about whether to pursue this or not."

Quinn smiled. "You're brilliant, Auntie Wang."

"I also wanted to tell you not to worry about tomorrow. You'll be in a public place, and it's a big step, but not a sure thing. This person might not even be related. Anything on the computer can be manipulated these days, Quinn."

"I know. I'm not getting my hopes up," she lied. If by some chance this was not a relative, Quinn was going to be devastated.

She took one more look in the mirror, hoping her makeup was right, then headed out the door. Outside the kitchen, Liam and a small group of painters were setting up tarps and stacking paint cans.

"Aloha," he called out, lifting a hand before turning back to the crew of men dressed in white pants and shirts. He'd brought help to finish painting while he rehung the kitchen cabinet doors. Quinn couldn't wait to see the old wainscoting polished up. Even the shiplap should be hung by nightfall.

"Morning," Quinn responded, then headed to her rental car. She hated that it felt awkward with him, and she wasn't even sure why.

But soon he'd be done, the family would move out, and she would go home. No sense in worrying about it, she reminded herself.

"Wait!"

Quinn turned around to find Maria hurrying toward her.

"Hi," Quinn said.

Maria had a huge smile, and when she got near enough, she hugged Quinn tightly.

"Well, you're in a good mood," Quinn said, feeling a bit awkward.

"I sure am," Maria said. "I've got a job interview lined up later."

"That's great!" Quinn smiled, watching the excitement play across the woman's face.

"And . . . are you ready for more good news?"

"Absolutely," Quinn said, almost adding that any good news would be welcome to offset what felt like months of the opposite.

"I've found a rental up on the north end of the island that we can afford. If I get the job," she added. "The landlord said he'd break my deposit up into payments too."

Quinn felt instant relief. Maybe it was all going to be okay after all. Maria and her family would get a new start, and Quinn's spur-of-the-moment house-buying adventure could be recovered.

"Oh, Maria, I'm so glad," Quinn said.

"You'll be proud of me for this, too, but yesterday I boxed up my entire room and even gave away a lot of it to the church for the summer yard sale." Maria rattled on about how it felt good to begin cleaning out the clutter; then she moved on to the kids changing schools and other details, but what Quinn noticed most of all was that Maria seemed to be taking everything in stride now.

"I'd better run, Maria," Quinn said. "I need to get to the airport to pick up my friend who is coming for a short visit. I want to make sure I leave early enough in case there's a traffic jam."

"Oh, that's nice. Is it your fiancé?"

Quinn felt a stab in her gut. "No, it's my best friend from many years back."

"That'll be nice," Maria said. "And you're right, one fender bender can put you back an hour or more. Be careful."

She waved and returned to the house. Quinn saw Kupuna standing in the doorway, and as she climbed into the car, she wondered what he thought about moving to the other side of the island. So far he hadn't mentioned much about having to leave his home, but he did give advice on the various projects that were going on. He said the house had needed a makeover for years. Quinn wondered how he knew, considering he couldn't see it, but obviously he knew every inch of it.

Yes, the house was finally coming together, and since the countertops were still held up somewhere, the plan was to tackle the floors next.

All the changes were going to look amazing.

At least one thing was going right.

Traffic wasn't too bad, and the drive gave Quinn a lot of time to think about her current state of affairs. She was so lost in thought, automatically following the GPS directions, that she was surprised when she arrived effortlessly. She found short-term parking, pulled in, and shut off the car.

She checked herself in the mirror, took a deep breath, and climbed out.

The sidewalks were busy, lined with cars and people checking luggage at the kiosks. The tourists were easy to pick out, as they looked confused navigating around in their flowered shirts or sundresses, the locals moving around them smoothly, wearing less ostentatious clothes and carrying plain travel bags.

Quinn went through the doors, and the atmosphere changed yet again. Inside, it was a mixture of vibes of elation from arriving passengers, happy and eager to have made it to Maui, and the disappointed and holiday-hungover people getting ready to make the sad trek back to reality.

As for herself, she was stuck between excitement to see Maggie and anxiety that their friendship wouldn't feel the same. That the easy and effortless vibe they'd always had would be gone, making the next few days even more stressful.

Quinn walked to the arrivals section and spent the next half hour staring out the window, too anxious to take out her phone. At two minutes until arrival time, she stood and went to stand near the door the passengers would be coming from.

It was a brutal combination of emotions that taunted her as she waited for her best friend to walk off the plane. She tried to calm herself by stroking the soft flower petals of the lei she'd bought inside the door. Maggie had never been to Hawaii, and Quinn wanted to try to make it special. Her thoughts spiraled out of control. They hadn't seen each other in a few years. What should Quinn say to her? Should she hug her? Apologize first? Avoid talk of the time they'd been apart? Quinn didn't know what to do. Other than her mother and Maggie, she'd never really been able to bond with other women. It was hard for her to open herself up, and she just never felt like she fit whatever it was they seemed to be looking for.

A few feet away, a mom sat beside two teenage girls, their heads down as they texted frantically. When she and Maggie were growing into teens, texting was just becoming popular among their crowd, but their moms were protective and didn't even allow them to carry cell phones. Quinn was glad they hadn't. She and Maggie had actually talked to each other. It was called *conversation*! With real words, her voice traveling into the wall phone and through a cord she'd stretched down the hallway as far as it would go. Their experience made for a deeper connection than she felt teens got these days with their chasing each other all over social media.

Quinn thought about their first prom and how quietly upset she'd been that she hadn't been asked. Maggie had her date secured before almost anyone. But at the last minute, she arranged for him to go with someone else so that she and Quinn could go together, claiming she didn't want to be stuck with the same guy all night anyway.

The next year both of them had dates, and they'd doubled. Quinn went with a long turquoise dress, and Maggie a short black stunner with sequins that showed off her amazing legs. Quinn's date drove, and they'd laughed like crazy when the two boys picked them up in his dad's pickup truck. Squeezed in like sardines, the four of them had the best time that night.

They'd ended it at Quinn's house, and her mother had arranged the ultimate sleepover for her and Maggie. She had ice cream laid out on the kitchen counter with every topping imaginable in tiny bowls around it. They'd rented movies—the old-school way, before internet streaming came along—and her mom had whispered to Quinn how thankful she was that they'd come home safely and not chosen to go party.

Quinn wasn't the type to put her mother through that kind of emotional distress, even when Maggie sometimes hinted they were missing out. Quinn was just glad to have gone to the prom at all, since she wouldn't have if not for Maggie.

As soon as the thought came to mind, Quinn lifted her eyes to see Maggie—first one off the plane, of course—making a beeline straight for her. She looked different—more mature and vulnerable, even—but those lively green eyes were the same. They practically danced with excitement.

Instantly all Quinn's doubts were gone. Nothing had changed. They still had their bond.

They met in the middle, and Maggie dropped her bags and enveloped Quinn in a bear hug, lifting her off the ground an inch or so. Quinn laughed through the tears that were falling and felt her heart rush with emotion.

When they let go, she put the lei around Maggie, who was also shedding a few tears.

"Your hair!" Quinn said, reaching for a long red strand. It fell almost to Maggie's waist in a dancing wave of movement, flowing like fire.

She laughed. "I know. I was trying to have a totally different look, so I stopped coloring it and let it have its way. And they were right— blondes do have more fun. I need to find my way back."

"No, you don't. It's beautiful this way," Quinn said. It reminded Quinn of the days before they'd both discovered hair color and highlights. "And you look great. You've lost a lot of weight, though." She couldn't get enough of looking at her, dissecting each change.

"It's been a stressful few years." Maggie lifted an eyebrow, reminding Quinn of their long conversation the night before.

"Well, let's get out of here," Quinn said, picking up the carry-on bag that Maggie had dropped. "Did you check luggage too?"

"Nope. This is it. You know me, I like to be free as a bird."

That was the Maggie Quinn remembered—the fiery redhead who had helped her through some of life's most angst-filled moments. She squeezed her one more time for good measure, feeling surreal that she was really there in the flesh, and they headed for the door.

～

Quinn slid her feet back and forth, letting the sand fall over them in little cascades before doing it again. Tonight the water was calmer than usual, rushing in to the beach and then easing back out in a seductive tease. Tomorrow was going to be a monumental day, but for now, she only wanted to concentrate on Maggie. They'd had dinner with Maria, Kupuna, and the kids—at Maria's insistence—and Maggie had charmed them all. Then on the way to the beach, she had exclaimed over how weird the situation was.

"You look really natural in this setting, you know," Maggie said. "I don't think I've ever seen you so relaxed."

Quinn hadn't thought about it, but Maggie was right. With each day she spent there, she was becoming more comfortable, despite the issues with the house and now the anxiety of finding a relative.

She stared out to sea. "I do feel different here. I love the sound of the ocean. It soothes me and reminds me of my mom. Since she was from Maui, I've always connected her with the sea but never actually felt her presence like I do here."

"Have you decided where you'll spread her ashes?" Maggie asked.

Quinn shook her head. "With all that has been happening, I haven't figured it out. I think my subconscious won't let me."

"It'll come to you," Maggie said, reaching over and rubbing her hand.

They'd grabbed a blanket, wine, and glasses, then found the perfect place just off the path from the cottage. They settled down on the sand with an amazing view of the water to finish filling in all the blank spots they'd missed in each other's lives. They'd started with the easy stuff. Quinn talked about the house, and Maggie told her about Charlie, beaming with adoration as she described a rough-and-tumble tiny boy who melted into her arms at bedtime. That led to the story about Colby, Charlie's dad, and how when she found out she was pregnant, he freaked out.

"I mean, I really can't blame him. I was a total nutcase when suddenly my belly outgrew my brain. One night he ate my leftover taco, and I sobbed like I was at a funeral. He didn't know whether to go get me another taco or have me committed."

Quinn threw her head back and laughed.

"Then when we brought Charlie home, I had a month off from work, but I felt like a complete failure. Colby would come home to find me still in my pajamas, my hair unwashed for the second or third day in a row and the house looking like a tornado had streaked through."

"I'm sure having a newborn is hard stuff," Quinn said. "I haven't even had a puppy yet."

Maggie laughed. "Oh, I'd say having ten puppies isn't as hard as having a baby. Some mothers talk about how heavenly it is and how they're filled with maternal bliss for years on end. All I could do was pray the little alien hanging on my boob would sleep for more than half an hour at a time."

"Did Colby help at all?"

"He tried. But it was awkward. One minute he's a sexy bachelor chasing after the girl of his dreams, then he catches her and—oops!— he has an instant family and doesn't have time to go out with the boys anymore. I felt like he was resentful. He claimed he wasn't. I told him I wanted him to leave, that I'd raise our son myself. I said it in anger, but we were both too proud to back off once we blew up."

That made Quinn sad. Maggie did have a stubborn streak.

"He really tried, though. He took me to every doctor visit," Maggie said softly. "He did the birthing classes, and he was there when Charlie was born, coaching me through it like a boss. I think Colby fell in love with him the minute the nurse placed him into those big, rough hands."

She sounded like she was still in love with him, but Quinn knew better than to push her. "It must be hard to be a single mom."

Maggie looked at her quickly, then gazed out to sea. "Yep. Even before the Ghost came along, this was the hardest damn thing I've ever done in my life. You don't realize it at the time, but the infant stage is actually the best part. I don't know how all these Instagram moms do everything so perfect and still look like a million bucks in all their photos. I'm almost glad I had to erase myself from all social media. At least I don't have that impossible depiction of motherhood in my face all the time, taunting me that I'm more or less a domestic failure. It's made it a lot easier when some days it's all I can do to thaw out chicken nuggets and give him his third Juicy Juice of the day."

"I bet you do just fine," Quinn said.

Maggie shrugged. "My mom thinks so. I hide all the sugary cereal and faux fruit snacks on the rare occasion she visits. For all she knows, I'm feeding him three servings of fruits and vegetables a day and washing him with homemade, chemical-free soap while we recite the alphabet backward and forward."

That made Quinn smile again. Maggie's mom could be quite type A when she wanted to. She had pushed Maggie into being an overachiever all the way until the tenth grade, when her daughter finally sat her down and told her to back off.

"Anyway, nuggets are protein, and ketchup is vegetables, right?" Maggie said, smiling again. "I don't give her enough credit, though. She's changed, Quinn. She's more relaxed with him than she was with us."

"I've heard that's how it is with grandparents." Quinn felt a catch in her breath when she thought of her own mother. She would've been such an amazing nana.

Maggie didn't notice, because she kept talking. "Having Charlie is still the best thing that ever happened to me. I talk like motherhood is torture, but really, when he lies beside me with his hand in mine, falling asleep as his beautiful eyelashes flutter gently, I melt. I feel this powerful love well up in me that is so big it could heat a nation. It's times like those that I realize I'm not just getting through the days, I'm soaking them up, collecting all his childhood memories and storing them safely in my jar of hearts. I stop worrying about the wet clothes I left in the washing machine or the foot-puncturing toys on the floor that'll greet me in the morning. I remind myself that my baby went to sleep safe and happy, and I tell myself I'm doing okay."

"Good. Because you know what? Okay is enough," Quinn said. "Some parents can't even reach that milestone. I'm sure Charlie is a great little boy, and I can't wait to meet him."

"Auntie Quinn." Maggie smiled. "You'll be all kisses, hugs, and story time. That'll be a big change from all the roughhousing he gets from his uncles."

"Do they see him much?" Quinn remembered Maggie's older brothers as being really protective of her, and always into outdoorsy things. At least Charlie would have some very macho male figures to look up to in his life.

"More now that the Ghost is locked away."

Quinn wanted to know more about Colby, because she could tell Maggie hadn't gotten over him yet. But Maggie changed the subject, refocusing the spotlight so it wasn't on her anymore.

"What are you going to do about Ethan?"

Quinn let all the air out of her lungs as she struggled for the right words to say. "I don't really know yet. I love him. Or at least I did. I think I still do. But I hate him too. At least right now."

"You know, I always felt like he'd do something like this," Maggie said softly.

That took Quinn by surprise. "You did? Why?"

Maggie paused, then released a long sigh. "There was a time or two he said some inappropriate things to me. Eased up too close in passing. He let his hands have a bit too much freedom."

"Why didn't you tell me?" It was a question tinged with soft accusation, but Quinn couldn't keep it in.

"I wanted to. But you acted like he was everything to you."

He was. He is. Still, she'd have wanted to know.

"I didn't want to shatter the illusion of Mr. Perfect," Maggie said. "You based your entire future around him. I just couldn't mess that up. I'm sorry. But I told him straight out he'd better never try anything with me again, or I'd go straight to you. That's when I guess he told you to stop spending time with me, because the calls started to get further apart. Then you started ignoring my text messages."

"I never received any text messages," Quinn said, turning defensive, even though her mind still reeled from the news that Ethan had put the moves on her best friend. Why she should be shocked, she didn't know.

"Well, I sent them."

Quinn knew then. Ethan had read the messages and deleted them. He was always picking up her phone, going through it. But God forbid she ever touch his. She should've suspected it before. She thought it was Maggie's outgoing personality he didn't like—but the fact is that it was her rejection that had turned him against her best friend. And she'd considered over the years that he might be too controlling, but she'd always pushed that thought away, because he really was a great catch, and she was lucky to have snagged him. She wasn't ready to even consider they wouldn't have a future.

"Let's not talk about him anymore," Quinn said. "Not for now. I want to focus on you. And tomorrow. I'm so nervous. But I can't believe you're here."

"Well, if not for me being stubborn, I'd be sitting on a balcony right now, not right here on the sand beside you. *I* can't believe you made me a reservation," Maggie said. "You know me better than that."

"Well, the cottage is so small. I didn't want you to feel closed in." She'd called the Maui location of her hotel brand and used her employee discount to reserve a room. Just in case.

But Maggie wasn't going for it.

"Actually, small is better. I like to know every corner of where I am. Less space to check out before I go to bed," Maggie said. "And of course I want to stay with you. It'll be like old times."

That it would. When they were younger, most of their overnights had been at Quinn's house, since she didn't have brothers to irritate Maggie. And their homes had always been small. Or cozy, as they liked to consider it.

But Maggie was referring to her stalker: the man who had made her last few years a nightmare. All from an online dating site, and one real date gone awry.

"It really sucks that you've had to go through that alone. I should've been there."

In the receding light she could see Maggie shrug.

"That's water under the bridge, Quinn. I would've liked to have had you to talk to, but to be honest, it wouldn't have been safe for me to be around you much. I have had to be so careful. If I visited someone more than once, I was afraid he might latch on to them too."

"You had to be so terrified."

"I was for a long time. And I was angry when I found out he'd been brought up on stalking charges before. Unfortunately, his two previous victims just wanted it over with, and they backed down easy. One of the trials was dismissed, and the other one got settled out of court. That just spurred him on to go after someone else. Just happened to be that I stepped into his radar."

"You're such a strong woman, it's hard for me to imagine someone like that targeting you," Quinn said.

"That's a good point. A lot of women have trouble with obsessive men because they are too kind and trusting. Or they're vulnerable, and the stalker picks up on that and uses it to his own benefit. As usual, I don't fit into a stereotype, but somehow I became his next target."

"I'm so sorry," Quinn said.

"Me too. I'm just glad that finally he's serving time."

"Are you anxious about when he gets out?" Quinn asked, worried for Maggie.

"Well, they're supposed to let me know, but I've set up Google alerts on his name just in case. And once a month I call the correctional center to be sure he's still listed. I still take a lot of precautions, but I know I'm safe now. And I have a dog that'll eat his face if he shows up."

"I just can't imagine someone like you getting tangled up with a crazy person," Quinn said.

Maggie took a long sip of her wine, then leaned back on one arm. "It happens more often than you'd think. He was a charmer at first—made himself look like a real catch. We talked for a few weeks before even going out. He sent me flowers twice."

"Before even meeting him?" Quinn asked.

Maggie nodded. "He saw online where I worked and sent them there. But when we did meet, he started telling me how he was all alone in the world. He'd cut ties with all his family, claiming they were the ones with issues. I asked him about close friends, and he claimed he didn't really have anyone to speak of, that he was a loner. He was really good-looking, but he talked himself up so much that immediately my college psychology class notes started swirling in my head. Narcissistic. Self-righteous. He gave me all the wrong feelings."

"He sounds like a real douchebag," Quinn said.

"You think? So after that night I tried to gently disassociate. He thought our date went beautifully. Didn't notice a thing and claimed it was love at first sight for him, that I was an answer to his dreams. I was like, whoa there, cool your jets, buddy."

Quinn laughed softly. She could just imagine Maggie's feisty side coming out.

Maggie waved her hand in the air in a dismissive way. "Talk about some alarm bells. I was nice, but I told him I'd decided I wasn't ready to get into another relationship so quickly after breaking up with Charlie's dad."

"He didn't take it well?"

"At first he said he understood, but then he sent me more than three hundred text messages over the next two days. When I didn't reply, he started coming to my job and leaving notes on my car along with a red rose. He kept sending gifts. Candy. Concert tickets. Once he even showed up at a restaurant I was having dinner at and invited himself to sit down. Thankfully it was with Trina from work and not a guy, which would've most likely set him off. Then one day in the grocery store, I turned, and he was there, silently watching me. It sent a chill up my spine. I got firm with him then and told him if he didn't leave me alone, I'd call the police. That's when he went off the deep end. From then on, he was leaving a black rose on my car. No notes anymore."

She paused and inhaled deeply. "Then he was in my house, Quinn."

"Oh my God. Were you there?"

"No. It was after days of rain, and Charlie was going stir-crazy indoors. So we went for a ride and were gone probably just over half an hour. When I got home, at first everything was fine. I gave Charlie a bath, put on his pajamas, and then carried him into my room so he could be close while I showered. I went to lay him on the bed, and there was a black rose."

"Maggie . . . ," Quinn said.

"Yeah, I know. You'd be proud of me. I stayed calm for Charlie's sake. I armed myself with my Taser and my phone, then barricaded us in the bathroom and called the police. They were there in ten minutes and couldn't find anyone."

"That's terrifying."

Maggie nodded. "You better believe it. I quit my job, traded my car, and took off. Oh, and I got my dog."

"What about Colby? He didn't try to step in?"

"Colby doesn't know what happened. He thinks I've gone crazy, leaving my job and moving from place to place. Or he thinks I'm doing it to make it harder for him to visit. I swore my mother to secrecy, because I thought he might use it against me and try to take Charlie."

"Why? Does he want custody of Charlie?"

"Not right now. He's too busy hunting, fishing, and sowing his oats like all the other country boys out there. But you never know when he'll meet some girl who thinks our son is just the cutest and would be better off with his dad full-time. Colby knows I'm a good mother, but women can make men do crazy things."

"So now what?" Quinn asked. "Your stalker is out of your life, so you can settle down again, right?"

"I don't know yet. I've got a lot to figure out. All I know is I'm tired of living in fear." Maggie used her finger to trace circles in the sand. "I'm not ready to go back to my old job and put myself out there so publicly yet, though."

"What about returning to animal medicine?" Quinn said. She remembered when Maggie had left her job as a vet tech to pursue more money in the public relations field. With her fiery personality, Maggie had shot up through the ranks quickly until she was one of the top-paid PR reps in her field.

Maggie shrugged. "I do miss working with animals. I just have to figure out if that's going to pay me enough to take care of Charlie. It's like I'm starting completely over with nothing from my past except for my son and my dog."

"And me," Quinn said. "I'm not going anywhere this time."

Even though she said the words, she wondered how much chaos it was going to add to her and Ethan's already crumbling relationship— that is, *if* she decided to work things out with him.

"And you," Maggie said. "But it's all a mess. I've been hopping around from one short-term rental to another. Charlie needs stability."

The photos of her son on her phone were just out-of-this-world adorable. He had his mom's freckles, though his hair was blond and didn't have the reddish tint. He was all kinds of cute, and Quinn couldn't wait to meet him.

"I think I've protected him from knowing most of what was going on, but he's getting old enough now that he needs friends. This year he should start some sort of preschool. And he doesn't understand why we had to leave the house we loved," Maggie continued. "I had hung train tracks around his room, and he loved to watch the little caboose go around as he went to sleep. I haven't been able to do that anywhere else. We've moved too much."

"That's so sad."

"Yeah, it was. But once I knew he'd been in there, it felt tainted. As though he'd marked it with his scent that no amount of bleach could clean away. But that's only a tiny bit of the aftermath. I also had to change careers, because mine depended on social media and put me in the public too much. Now that I don't have to worry about him breathing down my neck, I can finally work on setting up a new life and making new memories for Charlie."

"Where do you plan on living now?" she asked Maggie.

Maggie sighed. "I really don't know. I'm hoping my impromptu holiday from Charlie in this peaceful place can help me figure that out. And it really depends on where I can get work. I can't keep supporting my son on waitress tips. It's time to move forward and break up with the past."

Quinn couldn't imagine how hard it was for Maggie to go from making an executive-level salary to waiting tables. She had a new respect for her friend, who was definitely someone who would do what it took to survive.

Maggie stood. "On that note, we should probably get back. Decide what you'll wear."

Quinn joined her and brushed off her hands. "Are you sure you'll be okay sleeping with me? It's not too late to go to the hotel."

"Oh, shut up. When haven't I been okay sleeping with you? What, have you become a massive snoring machine now? Do you fart in your sleep? Do you sleep naked now? Or is there something else you need to tell me?"

Quinn laughed. She'd forgotten how much she loved Maggie's sense of humor and her ability to turn every sad moment around. "Fine, but I don't care if you are company—I call the shower first. I remember how you don't clean your hair out of the drain."

Maggie was bent over picking up the blanket and wiggled her butt at Quinn before standing and facing her. "Yeah, well, you'd better cut it short, sister. We all know how you like your bathroom time to make sure you look perfect before even going to bed. How long does your nightly regimen take these days? An hour?"

They knew each other so well. It was a priceless gift. One they'd almost lost. Quinn felt a rush of emotion and reached over and took Maggie's hand. "Thank you for coming, Maggie. We'll get through this, and then, I promise, I'll be there for you too."

Maggie squeezed her fingers and held on, a silent pact that this time, they wouldn't let anything come between being there for each other.

Chapter Eighteen

Quinn was up before dawn. It had taken Maggie a long time to fall asleep. Before getting into bed, she'd insisted on checking every inch of the cottage, then went back to the door and windows at least three times to make sure the locks were engaged. Though she claimed she felt comfortable there, she acted like someone was waiting just outside to get them. Quinn was really patient with her, considering all Maggie had been through. It made sense that she was paranoid or maybe it was just proactive—but getting to sleep so late made her feel hungover.

Ethan had sent more texts. He said he'd booked a flight over.

Quinn broke her commitment not to respond and sent him back a message telling him not to come, that she wouldn't see him. Then she turned her phone off.

She pulled some leggings on, not even caring that they didn't match her long sleep shirt, and made herself a cup of coffee. She slipped quietly out the door so she wouldn't wake Maggie. She settled herself on the lanai, grateful she'd left her yoga mat outside so she could do some stretches and meditation when she finished her coffee.

Before she could get to it, Liam showed up. She forgot he was supposed to be there bright and early to start sanding the floors. If Quinn had seen him coming, she would've snuck back in, but for a big man he was as light-footed as a deer.

"Good morning," she said as he crossed the courtyard to her lanai. She wanted to cover her naked face and smooth her hair, but he was watching.

He raised his eyebrows. "For some."

"Grouchy today?" Quinn asked, noticing an uncharacteristic frown. She'd also never seen him look so disheveled.

"Tired. I take it you haven't talked to Maria." He leaned on the porch rail and sighed.

"No, what's wrong?"

"Good news and bad news. Which one do you want first?"

"Please tell me something good. I need it," Quinn said.

"After hearing nothing back from her job interview, Maria took a chance. She made up some of her famous shortbread cookies and took them to the bakery. The owner went nuts over them and wants to stock them. She's going to let Maria work from home so she can still be here for the kids and Kupuna."

"That's fantastic! What a genius move!" Quinn was so happy for Maria.

"Yeah, her generation always connects those cookies with their childhood, but not many can make them just like the old recipe. I predict that Maria will be swamped with orders within a few weeks. She has to let that bakery have the cookies exclusively for six months, and then she can start selling them to other bakeries and hotels if she wishes."

"I'm thrilled. Maria needed this so bad. Not just for the money, but for her self-confidence," Quinn said. "I'm scared to ask, but what's the bad news?"

"Pali. He missed a winning pass at the game last night when he tripped and somersaulted. He got to his feet, and I saw him look up at someone in the stands then stomp off the field. We couldn't find him anywhere after the game. I went to all his friends' houses and every beach he likes to hang out at. He won't answer his phone and turned off the cell phone locator. We had to give up when it hit three in the morning. Maria was beside herself when I finally left."

"Oh no," Quinn said. "Are you sure he didn't maybe slip in?"

"Nope. I just checked. I'm about to call the hospitals. Make sure he wasn't involved in some accident or something."

"Did you see what caught his eye in the stands?"

Liam nodded. "Yep. But don't tell Maria. She's got enough on her plate right now worrying about Pali."

"What was it?"

He leaned toward her and whispered, "His dad was there. I spotted him just before he turned and disappeared. I guess they were both scared off after they saw each other."

"I don't understand. I thought Pali was upset at his dad's sudden absence?" Quinn said. "At least now we know the man is alive. Wouldn't Pali be glad he came to the game? Relieved he finally showed up?"

"Normally, yes. But the love between a father and son is a complicated thing. Pali screwed up last night, and for Jaime to choose that moment to be there and witness it . . . well, that hurt Pali's pride. And it probably brought all his anger to the top. He's a good kid. But he's confused. The kind of mental turmoil he's been through will make you do stupid things."

"Maybe you need to check the police station first then." Quinn drained the rest of her coffee. "Is there anything I can do?"

"No. You've got your big meeting today, right?"

"I sure do." She got a queasy feeling in her stomach.

"Are you nervous?" he asked, sitting down on the step. "Want to talk about it? It might help."

She hesitated.

"You don't have to," he said. "But I'm here if you need me." He looked wounded.

"It's not that I don't want to talk about it. I just don't know what to even feel. I guess I'm nervous. Excited. But scared too."

"What about it scares you?" he asked.

"If this person is really related to me, then my whole life changes today. I want to know where I come from, but now that there could be something concrete, I don't know if I'm ready. Change has never been easy for me. To tell the truth, someone has always stepped up and done the hard stuff for me."

"You're braver than you think, Quinn. I mean, you up and bought a house an ocean away from everything and everyone you know. You came here, and you took control and made a plan. And one with compassion, I might add. Give yourself some credit. You can do this, and if this person is someone you don't want to claim, then walk away with your head held high, but at least you will know something one way or another."

"You're right," she said. God, he was so right.

"I would offer to come with you, but I heard you have a sassy redhead holed up in there," he said, nodding toward the cottage.

Quinn laughed. "Yes, and I want you to meet her. Maggie is my best friend but also the closest thing to a sister I've ever had. She's a take-no-lip kind of girl, and I think she's just what I need beside me. I have a feeling every question I've planned to ask will disappear from my train of thought, and Maggie will be able to step right in and take over."

He nodded. "Good. I heard she took the red-eye over here just to make sure she'd make it in time. That's a great friend to have."

"Yeah, she's something. But I appreciate your offer. Or, um . . . the sorta offer."

"Anytime, Quinn." He stood and headed for the main house. "I hope you'll let me know how it goes."

"Of course," Quinn said. "That is, unless the coconut wireless informs you first."

She loved the sound of his laugh as he disappeared through the kitchen door. He had an uncanny way of saying just a few words and making her open up. Though she was glad Maggie was there, a tiny part of her would've been happy to take Liam with her to her meeting too. He just gave the kind of quiet support that was so rare these days. No judgment. No opinions. Just support.

~

With an hour to go until they needed to leave, Quinn was so nervous about the meeting that she made Maggie crazy with her pacing around the cottage.

"I'm going to take a quick walk down to the beach," she said, sliding her feet into her sandals. "I'll change when I get back."

"Yes, that's a great idea," Maggie said. "I'd come with you, but I think you need to be alone for a few minutes. Go do some yoga poses. Breathe the salty air. Anything and everything you can think of to burn off that anxiety."

Quinn laughed, grabbed her sun hat and a towel, and then headed out the door. She made a quick detour for the path, avoiding the back door of Maria's house.

Five minutes later she approached the water. She leaned her head back, closed her eyes, and breathed deeply.

"It's serene out here, yes?" a voice called out.

Quinn jumped. She turned to see Kupuna sitting on a small foldable chair, just a few feet to the left of the path she'd come down. She'd been in such deep thought she hadn't even seen him.

"Yes, it is," she called back, then walked over to him.

She lay her towel on the ground beside his chair and sat down, bringing her knees up and wrapping her arms around them. She couldn't say what moved her to join him, especially when she had wanted to be alone, but she was drawn to him.

He sat staring out to sea as though he could really see the waves crashing upon one another. His face intrigued her; the nooks and crannies held so much wisdom. She found herself wondering what his life story was about.

"Maria said that today is a big day for you," he said, breaking into her thoughts, his voice low and calm.

She nodded, forgetting he couldn't see her.

"Yes, it is. But I'm afraid." The words came out nearly without her knowing it, startling her with the truth she spoke.

He reached over and took her hand. It should've felt awkward, but somehow it didn't.

"Whatever you find at the end of this day, it will not change the person you are. But you may need to dig deep and find forgiveness for all that has transpired. The Hawaiian tradition teaches that all life is connected. *Ho'oponopono* means 'forgiveness' and is not only a way of healing ourselves but others and our world as well."

Such profound words that they kept her silent. What did he know that she didn't? What was going to require this forgiveness that he spoke of?

There really wasn't much to say after that. When he let her hand go, it tingled where he had held it.

She watched the waves for another minute or two, then rose.

"Thank you, Kupuna," she said, gathering up her towel. "I'll think about your advice. I'm sure it will come in handy."

He nodded solemnly.

"Did Pali come home?" she asked.

"No, but he will," Kupuna said. "He's a good boy. Confused, but good all the same. I expect to see him by nightfall."

"I hope so. Well, I need to run. I hope you have a good day."

He nodded and held up a hand. His farewell. Or dismissal.

Quinn trekked back up the path, feeling lighter.

When she returned to the cottage, Maggie was on the porch, her arms wrapped around her knees while she perched in the chair. An unusual scowl covered her face, furrowed eyebrows and all.

"I'm glad you finally came back. We need a blowtorch," she said. "Or a gallon of gas and a match. Hell, bring me a stick of dynamite. The cottage has to go."

"What's going on?" Quinn asked.

"There's a damn centipede in the shower, and we need to burn this sucker down."

Quinn laughed as she went inside to take care of the centipede, explaining to Maggie, who followed her like a scared child, that Hawaii is in the tropics, and the tropics have scary bugs sometimes.

That didn't relieve Maggie, and as soon as Quinn hurried into the outfit she'd chosen, applied her makeup, and fixed her hair, Maggie nearly dragged her out to the car, saying they'd leave early and take the scenic route. Quinn didn't tell her there was only one route to Napili, but luckily all routes were scenic in Maui.

"I should've gone in and talked to Maria," Quinn said as they backed out of the driveway. Not checking in made her feel like a horrible person. She'd told Maggie about talking with Maria's father, that he said Pali hadn't come home. "And I'm sure Alani is beside herself. She adores her big brother."

"I told you, he's probably sprawled out at some girl's house. At his age, it's a miracle he's not sneaking off all the time. He's a teenage boy. He cares only about football and girls."

"And surfing," Quinn added. She hoped that Maggie was right. Pali wasn't the typical teen. Yes, he had an attitude, but he usually wouldn't do anything to disrespect or disappoint his grandfather.

"Not your circus," Maggie said.

"Not my monkeys," Quinn finished, smiling at their old game.

But in a way, they were her monkeys. She hoped Pali made it back without any scars. He might despise her for taking their home, but she secretly had a soft spot for him. Despite his seemingly endless supply of angry hormones, he was good to his mom and respectful to his grandfather, and just a few days ago, Alani had told her that Pali had taken her out on the water for some surfing lessons. What teenage boy did that for his little sister?

She put her foot on the brake to let a family cross the road. A dad led the way to the other side, with the young mom and three small girls padding along behind him like a line of ducklings. He pointed to a coconut lying on the sidewalk and said something, and the girls laughed. The dad also carried a baby in a pack on his back. For having four children, the parents' faces looked awfully relaxed. She thought of Ethan and how he'd handle leading the pack. He'd probably be calling out orders like a drill sergeant, his focus on the destination rather than everything around them as they went.

That could be a good thing, though. Couldn't it?

Enough thinking about Ethan. He made her thoughts even more chaotic. Quinn shut down mentally and listened to Maggie chatter.

It didn't take long before they saw a sign that said NAPILI.

Basically just a residential neighborhood dotted with boutique hotels and upscale vacation condos, Napili was much less crowded than the Ka'anapali and Kapalua areas it lay between. Quinn wondered if her relative lived in one of the swanky gated neighborhoods or if he'd chosen a place to meet far from his home.

"Wow, look at that." Maggie pointed across the road at the view of the ocean. "I can't even describe that color. Blue? Green?"

"Azure?" Quinn offered. Whatever it was, the waves were beautiful.

Maggie bounced in her seat. "Quinn, we still have forty-five minutes. Let's walk down to the water."

"I'm not really dressed for the beach." After sorting through her clothes a million times, she'd finally settled on a white sundress and strappy brown sandals for the meeting. She put her hair up in a twist and added silver hoop earrings. She didn't want to look sloppy or too casual. She thought about her billowy white pants but then decided they might make her look too pretentious. Every other outfit was wrong for one reason or another until Maggie finally pointed at the sundress, and Quinn reluctantly stopped obsessing and put it on.

"You're fine," Maggie said. "We'll take our shoes off when we get to the sand, anyway. I just want to get my toes wet."

Easy for her to say. Maggie wasn't in a dress. She'd donned a cute pair of khaki shorts with a bright-yellow shirt. Her feet were nice and relaxed in flat beige sandals. Maggie could pull off any clothes in any setting. She had the confidence. And she did just come all the way to Hawaii for Quinn and hadn't yet touched the ocean.

"Fine," Quinn said. "Help me find a place to park."

She really didn't want to do anything but get to the restaurant and wait, but maybe a distraction would help her nerves, so she followed Maggie's directions for parking and pulled into the last available space in sight.

They jumped out and trailed a beachwear-clad trio down a long staircase that led to a crescent-shaped beach bordered by lots of palm trees. A woman and her dog went jogging by, the dog in perfect step with his owner and looking deliriously happy to be out there.

Just as Quinn and Maggie took off their shoes and stepped out into the sand, they saw a group of sunbathers gathered at the water's edge looking out toward a dark spot, which was most likely a reef.

Maggie ran out to see what was happening. Quinn was right behind her and heard a tall golden-boy type near them say it was turtles.

"Wow, I see them, Quinn!" Maggie pointed and grabbed Quinn's arm, squeezing the life out of her.

"Where?" Her question sent about three fingers in the air from people pointing where to look until Quinn also zoned in on them.

"I didn't realize sea turtles were so big," Maggie said.

Her eyes were huge with excitement, and Quinn thought of her experience in the water with Liam. The sea turtle that had calmed her and then guided her up. Quinn was sure of it. However, she wasn't sure if she was ready to share that with even Maggie.

The turtles ducked back under the water, and Quinn watched as Maggie waded in deeper, laughing as the water swirled around her feet.

"This is making me dizzy," Maggie called out.

"Don't look down." Quinn gave her another minute or so, then called for her to hurry. The anticipation of the meeting made it hard for her to concentrate on anything else, and she wanted to get it over with.

Maggie joined her, and they left the beach, coming back up onto the street.

"I saw the sign for the Sea House. It's practically across the street," Maggie said, pulling Quinn along.

They both heard a catcall and turned to see two guys some yards behind them. One of them waved, and Quinn returned the gesture.

"Better not encourage your admirers if you don't know them," Maggie said nervously.

"Oh, sorry, Maggie," Quinn said, realizing that strangers now made Maggie nervous. "But they were just kids. I mean, come on. And obviously they were looking at you."

Maggie laughed. "We need to get your self-esteem up, girl. That tall guy was all googly eyes at you. Are you blind?"

Quinn didn't believe it for a minute. Yes, she could put herself together pretty well, but there was no camouflaging the extra pounds she needed to lose or the fact that she was over thirty. Maggie was different. With her long, gorgeous hair and lithe body, she could pass for twenty.

"You worry me with your lack of self-confidence, Quinn. Before you came here, were you and Ethan still okay *in the bedroom?*" Maggie asked, wiggling her eyebrows up and down in a provocative way.

Quinn could feel her cheeks heat. They'd always been open about everything, but now she felt uncomfortable. But Maggie was the one person she didn't want to keep secrets from.

"We've had a dry spell," she admitted.

Maggie reached over and patted her leg, then smiled widely. "Well, I think you could use a little rain, sister."

They both laughed.

"You might be right," Quinn said, "but right now we need to get over to the restaurant. I feel like I'm going to be sick, and I need to get to the restroom before noon." Quinn could hear a clock ticking in her head, each second pounding after the other, moving her closer to the meeting and, finally, to some answers.

Chapter Nineteen

The Sea House was a gorgeous venue to make a memory in. At least that was what Quinn kept telling herself as the designated time slipped by and still no one showed. It was more than forty-five minutes past their set meeting time now, and she was beginning to give up hope. She had to admit, in the last two days she'd built up quite a fantasy in her head about the possibility that she would be meeting her long-lost father and that they were going to hit it off splendidly and live happily ever after.

That fairy tale was dissolving with every minute that ticked by.

"Maybe there was a traffic accident," Maggie said. She twirled the tiny umbrella between her fingers.

"Or maybe this was all a big joke," Quinn replied, her eyes on the cuticle she'd just ripped to shreds.

She wasn't too savvy about the Lineage site and didn't know if it was possible for someone to fake a connection. Even Auntie Wang could've messed something up, opening her account to someone who would eventually claim to have half a million dollars waiting for her if she'd only wire them a transfer fee first. But what would he gain by not showing up?

Confusion was beginning to be her most constant companion. She was so rattled that she'd bumped into a man coming out of the bathroom. Her embarrassment was such that she was glad he wore a baseball hat and she couldn't see if his eyes were making fun of her or not. Then, in her hurry to get away, she almost took out a teenage girl on the other side.

She needed to pull herself together.

A waiter approached and put their second round of drinks on the table.

"With an extra umbrella," he said to Quinn, smiling down at her.

"Thank you," Quinn said, then felt awkward as he looked at her for a long moment. He was probably a bit older than she was, and his prolonged attention felt weird.

"You're very welcome," he finally said, then moved away.

Maggie raised her eyebrows at Quinn.

Quinn shrugged back with a silent don't-ask-me look.

"I saw Liam this morning," Maggie said, breaking the silence.

"And?"

"You were getting dressed, and I saw him keep peeking at the cottage, watching to see if you'd come out again."

"Don't get excited, Maggie. It's not like that."

Maggie gave a knowing grunt.

"Maggie, don't," Quinn said. "He really has become a great friend, but I'm still not sure what I'm going to do about Ethan."

"I can't believe you're still thinking of forgiving Ethan. Once a cheater, always a cheater. That's what they say, Quinn. He's not a good guy. You need someone who will appreciate what a great catch you are."

"He's not a bad guy, Maggie. And Ethan and I have a lot of history. I'm not going to just throw it all away without at least hearing him out."

"So you are going to take his call? Or did you already? At the beach this morning? That's why you wanted to go without me?"

"No, I haven't talked to him," Quinn said. "I guarantee he's steaming because I won't respond to his calls or texts. I'm not ready to hear what kind of excuse he has. Not when Gina pretty much admitted why she was there. I might just wait until I get home. But let's talk about you. Are you ever going to give Colby another chance?"

"Deflecting, are we?" Maggie teased.

"Well?"

"At this point, we're friends just working on coparenting the best that we can."

"That sounded rehearsed, but I'll let it pass," Quinn said. "Does he get to see Charlie often?"

"Well, he wasn't seeing him much at all while we were on the run. But in the last month or so, he's come by a lot. Charlie is obsessed with his dad. He even wants the same kind of boots. I told him maybe for Christmas Santa will bring him his own shit-kicking, steel-toed clodhoppers."

"You didn't," Quinn said, her eyes wide.

Maggie laughed. "Of course not. But I did say if he's good, then Santa might bring him some boots. I'm sure Colby is already looking for the right pair."

"You don't think it will ever work out between you two?"

Maggie shook her head. "I think that ship has sailed. He's a great guy. But we were like oil and water when we lived together. It wouldn't be good for Charlie to see that."

"But what if it was just the pressure of being pregnant and Colby afraid of being a father? Lots of couples struggle when that happens."

"I don't know, Quinn. I can't even think about all that right now. I've got to get my life together now that I'm free from looking over my shoulder."

They let the conversation trail away. Relationships were hard, and it was even harder to try to explain them to someone else.

"This guy is really pissing me off," Maggie said, looking at the time on her cell phone.

"Why would he make us sit here and wait?" Quinn asked. At least they had something to look at. The restaurant sat right on the beach, and she kept her mind busy by watching the people lying in the sun or playing in the water. Out a bit farther, what appeared to be a father and his teenage daughter were paddleboarding, and their exchange was amusing as the girl clumsily followed her father's instructions on how to maneuver the board. She almost ran over a swimmer, and the father's helpless expression was priceless.

"Look at that sweet girl. She's making me miss my boy," Maggie said, pointing at a tiny toddler frolicking in the waves with her mom hovering over her. The girl wore a frilly pink swimsuit—ruffles on the butt!—and a pink hat tied under her chin. She was all chubby rolls and blonde hair and was so adorable that Quinn's heart skipped.

Maggie laughed. "When Charlie was that small, he refused to wear a hat in the sun. Now he's old enough that I can negotiate terms. A hat means half an hour more. No hat means we leave right away."

Quinn could just imagine Maggie standing over a tiny boy with her poker face on as she laid out the terms of their negotiations.

The waitress approached, carrying a tray. She put a plate of pancakes in front of Maggie, then a smaller one with bacon on the table before leaving them again. After sitting there for nearly an hour, they felt food had to be ordered or they'd be asked to move to the bar.

Maggie was glad to oblige.

Quinn couldn't eat, but while she left the drink with the umbrellas on the table, she'd ordered a tall glass of tomato juice to settle her stomach.

"These are great," Maggie said. "Sure you don't want a bite?"

Quinn shook her head. The pancakes were topped with fresh bananas and toasted macadamia nuts, and just looking at them made her feel queasy.

"Did you hear about the angry pancake?" Maggie asked, her mouth full.

"No."

"He just flipped," Maggie replied, laughing.

Quinn smiled weakly.

"Sorry. But you're so tense you look like you might just break in half," Maggie said. "Please, try to take some deep breaths and relax. You're going to give yourself high blood pressure."

"I know. I'm trying." Quinn knew she wasn't very good company, but Maggie couldn't possibly understand. Maggie knew her entire family history. How could she know the deep sense of longing that came with feeling as though you had no one in the world who shared your blood? Or they were out there somewhere, but unreachable?

This wasn't just a regular meeting for her. It was everything.

Unless it was nothing.

Quinn's phone rang, and she jumped. She fumbled in her bag until she found it, then looked at the screen. It was Auntie Wang.

"Hello?"

"Quinn, this is Wang," the old woman said. "Are you still at the restaurant?"

"Yes. He hasn't shown up," Quinn said, trying to keep her voice steady. Something about the motherly figure Auntie Wang presented made her emotions bubble to the surface.

"I know," she said. "He sent me an email. He came, saw you, and then left."

Quinn didn't know what to say. He had been there? Watching her? Her skin tingled eerily.

"Why did he leave?" she finally asked. She scrolled through images in her head, trying to remember every male who had come around their table or walked up the ramp. No one had looked suspicious. She hadn't caught anyone staring at her. And she'd been looking, scrutinizing every man.

"He just said he wasn't ready," Auntie Wang said.

He wasn't ready? What about her? If he was her father, he was abandoning her once again. How many times in her life was she going to have to experience that feeling?

Auntie Wang cut into her thoughts, breathless as she spoke faster than normal. "But listen, Quinn. It doesn't matter. I think I stumbled upon the direct path to the truth."

The truth.

Two words that held so much promise. And this time, Wang's words sent goose bumps creeping up Quinn's arms. Could that mean something? Was the universe trying to tell her that this was really it this time?

"Just a minute, Auntie Wang, I can't hear you well enough."

Quinn signaled to Maggie that she was going to walk outside, away from the clattering sounds of dining around them. When she got outside, she turned away from the beach and went to stand under a huge banyan tree on the path leading to the parking lot.

"What do you mean by the truth?" Quinn was beginning to believe she'd never know the truth of who she was. And this person claimed to have it? Sounded too good to be true.

Auntie Wang sounded breathless when she answered. "This is much more complicated than I can tell you on the phone. I spoke to Carmen Crowe. She's the right age, and though she's aged not so gracefully, I can tell she's the one in the photo with your mother. I told her all about you."

Quinn's heart was beating fast. "So now what?"

"She was very resistant at first. I thought she was going to shut me down. But she finally said it was time to talk. I think this is it, Quinn. She wants to meet with you today. Just you, though," Auntie Wang said. "She said she'll take you to someone who will give you the answers you need."

Immediately, Quinn knew Maggie wouldn't go for that. But her gut told Quinn that Wang was onto something. This might be the lead she was looking for. She felt more excited about it than she had even about this so-called connection who hadn't shown up. This woman—this

Carmen Crowe—had known her mother back in the day. They looked very close in the photo. And if that was the case, then she had to know something about Quinn—and her birth father too.

"Call her back and tell her that I'm not coming alone. I'll have my best friend, Maggie, with me. If she doesn't like that, then she can hold on to her secrets."

Of course Quinn didn't mean that, but she could bluff as well as the next person. And she wasn't going anywhere without Maggie.

"I'll see what I can do," Auntie Wang said. "You be here at half past five. I told her to pick you up from my house."

Chapter Twenty

Only minutes after Quinn and Maggie arrived at Auntie Wang's house, Carmen Crowe arrived in an extended cab pickup truck. After quick introductions and an awkward pause, they were on their way.

"It's not my story to tell," was the only thing Carmen would say when Quinn and Maggie peppered her with questions before they'd gotten in the truck and after, on the way up the road to Hana.

"I find It totally ridiculous that you know something and won't give us some insight on what Quinn is about to face," Maggie said from the back seat.

"It's fine," Quinn said. "Let's just get there, and then we'll sort it out."

Carmen gave her a grateful look, then thankfully put her eyes back on the road. The road winding through the Upcountry was just as dangerous as Quinn remembered from when she and Liam had taken it.

And the woman wasn't the best driver. She drove with both hands on the wheel, leaning forward as though she could barely see the road. A few times she pulled over to let someone go around her, refusing to pick up speed.

"So, are you married?" Quinn asked, breaking the awkward silence.

"Nope," Carmen said.

"No children?"

"My pets are my children. I have dogs and horses. Half a dozen cats in the barn. Even a few tamed rabbits."

Quinn wondered why Carmen had never married, but then, it wasn't her business. She couldn't think of any other questions that weren't intrusive. They took the rest of the trip in silence, other than a few words from Maggie now and then.

Quinn got more nervous with every mile. The entire event was unfolding like some sort of movie.

From the road, the house looked imposing, and as they took the winding driveway, Quinn noted it also looked empty. Lifeless. As far from welcoming as a home could get. Built in a mountain retreat rustic style, the house boasted tall matching front windows that looked out over the land. To Quinn, they reminded her of two bottomless eyes watching them approach.

"Who owns this house?" Maggie asked.

"You'll know soon," Carmen said.

That appeased Quinn for the moment.

Maggie, not so much. She was very unhappy about the secrecy. Quinn already had to shush her a few times when her temper started to show.

They parked as close to the door as possible and followed Carmen to the porch. Quinn noted how bent over she was, as though she held the weight of the world on her shoulders.

It was hard to believe that Carmen was the same age as Quinn's mother. Carmen could've passed for at least a decade older, the lines and grooves around her face belying a woman in her late sixties.

Even so, she looked strong. Not physically so much. It was more of a mental strength that she carried. She was sharp, and Quinn could see the stubborn streak that must have defined her throughout her life.

Quinn could feel the racing of her heart, and the pounding of her pulse alerted her that whatever story it was that Carmen wanted someone else to help her tell, it was huge.

Carmen reached the top first, and she went to the door to knock.

"Wait," Quinn said.

Carmen's closed fist hung midair as she turned around.

"I need a moment," Quinn said, then sat down on the top step, dropping her head into her hands. Everything was moving so fast, she felt like she needed to step back and take a second.

Maggie sat down beside her, and Carmen lowered herself to the other side. The three of them sat there, silent, not touching, but there.

"You can do this, Quinn," Maggie whispered.

Quinn squelched the urge to run, visualizing Kupuna's kind face and the words he'd shared with her that morning. Perhaps the answers she was seeking were not about discovery at all but about forgiveness. Above all else, Quinn wanted healing. She needed to feel whole inside. Her entire life there had been a void—some deep, dark, empty place that was too unreachable to even begin to try to heal it. Even under the loving and devoted care her mother had given her, there was something missing. If her healing would only come about from forgiveness, then that was what she'd have to muster up, no matter what the story was.

She took a deep breath.

"Okay, I'm ready."

Carmen nodded, then stood and held a hand out for Quinn.

Quinn took it, noting the surprising strength the woman had. When they stood and turned, the door was already open.

A woman stood there. She clutched the doorframe with one hand, her gnarled fingers like claws as she stared first at Maggie, then Quinn. She was old. At least in her eighties, if not beyond. Her white hair was pulled back in a severe bun that showed the large pearls weighing down her earlobes. Though her house was up high on the mountain and nearly backed into the jungle, she was dressed more like a socialite, a black sweater shell over a white blouse, her slacks showing a spiffy pressed crease. She wore one diamond ring, and the stone looked too heavy for such an old woman to bear.

Her expression was intense as she searched Quinn's eyes.

Carmen nodded toward Quinn. "This is her."

The old woman nodded back and stepped inside, a silent invitation.

It was an uncomfortable moment. No niceties. The silence was deafening, setting Quinn even more on edge.

"I'm Quinn. Thank you for seeing us."

The woman nodded. "I'm Helen. Let's sit down."

With Maggie right behind her, Quinn followed as the old woman pursed her lips and held her shoulders as upright as she could manage, then led them to a family room.

She gestured for them to take a seat on the couch before disappearing down a hallway.

"This is all too mysterious, Carmen. Can we just—"

Carmen held her finger to her lips, shushing Quinn.

They heard some noise from a room down the hall. Some muttering and sliding of what sounded like boxes across a floor. Finally, Helen emerged again, carrying what appeared to be a boot box. She crossed the room to the rocking chair, set the box on the floor, and then took a seat.

She turned her attention back to Quinn, and her stare took on an intensity that Quinn had never experienced.

"Do you have a birthmark?" she asked.

Quinn nodded.

"Where is it?"

"Behind my ear."

"Is it shaped like anything in particular?" she asked.

"Yes, it's shaped like a sea turtle." She tried to keep her tone in check, but it was obvious if the woman knew she had a birthmark behind her ear, she probably also knew what shape it was.

The woman nodded solemnly. "You are well?"

Quinn nodded. "I am."

"I have a story to tell you," she said. Her voice sounded shaky. Uncertain.

"That's why I'm here, I suppose," Quinn said, looking at Carmen for confirmation. Maggie took her hand and squeezed it.

"We all have our own story," Carmen said. "But what you will see is how it all fits together in the end."

The old woman rocked back and forth, her chair creaking eerily with each pass.

"I would like you to reserve your questions—and your judgment—for when I am finished telling. Can you do that?" Helen asked.

Quinn hesitated. "I'll let you speak." She wasn't promising she wouldn't judge, though. That much she probably couldn't control, depending on what the woman had to tell. And she sure couldn't guarantee that Maggie would stay quiet.

Helen closed her eyes and took a deep breath. When she opened her eyes, they were boring a hole through Quinn. "I've had a troubled life, and an unfair one at that. I did everything right, and still the universe tried to punish me. As a child I listened to my parents, respected my teachers, and did what I was told. I graduated high school in Oahu at the head of my class and then moved to Maui with my parents and siblings. I never chased the boys, but one chased me, and I made him marry me before trouble could find us. We built a house on the same property that my parents owned, and he went to work for my father. He worked hard, and we had four children. My sister also married and began to raise her family on our family land, all of us together like our culture is meant to be. Soon my sister had five mouths to feed, and the place was filled with the sound of children. The kids grew up like siblings, and we cared for them as a group, sharing the work between our two families and their very hands-on grandparents. The children were together for meals, homework, and especially playtime." She paused to catch her breath.

Quinn didn't know where this was going, but the woman was describing an idyllic life, something akin to how Auntie Wang had described her own childhood. Once again, Quinn felt a longing stir for what might have been had her mother not decided to leave Hawaii. The family life was so strong here, but her own childhood had been more than a little lonely.

"It wasn't only to build strong family bonds that we lived our lives so closely. It was also for protection. Our family was met with more than its share of bad luck, but we tried to shield and protect the children from it as much as we could. Some of it they understood, but much of it we were able to hide from them. Despite some bumps in the road, most of them did well. But a few had their troubles, and let me tell you, do you know what it's like watching your child grow into adulthood and fall into the wrong crowd? Or to see them follow some ignorant way of life—the morals and values we instilled in them just dropped by the wayside like a bag of trash?"

She continued, her voice escalating, becoming harsher, "You feel helpless, that's how you feel," she said. "It tears your heart out to watch them make mistake after mistake, knowing that the damage they are doing can follow them for the rest of their life. We spent their childhoods emphasizing family loyalty, and then in a wink, when things get gritty, they couldn't care less."

"Skip ahead, Helen," Carmen said. "She doesn't need all that background."

Helen calmed down and lowered her voice. "My sister's children didn't give her half as much heartache as mine gave me. I feel like I spent most of my time apologizing to school administrators and other mothers, always defending my kids for whatever mess they found themselves in. You see, I knew they were rebelling because things at home weren't what you'd call pleasant. Their grandfather was an angry man. A righteous man. And bad luck followed him everywhere he went, with much of it trickling down to those of us under his care. We all lived on the family land, but no matter that my husband was also a strong man who tried to rule his own household, my father refused to step aside and let us raise our own families. He ruled everything, and I wanted to move away. But everyone else wanted to stay."

She paused, looking lost in a memory before she focused again. "Finally, after high school my oldest two straightened out and began to fly right. My father found a way to get through to them when their father and I couldn't. I think it was the threat of losing their inheritance, but however he managed it," she said, waving a hand in the air, "it worked. But that left Jules, my youngest and most stubborn child. She hated how the community judged her and the way her classmates considered her a spoiled rich kid; therefore, she rebelled more than all her siblings put together. When she was eighteen, she met a boy who came from the mainland. Noah. At first I thought it was a relationship that would pass quickly. But with his free-spirited ways and reluctance to follow society's rules, he won her over immediately. A few months later she snuck off and joined him in one of those tent colonies along the beaches.

"But I found her. You should've seen her face when I lifted the flap of their tent and saw her all tangled up with that boy, looking like some kind of ragged drifter. I know exactly what they were doing in there, and she'd never seen me so angry. I'm sure my eyes were flashing fire when I jerked her out of there."

She paused for a breath.

"We argued, and from somewhere deep inside her, she matched me flame for flame, barb for barb. Everyone around us was afraid to step in. I think there on the beach with the waves roaring behind us, our hair whipping in the wind, and both of us trying to outscream the other, we looked like two enraged witches. I've never been one to hang our dirty laundry in public, but I was so mad—and she was too—that we laid out every single grievance against each other we'd been harboring since she was old enough to walk.

"It went on for far too long, but finally we both ran out of steam. When I begged her to come home, she refused. I couldn't drag her back, so I left her there. I hired someone to check in on her frequently, just to make sure she was okay. It was humiliating. The whole town knew our daughter was down there living like a homeless person, and I couldn't do a thing about it.

"That boy convinced her that she didn't need us or our money—that all she needed was the clean ocean air and the freedom of the water, and they could live happily ever after on Spam and rice."

Helen took a drink of her water and cleared her throat, but it was getting raspier the longer she talked. She looked quite ill.

"Do you want to take a break?" Carmen asked her.

"No. It's too late to stop now," Helen said. "So Jules might have been the most free-spirited of all my children, but she was also the most stubborn. Her father said she was just like me, but she'd rather spit in his eye than acknowledge that truth. We thought once they went hungry for a time that she'd come crawling back, but she and that boy figured out a way to make a living without our help. They both loved the water, and Jules had a way with people. Soon they went from giving surfing lessons to owning their own small boat where they led scuba-diving charters. But even with some decent money coming in, they still lived a free-spirited kind of life. Finally, they moved up from a tent to a camper, but I still kept tabs on her, because despite the way she turned her back on all of us, we loved her."

The old woman looked away when she spoke of love. Maybe she wasn't as hard-hearted as she appeared.

Helen swallowed visibly, then continued, "When she had her first child, Jonah, she brought him to see us, and we tried again to get her to come home, to raise the boy here in a safe place with his cousins and other family like she'd been raised. But she refused. Her visits were infrequent, but she wasn't cruel enough to completely keep me from my grandson. We called a silent truce so that Jonah could know his grandparents and other family. A few peaceful years went by, and then she had her second child."

Helen paused, her expression lost in a memory they couldn't see. Quinn could swear she saw a few tears glistening in her eyes, but if they were there, they were blinked away quickly.

Then she stared at Quinn again. "Her second child was a girl. A tiny snip of a thing she was, her features a blend of her mother's Native Hawaiian heritage and her father's Scandinavian one. From the very first week they brought her home, that child took to the water, and her father called her his little Nama, short for Namaka, who was a water spirit and the god of the sea. She was the center of their world, and having her softened them both. My daughter had matured, and her sense of *ohana* was coming back. She couldn't resist the pull of family, and, finally, I felt that we were in a place of healing. After some convincing, I even managed to pull together a small wedding so that Jules and Noah would be legal and the children could have his name without complications. As a wedding gift, we bought them a small piece of property near the beach, where they built a humble house. They did nearly everything themselves, insisting it would be their forever home and they wanted their mark on it. Their goal was to be self-sufficient eventually, so it had solar panels and all that other stuff those off-the-grid people do. They planted fruit trees, and last I saw, they had a huge garden."

Quinn had to admit, the story that Helen was telling about her daughter may have been unsettling to her as a mother, but it sounded very romantic from the viewpoint of Jules and Noah.

Helen rocked back and forth for a moment, catching her breath.

"Life went on, but our relationship was still tenuous. Jules and Noah didn't want to accept any more gifts and strove to maintain their simple life. They embraced the land we'd bought them but turned away from any other offerings. They wanted to do things on their own, and their visits were few and far between as they worked to build their business."

She stopped talking and moving, sitting completely still. Her eyes on her hands clasped tightly together in her lap.

"Tell her the rest, Helen," Carmen said.

Helen looked up again. "I didn't hear from my daughter again until months later, when she called me, hysterical and begging for my help. Nama was missing. She and Jonah had fallen off the boat when an unexpected squall came up during a scuba tour. Her brother was found immediately, but Nama had disappeared, and, at less than two years old, was thought to be drowned."

Both Quinn and Maggie gasped at the same time.

"With my daughter on the other end of the phone, I fell to my knees, broken in the knowledge that the curse had found my grand-daughter, and this time it was exacting the ultimate punishment for deeds done long before she was born."

Chapter Twenty-One

Quinn watched Helen closely. The woman looked drained, her complexion now a pasty white, the circles under her eyes darker.

Carmen went to her and knelt, searching her face as she took her hand. "How do you feel?" she asked her.

"Relieved," Helen said. "But also afraid. Very afraid."

"You rest now," Carmen said. "This is almost over. It's my turn."

Helen nodded, then laid her head against the back of the rocker. She didn't move, seeming too exhausted to even find comfort in rocking back and forth.

Carmen returned to the couch and removed a colorful crocheted coverlet from the back, then took it over and spread it across Helen's lap.

When she took her seat again, she leaned forward. "I'm the same age as Jules, but my life was as far from her kind of lifestyle as one could be. Jules was born into money, and her family had it scattered in many investments in every direction, while the Crowes' net worth was and remains tied to the land. We owned a small ranch in Hana, and we paid our bills by raising cattle. We also had horses, goats, and all the things a child loves to grow up around. To me it was the best place on earth."

So she was just a country girl at heart. That explained the boots, pickup truck, and her scuffed-up jeans, as well as the rough way she carried herself. Quinn couldn't even imagine her in a dress or wearing a ring the size of the rock that Helen wore.

"When I was about seven or eight, I was given a horse. From the moment we saw each other, we had a bond that transcended explanation. His name was Wiley, and I woke each and every morning hours before school would begin so that I could start the day with him. My other love was for the land our family owned. Wiley and I rode every trail around our ranch and the mountain several times a week, imprinting our presence into the soil. He loved it there as much as I did, this I instinctively knew. Once, Wiley caught some sort of virus that was rare but deadly among the herd. I slept with him every night until he finally recovered. My parents said he should've died, but he couldn't find the will to leave me, so he carried on further than what most animals could've done."

She paused, lost in thought for a moment.

"When I was eleven, our barn was set on fire. It burned for hours before we even woke and sounded the alarm. Wiley died before we could get him out. He would've lived another twenty years if it weren't for the hatred of a reckless human. I knew I had let him down when he needed me the most, and I slipped into a terrible depression that took far too long to overcome."

A tear ran down her face, and Quinn felt moved to comfort her but refrained. She didn't look like the type to want anyone's pity.

"I never really got over it, even when my parents gave me another horse. I loved him, but we didn't have the bond that Wiley and I did. When I got older, I heard the rumors that the fire was no accident. My brother told me he thought it was probably set by one of the Rochas, the family who'd lost their barn and part of their house in a fire years before and blamed our family."

Helen looked pained before adjusting her expression again.

"I was shocked at the story my brother told me. I hadn't even known about this vendetta until then. I understood then that Wiley's death was some sort of eye-for-an-eye act of retribution. But what the

Rochas didn't understand is that we didn't set their fire, and their act of revenge took away my best friend and made them an enemy for life. I'm ashamed to admit it, but a seed of hatred for the Rochas sprouted in me and grew fast and hard. It was an uncontrollable kind of hate, and I longed to find a way to make them pay for what they did to Wiley. One day when I was out walking by the sea, the universe delivered an answer to my prayers."

"What was it?" Quinn asked.

"I was looking out across the water, searching for marine life and hoping to see a whale or at least a dolphin, but some movement in the high grass on the dunes caught my eye. I went over, thinking maybe it was a stray dog, but it was a child. A pale, shivering little girl. She'd dug herself a hole and lay with her legs pulled up to her chest."

"You found Nama?" Quinn asked, putting the two stories together. Carmen nodded. "Yes, I did."

"How did you know it was her?" Maggie asked.

"It didn't take a rocket scientist to figure it out," Carmen said. "I'd seen the news and read the papers. The headlines were everywhere: 'Young Heiress to Rocha Estate Lost at Sea.' And I'll admit, every time I saw the words or listened to a new report, I felt a stir of triumph. I didn't want a child to die, but I'm ashamed to say that I was enjoying the fact that the family was suffering."

"I'm sorry, but that's just sick," Quinn said, unable to stop herself. She looked at Helen, who sat rocking with her eyes closed.

"I know it is," Carmen said, choking over the words. "I'm not that person now. But back then I was young and stupid, barely twenty years old, and you have to understand, not only had the Rochas taken the life of my horse, but I had also learned that the land I so loved was only a tiny portion of what was really ours. The great-grandfather of that missing girl had stolen my legacy. *My* land. And I was livid."

"Tell the rest," Helen said, opening her eyes weakly.

"I bent down and tried to talk to her. At first she didn't respond. She wouldn't even open her eyes. My mind was spinning; I couldn't believe the luck that I, of all people, was the one to find the Rocha child, and now she was going to die anyway. I felt sad for the impending loss of such a beautiful being." Carmen paused, looking pointedly at Quinn. "But then she opened her eyes and looked up at me."

Quinn had a feeling she wasn't going to like what was coming next.

"I argued with myself on that beach as I comforted her," Carmen said. "I knew the right thing to do, but that deeply cultivated hatred burned in me, and I wanted to make the family suffer just a while longer."

Quinn looked from Carmen to Helen, amazed that they could even be in the same room together. How could Helen just sit there and listen to Carmen talk about finding her granddaughter and deciding to make them suffer longer? What kind of people were these? Something really strange was going on between the two of them, and Quinn couldn't figure it out.

"Wrap it up, Carmen," Helen said. "It's my turn, and we need to finish this."

Carmen nodded. "I only kept her a day until my conscience got the better of me. For all she'd been through, she bounced back fast. Sure, she was weak and dehydrated—even sunburned—but after some food, water, and rest, she seemed okay. I was so relieved that I almost went straight to the police with her, but I just couldn't do it. I thought somehow once the Rochas heard that a Crowe had found Nama, they'd accuse me of kidnapping her. I could just imagine the news picking up on our 'Hatfields and McCoys' story and splashing our family name all over the headlines, right alongside a snapped photo of them walking me into the jail with handcuffs."

"So what did you do?" Maggie asked. Quinn could tell by her voice that she was getting very impatient.

"What I wanted to do was hand her over without any media involved, so I tried to find a number to call the child's mother. She didn't have a phone listed, so when Nama was asleep, I snuck out and went downtown. I looked for one of the posters with her face on it, then called the number."

She looked at Helen pointedly.

Helen picked up the story. "Jules and her husband wouldn't leave their boat. Night and day they were out searching, so the posted number was mine. I was alone the day that I got the call. At first I thought it was another prank. We had listed a substantial reward to anyone who found Nama, and most of the fishermen had set aside their work to hunt for her and grab a payday that was probably more than they made in a year. We had a few false leads, people trying to weasel the money out of us before handing over our granddaughter. When Carmen said she had her, I was so tired of it all that I called her a liar."

"I didn't want her money," Carmen said. "When I told her that, she was taken aback. But when I mentioned the tiny birthmark behind Nama's ear, she shut up and started listening."

"The officials didn't release that information in case we needed something to identify her that no one could replicate," Helen said. "When Carmen said something about it, I knew that she might have really found our Nama. When she told me she was a Crowe, I was stunned, and then I was terrified. It was the curse that had dropped Nama into the sea and then hidden her from all the searchers only to deliver her to our family's biggest enemy."

"So you returned her?" Quinn asked Carmen.

"No, she didn't," Helen answered for her. "Nama had survived the unsurvivable, and I felt that if we took her back, something worse would happen to her."

"What the hell kind of messed-up story is this?" Maggie said.

Helen nodded. "Back then, my thoughts were that this event had happened this exact way for a reason. Fate had delivered one of ours straight into the arms of a Crowe. That meant we should give Nama up as penance for the wrongs our family had done to the Crowes. If we did, the curse would end, and my remaining and future grandchildren wouldn't be in danger. I thought that eventually the loss of Nama would bring us all together again as a family. We'd gather to grieve, and then heal."

Quinn could feel herself getting angry. "Do you know how absolutely insane that sounds?" she asked the old woman.

"I do. But by the time I realized how wrong it was, the deed was done."

Quinn stood and Helen did, too, facing her, suddenly strong and imposing. "You've known where this story was going all along, Quinn. You could've stopped it at any time. You wanted to know the truth."

Quinn reached up and felt behind her left ear, her finger rubbing the birthmark she'd hated her entire life. Yes, she'd known it at least halfway in. But that lost child didn't exist anymore. *Nama*, Quinn thought, finally admitting it to herself. I'm *Nama*. She sat back down, weak in the knees. She closed her eyes and tried to process the sudden realization. If she belonged to Jules and Noah, then Elizabeth wasn't her mother?

"I want to hear the rest of it," Quinn said.

"I tried to bribe Carmen to take you to the mainland," Helen said. "I told her I'd give her enough to get a new start, and I'd arrange for the best identification documents that could be had, that she'd never be found out. I just wanted her to keep Nama safe until she was older. I planned to also set aside a trust for Nama that she would get one day when I was gone. But Carmen wouldn't leave Maui. She couldn't break the connection to her people's land for any price."

Quinn's anger was chased away in a rush of adrenaline and realization. She couldn't pretend she didn't know who she was anymore. But their stories still didn't answer everything she needed to know.

She locked eyes with Carmen. "So tell me, who is my mother? Not my biological mother, because obviously you think that was Jules, but Elizabeth, the woman who raised me?"

"Beth was my best friend," Carmen said. "I chose her because I could trust her, and I knew she could disappear without it looking suspicious."

Chapter Twenty-Two

Helen got so weak she nearly crumpled over in the rocking chair. Once they determined she was okay, Carmen called off the rest of the meeting, saying she'd fill them in on the last details as they drove home. Helen didn't argue. She actually seemed relieved.

"Before I leave, what about Jules and Noah? Are they both still living?" Quinn asked, nearly holding her breath as she waited for the answer.

"They are," Helen said, her voice now a hoarse whisper.

She allowed Carmen to help her to her room, settle her into her bed, and bring her a hot cup of tea before they locked up and left.

Though Quinn felt a slow stirring of anger at the old woman, she felt bad for leaving her all alone in the spooky house so far up and away from everyone.

The thought that Helen was her grandmother was one that still felt bizarre, and Quinn barely said goodbye to her as Carmen walked her down the hall.

Once in the car and on the way back, Carmen picked up the story. There had already been so much said that Quinn struggled to stay focused. Her head was reeling with information overload and the huge secret her mother had kept her whole life. Now so much of it made sense. Her mother had never wanted her picture taken. She avoided social networking like the plague. She'd never bought a house, a new car, or anything that required credit. She worked housekeeping and nanny jobs that paid under the table so no one would ever scrutinize her credentials. She didn't make friends, rarely had a boyfriend, and of course never claimed any relatives.

Knowing all this, it was still hard to connect the sweet, doting mother to the profile of a criminal, but Quinn had to admit, her mother had pulled off a crime that not many could. Her mother was a kidnapper. Or was she? They'd given Nama to her. But then, Nama wasn't theirs to give. If the child hadn't been declared dead at sea, Quinn could just imagine her mother's face plastered all over post offices, listed as one of "America's Most Wanted."

It was too much. This couldn't be real.

But it was.

She still couldn't think of herself as Nama. It was as though the story was about some child from Maui. From a family she didn't know. A tragic tale but one not connected to her.

Maggie was silent in solidarity, somehow knowing that all Quinn needed right now was time to process the new past laid out in front of her. Everything she'd ever known was a lie. The only family she'd ever had was a fraud. And that was a hard discovery to reconcile with the woman she loved more than anything in the world.

Elizabeth Senna—or Elizabeth Makena, whatever her name was—was just someone Carmen and Helen had talked into doing their dirty work. A paid criminal who took Nama—*took her*—to the mainland to hide her. According to Carmen, Beth was a good girl from a bad family, the only child of a couple embroiled in a dysfunctional marriage too chaotic to think much of the daughter they were neglecting.

When Carmen and Helen presented the idea to Beth, they told her she'd never be able to contact her parents again.

No love lost there, she'd told them. *They wouldn't know it if I fell off the earth and my ashes blew back in their faces.*

What they hadn't planned for was Beth falling in love with Nama and the role of motherhood. Carmen said that the day she'd handed Nama over to Beth, there had been an uncanny affection between the two.

Nama had nestled into Beth's softness, preferring it to Carmen's more matter-of-fact way of handling her.

In the days leading up to their departure, Beth's complete attention to Nama showed Carmen she'd made the right choice. When she conveyed this feeling to Helen, the woman arranged for new identification documentation, set up a healthy, anonymous account for them to live off, and then tried to push it to the back of her mind and help her daughter deal with the tragedy.

Carmen took care of getting Beth and Nama off the island. It was a stressful situation, as at any moment they expected Beth to be arrested for kidnapping, but they looked the part of mother and daughter and made it through security without any trouble.

As Carmen talked, Quinn let her head lie back on the headrest, watching the road ahead of them. Maggie asked a few questions here and there, but Quinn was too drained. After the first few miles, she felt like she was outside of her body, listening to a horrifying story being unraveled but not really being there. For some reason, the thought came to her that it was no wonder Carmen hadn't married or had children. She probably thought she didn't deserve them after what she'd done.

According to Carmen, she was the only one to keep in touch with Beth, since Helen was too afraid to be connected to her. Helen had hoped that they could all move on and her deed would prove best for everyone.

But after only a year, Helen had second thoughts when her daughter Jules couldn't overcome her grief. She talked to Carmen, who relayed to Beth that she should bring the girl back. They created a scenario in which Beth would leave Nama somewhere safe and then make the call for the family to find her. They gave Beth a month to come to terms with it and make the drop. She was promised that no one would ever know she had taken the girl and told there'd be another deposit of a substantial amount of money—a gesture of gratitude for keeping Nama safe.

"Beth told me she needed some time to think about it," Carmen said. "But when it came down to the last days, I only got one more call from her. She'd completely panicked. You would've thought I was asking her to give up her own flesh-and-blood child. She said she didn't want Helen's money. She wanted to keep Nama."

"How did she think she'd get away with it?" Quinn asked.

"She *did* get away with it," Maggie answered.

Carmen nodded. "Yes, she did, didn't she? At least until now. I assume she knew Helen wouldn't involve the law. She packed you up and just dropped off the radar. Disconnected her phone number and moved to an unknown address. She also drained the bank account Helen had set up for Nama's ongoing care, though she'd claimed not to want money."

Quinn thought of her inheritance and now knew how her mother had accumulated such wealth and hidden it for so long. It must've been Helen's money, invested from the time Quinn was a small child.

"I don't think she used much of it," Quinn said.

Carmen said they tried with all they had to find Beth and Nama. Carmen even went to Beth's family. She didn't tell them their daughter had Nama, just said she needed to get in touch, but they claimed they hadn't heard from her. Her mother had the letter that Beth had left them, saying she was going out to make her own way, and then nothing else. Her father said he hoped she never came back, that she was just a drain on his bank account.

Helen hired investigator after investigator, but they couldn't find any trails leading to Beth or Nama.

"Obviously, since now we know you've been in school and work, and even have a driver's license, she did away with the documents that Helen provided her and arranged for new birth certificates and social security numbers," Carmen said. "So she definitely used some of the money."

"But when Beth wouldn't bring her back, why didn't Helen tell Jules her daughter was still alive?" Maggie asked Carmen right before they arrived at Maria's house. "She could've at least given her that."

"Yes," Quinn added, still unable to connect with Jules as her mother but feeling pity for the woman anyway. "Why make Jules suffer even more?"

"Because unless Helen could deliver Nama back to Jules, her daughter would hate her forever. She'd helped her disappear and now was nowhere to be found. It was better to let her think the girl drowned. Not only that, but I was complicit. I had found the girl—you, I had found you!—and I tried to end the battle with the Rocha family, only to become part of something that could get me thrown in prison forever. Helen thought her family had done enough damage to ours without adding more to it. She was also convinced that the curse was the reason we couldn't get to you, and it was stronger than our will to find you."

"You were afraid of involving the authorities," Maggie said. "Of going to prison."

"I was more afraid I'd never see you alive again," Carmen said, taking her eyes off the road to look at Quinn.

"Please don't. That girl isn't me. She was Nama," Quinn said. She felt as though she were awake in a dream—or some sort of nightmare. She wondered about Jules, the woman who was her first mother, and felt a small rush of guilt that she didn't feel any sort of longing to see her or know her.

"Maybe they should take a DNA test," Maggie said. "What if Quinn isn't even Nama?"

Carmen was shaking her head even before she answered. "What are the chances I would find a girl the same age and identical to the daughter Jules and Noah lost at sea? You don't need a test. If you take one look at Jules and her other daughters, you'll know. And she has the birthmark."

Other daughters. Quinn had sisters. And a brother. The one on the boat with her. Jonah. "What about their son? Surely they were glad at least one child was recovered," she asked.

Carmen nodded. "Of course they were. But that's a whole other story. Jonah never forgave himself because he was supposed to be looking out for you. He was already a sensitive boy, and his childhood was ruined. He enlisted and came back from Iraq a broken man. Got tangled up in drinking and drugs too. He lives on the streets most of the time."

Quinn was taken aback. "He comes from a family with the resources to put him in any kind of program, and he's on the streets? I don't understand."

"The human mind deals with tragedy in different ways," Carmen said. "Jonah decided to walk away from those who can help him. He chose to fight his demons alone. But he comes around his family occasionally. Just like any Hawaiian, the tie to family is a hard one to cut permanently."

Was that the reason Quinn had always felt a pull to go to Maui?

"Quinn, their home is only a few miles away. You could see your mother and father tonight."

Father. Quinn couldn't believe she'd started this crazy journey simply to find her real father and possibly some of her mother's family. If she'd known her mother's deathbed confession would lead to all this . . .

"No, I want to go back to Maria's right now," Quinn said. She couldn't even think about meeting anyone else right now. It didn't feel right yet. It felt . . . disloyal, she supposed. Not that Elizabeth was really her mother, but then, she was. And despite the complete wrongness of what she'd done, she'd given Quinn a good life and had loved her with every fiber of her being. Whatever her reasons for doing what she did, Quinn knew that love was at the root of it.

"This is enough for one day," Maggie said. "Please just get us back so that Quinn can rest."

Quinn was glad that Maggie was there and that she wouldn't have to face the empty cottage alone with her thoughts.

Both Helen and Carmen had promised not to say anything until Quinn was ready. It might not be soon, either, because she needed to take some time to process everything. If they were expecting a big, joyful family reunion, they were going to be sorely disappointed.

Helen warned her that she might not be there if she waited too long. Her health was bad, and she admitted that she always hoped she'd be long dead before Nama was found. She dreaded facing her daughter when she learned what she had done, and Quinn couldn't blame her. If Helen wasn't already dead, she might be after Jules and her husband learned the truth.

Jules's husband. Quinn's father. She still couldn't believe it. A real, live father, her own flesh and blood—something she'd longed for her entire life. They'd barely said anything about him other than the fact that he'd grown into a decent person who had built his own legacy for his children, a legacy that wasn't dependent on the Rochas' money.

"What's their family name?" Quinn asked as they drew near to Maria's house.

"Monroe," Carmen said. "Jules and Noah Monroe."

So her name was Nama Monroe. Or at least it used to be. What a day of discovery. She had a lot of information—and suddenly she had parents, siblings, and a grandmother—but now what was she supposed to do with it all? She simply wanted to get back to her cottage and find some privacy to make a call. There was one person she needed to talk to right away.

Chapter Twenty-Three

Quinn wasn't going to find the privacy she needed anytime soon because when they pulled up to Maria's house, there were at least half a dozen cars parked in the driveway and lining the street in front of the yard.

"Something's happened," she said, feeling nervous as she thought of Kupuna. He wasn't really a frail man, but he was the oldest person in the home. "This isn't the night for Maria's dinner."

"It's probably about Pali," Maggie said.

"Do you need me to come in with you?" Carmen asked.

"No," Quinn and Maggie said at the same time.

"Thank you, but just drop us off right here." Quinn pointed at the corner. She spotted Liam's truck and felt a rush of relief that he was there.

Carmen came to a stop.

"Listen," she said, and Quinn paused, her hand on the door, "I know you say you aren't ready to meet your parents. But please don't leave Maui without letting Helen have closure for what she's done. I can live with it either way, though I wish I could take it back. But that old woman has suffered for nearly three decades over her deed. The Rochas are a huge name in Maui, and when this gets out, she'll probably do something rash out of shame, but it's her last wish on this earth to see her sins undone."

"I still don't see why you care," Quinn said. "So much for sworn enemies."

She opened the door and climbed out.

"Because I finally learned that revenge tastes bitter," Carmen said. "Forgiveness is a much sweeter way to live, Quinn. I'm not asking for it from you, but I've given it to the Rochas from the Crowes. I'm willing to pay for my part in what we did. But Helen is frail. I beg you not to send her to jail."

Quinn shut the door without responding. Let Carmen have a night to worry about it. This wasn't some practical joke gone awry. It was her childhood. Her life. And it had been taken from her. Even if Quinn felt sorry for the old woman, the emotion was buried under a simmering anger.

Maggie was already out of the truck, headed up the driveway. Quinn knew she was exhausted too. And she could never thank her enough for sitting through that with her. She followed just as Liam was coming out of the house. When he saw them, he approached.

"How did it go?" he asked, his voice sincere and full of concern as he examined Quinn's face.

Maggie let out a harsh laugh. "Like a Lifetime movie. I'm going to take a shower. I feel dirty." She continued around the house to the cottage.

"I have a lot to tell you, Liam, but first, what's going on here?" Quinn asked.

"Pali's been in an accident. He was just released from the hospital."

"Is he okay?"

Liam nodded. "He's alive. But he's got some really serious injuries. He tried to surf Jaws alone, and at night."

"What's Jaws?"

"It's the most dangerous place to surf on the island. Just paddling through the explosive shore break is a feat in itself. Then riding the mountain of water that moves as fast as Jaws is usually reserved for the professionals, especially now while the swell is huge. Pali isn't even near ready for something like that, and he might never be. I guess in his first major act of rebellion, that was where he had something to prove."

"Well, that was reckless," Quinn said.

"Yeah, exactly, but that's what happens when you have a boy keeping everything bottled up, and that anger, humiliation, and testosterone raging through his veins finally erupt. But he'll be okay. He's resting now."

They began to walk up to the house.

"So how did he get injured?" Quinn asked. "And how did he get out there?"

"He hitched a ride with some older boys who were going out there to drink some beer and watch the waves. When they were ready to go, he borrowed a board, and they left him there, probably thinking he'd never have the guts to really try it. But he did. And according to him, he got dumped off while attempting a barrel."

"A what?"

"Hard to explain, but it's the most violent part of the wave where you have the least control. Think of it like a rag doll catapulting through the air. He's damn lucky he was leashed, but during his spiral he injured his shoulder, broke his right leg, and dislocated his left kneecap. I'm surprised he didn't amputate a finger with that leash too."

Quinn felt sick to her stomach. They approached the front porch and sat down on the top step. At first their knees were touching, but the sensation was so unsettling that Quinn moved over a few inches to put some space between them.

"How was he rescued?" she asked.

"That's the miracle. He still had his board, but with his injuries he couldn't get to shore. Jaime got word that Pali was missing, and he went to every beach, searching for hours. By the time he found him, Pali was clinging to the board hundreds of feet out."

Of all the people to find Pali, Quinn had to think it was divine intervention for his dad to be the one.

"To beat all, Jaime can't swim," Liam said. "He's probably the one man in our family who wasn't obsessed with the ocean growing up. At least that I know of."

"Then how did he get him in?"

"He had to learn real quickly."

Quinn felt goose bumps crawl up both arms.

"It's true," Liam said. "He saw someone clinging to a board out there and knew in his gut that it was Pali. He said there wasn't time to call for emergency services. He jumped in and floundered for a minute or two; then his reflexes kicked in, and it was either swim or drown. He made it out there and pulled Pali to the beach."

"That's absolutely amazing," Quinn said. "Where is he now?"

"Jaime?" Liam nodded toward the house. "Inside. Probably trying to pry Alani off the back of his neck, where she's been hanging like a monkey for the last half hour."

"How's Maria taking his sudden return?"

"They aren't talking about it right now. Pali is their priority. He's going to be incapacitated for a while."

Quinn felt ashamed that her next thought was that she'd never get them out of the house now. But it fell to the bottom of her pile of troubles when she remembered that she wanted to tell Liam about Carmen and Helen and the discovery about her identity.

"I've got a lot to tell you, but do you think I should go inside and see Pali first?"

"No," Liam said. "He's sleeping. Everyone else is about to head out. I don't know if Jaime is staying or what. Let's give them some time to talk. Want to go to the beach?"

"That sounds good. Let me just pop in and tell Maggie."

Chapter Twenty-Four

Liam grabbed a beach towel off the line as they walked through the back courtyard to the beach path. Quinn followed, staying close to him since he knew the trail and it was dark.

Five minutes before, she'd felt absolutely physically and emotionally exhausted, but now she felt a burst of energy. Since Maggie had arrived, she hadn't seen much of Liam, and she had to admit she missed him.

They settled close to a dune, adjusting the towel so they could recline and either look at the waves or the stars. At first they were quiet, and that was something she appreciated about him. He never wanted to miss the beautiful things. Sitting there with the breeze coming off the ocean and the moon shining down on them definitely qualified as a special moment.

"So where do we start?" he finally said.

"It's probably going to be the craziest story you've ever heard."

"It'll do you good to repeat it, then. Get it out of your system before it begins to poison you."

"I agree, but first, I'm dying to know about Jaime. Where's he been? Why'd he leave?" Quinn knew it was none of her business, but she felt such a fondness for Maria that she just had to know. "Or did he tell you anything?"

"He did. We had some time alone together after we got Pali situated. Remember I told you Jaime worked at the lumberyard for decades?"

She nodded.

"Well, it was sold last year when it started losing business to the big-box stores. First it was just Lowes, but when Home Depot came in, the lumberyard owners jumped ship and sold to a family that owns a lot of stuff on this island and could afford to bring it up to scale to compete."

"Jaime didn't want to work for the new owners?" Quinn asked.

"He tried. They installed some high-tech computer system that everyone had to learn to use. Jaime had problems catching on, and they put him on probation because he made some mistakes. Computers aren't his thing. He tried, but they eventually let him go and refused to give him his pension due to some legality he didn't understand."

"They fired him because he can't understand the technology?" Quinn thought that was beyond unfair. From what she'd seen in the photos, Jaime was about the same age as her mother, who also had trouble figuring out technology. Quinn had spent a lot of time convincing her to switch to a smartphone but didn't even try to talk her into letting go of her mistrust of the internet. Jaime probably just needed more training. Better training, even. She felt guilty considering she'd mentally branded Jaime as a loser who'd abandoned his family.

"Yep. Jaime heard they filled his position with two college kids who alternate shifts. They can pay them cheaper and can skip paying benefits."

"Why didn't he just tell Maria? They could've done something about it together. He didn't have to leave them," Quinn said. She felt so sad for them.

"Pride. Again, in the Hawaiians it's a very noble attribute, but can also be a serious thing. Jaime was able to keep paying the bills for a while by getting a loan on the house, but that just put him deeper in debt. When it ran out, he left. He said he couldn't face the kids and Maria and tell them the house was going to be taken by the bank. He really couldn't stand the thought of telling Kupuna either. He thought he could figure something out."

"So he was coming back?"

"He did plan to come back when he got a new job and was making regular money. But all he's found to do is some roofing and a few landscaping jobs. Nothing permanent."

"That's heartbreaking. So now he'll leave again?" Quinn couldn't imagine what Maria would do if Jaime disappeared again.

"I don't think so. I talked to him about having enough faith in Maria to know she'll stand by him no matter what. I told him he should appreciate that he has a wife and kids to come home to. Some men don't have that anymore, or never did."

Liam got quiet then. Quinn didn't turn to look at him; his voice was heavy with emotion, and she was afraid she'd see tears.

"I hope he'll stay. She's going to need help with Pali," she said.

After a minute or two went by, she broke the silence. "Well, let me tell you about my saga. I found out who my father is today."

"That's great, Quinn!" He sat up straight and rubbed her arm. "I told you it'd all work out."

She didn't know about working out, but at least she knew her identity now. Though, given the choice now, she wasn't sure if she'd ever come to Maui.

"Do you know a man named Noah Monroe?" she asked.

"Of course. He owns Monroe Maui Excursions down on Front Street. I think his daughters and their husbands run it most of the time now. His wife is a Rocha, but she doesn't have much to do with them. She and Noah spend a lot of time helping the homeless who hang out on the beach. They provide sack lunches and sleeping bags. Help some of them get started again. They're good people."

"They're *my* people," Quinn said, saying the words slowly as though they'd sting coming out. It still didn't sound true.

"I don't understand."

"Did you know that they lost a little girl a long time ago?"

"Yeah, I did know that. I went to school with Jonah. Everyone said the loss of his sister was why he was so hard to get along with. He felt responsible. Growing up he was always fighting or skipping class to go to the water. He bought his own small boat when he was fourteen and used to go out alone, just cruising the waters. He joined the service when he was eighteen. And I haven't seen him in years, come to think of it."

Quinn breathed in and out, trying to still the explosive thumping of her heart. There was so much to explain, but how could she tell him that everything she thought she was . . . wasn't? Finally, she was able to whisper three words.

"He's my brother."

Liam looked her way, trying to see her face in the dim moonlight.

"What are you saying? Are you that girl? The one lost at sea?"

She nodded, unable to speak past the lump in her throat.

"That can't be possible. How? I—I don't understand."

"I don't either. It's really complicated. The story sounds like something out of a fantasy book, but according to what I know so far, it fits. I'm her, Liam. I'm Nama Monroe. Or I used to be. Of course, I'll want proof."

She could tell by the increase in the speed of his breathing that he was having a hard time processing what she'd said. She didn't blame him. She hadn't processed it herself.

"Quinn, if that's the truth, I need to tell you something right now before someone else does. The lumberyard that Jaime worked for that was bought out? The new owner who fired him? It was Noah's brother-in-law, Todd Rocha. That's Jules's brother. He bought the lumberyard."

The shame that Quinn instantly felt threatened to engulf her and smother her last breath. She was connected to this family who had caused so much pain to other people. To Maria. And her children. And God only knew what other locals were innocent collateral damage to her family's greediness on Maui.

She choked on sudden tears, trying to will them back. But they came faster, leaving hot tracks down her cheeks, backing up in her throat.

He put his arm around her and pulled her in close. "You're okay, Quinn. It's a lot to take in, but you're going to be just fine. And you're right—this is going to be a hell of a story. But I've got all night, and we're going to talk this through."

Quinn hated being so weak. She hadn't even whimpered when Carmen and Helen told their stories. She hadn't shed one tiny tear. She'd held it together pretty damn well, she thought. Now she realized that, more than anything, what she'd been fighting in front of them was anger. She hadn't said it, but how could she not feel resentment about the family she'd lost? A lifetime set out for her with two parents and siblings and extended family. Something she'd dreamed of her entire life. And that made her feel guilty. She loved her mother. Her mother had sacrificed everything for her. Had given her more love than most children ever experienced. She'd been strong in front of the women, but here in the safe circle of Liam's arms, she couldn't stop crying.

The emotion came from deep inside, flowing from her heart and emptying her very soul. She cried for Nama. She cried for the mother she didn't know who'd lost her. For the father she'd never had, and for Jonah, a child racked with guilt his entire life. And the mother she had known—Beth—she must've lived in a state of terror that they'd be discovered. Then while she was at it, she cried about Ethan. And the loss of their trust. Maybe even of their future.

The keening that came from her sounded like a wounded animal's. She knew this, yet it was out of her control. Quinn cried until she had nothing left. And still Liam held her. Quiet but solid. And like a ship on the rockiest waves in the sea, he rocked her back and forth, bringing her comfort and a sense of peace with his touch. So she simply let go, an unfamiliar endeavor for her but one that was past due.

Chapter Twenty-Five

Quinn opened her eyes and saw that her nose was literally inches from a familiar spattering of freckles. Maggie snored lightly. Quinn turned over and looked at the clock, then remembered the night before. Liam had walked her back to the cottage, making sure she was inside with the door locked behind her before getting into his truck and pulling out of the driveway. Maggie was still up, nervously waiting for Quinn to be in for the night so she could go to bed too.

As soon as Quinn's head hit the pillow, she was out.

What an astounding day she'd had, though. She felt like she'd been to hell and back, but then she remembered the evening spent under the stars, feeling less alone than she'd felt in years. The experience with Liam left her feeling slightly embarrassed but also unexpectedly refreshed. She'd needed the judgment-free outlet that he gave her so easily. He hadn't tried to talk her down from her emotional cliff dive. He'd chosen not to use any clichés or words of wisdom to make her feel better, somehow knowing that what she needed most of all was to let it all out, to release the pain of finding out she was never who she thought she was.

For that, she'd always treasure their friendship.

She sat up and checked her phone. Fourteen unread emails from work.

Nothing from Ethan.

Relieved that she wouldn't have to read any begging or accusatory texts so early in the morning, she quietly untangled herself from the bedcovers and headed for the bathroom.

After a quick shower, she dressed in a shirt and well-worn shorts she normally saved for indoors only, then put on just the lightest touch of sunscreen and makeup, pulled her hair up, grabbed her bag, and slipped out the door.

She considered her sandals outside on the porch but left them behind as she headed for the trail. The beach beckoned her to return, and Quinn was ready to comply. At the water's edge she found she could think more easily. The soft sound of the waves lapping at the shore calmed her soul, allowing her to work out the priorities in her mind.

Arriving at her favorite spot, she sank down in the sand and slipped her sunglasses on. The ocean was calm today, and she stared out, imagining she was on a boat that would take her far away from all her responsibilities. There were so many decisions to make now, with the first and most important one being which and how she wanted to make contact with her biological parents.

Of course she was curious about them. Just like any child who hadn't known their mother or father, she wondered if she looked like them. And who was she most like in her personality? Did her love of reading come from her mother, and was her tendency to bottle up her feelings something her father had handed down?

Carmen and Helen said she looked just like her mother, but were there any physical traits from her father? Her nose, possibly? Or the shape of her ears? She thought about Maggie's feet and how she always bemoaned that they were exact miniatures of her father's and brothers' wide ones, with long toes, a paternal trait she hadn't particularly wanted.

Quinn worried that her parents wouldn't be impressed that she was their daughter. Of course, realizing their child hadn't drowned would be a relief that had been a long time coming, but once that faded, would she be able to measure up to their expectations?

Down the beach a man jogged, his dog keeping stride with him, their joy at the freedom they experienced evident with every strain of their muscles.

Would she ever feel that way?

Or was her life destined to be one of questions and confusion? One of always trying to present a better self to the world, of feeling judged and alone?

She took her phone out, preparing herself to read the work emails, knowing she was really pushing things with the absence from her job. Would she find an ultimatum? Was she already fired?

She leaned her head back and closed her eyes, filling her lungs with the delicious air of Maui, reminding herself to relax and stop worrying. Slowly, under her breath, she counted backward from ten.

She felt a shadow block out the warmth of the sun, and when she opened her eyes, she thought she was seeing things.

A man stood there, standing over her, just as Liam had done that first day they'd met on the beach.

But this wasn't Liam.

Even with the darkness across his face, Quinn would know that profile anywhere, as well as that confident and provoking stance. Even the body language that seemed to silently challenge as he stared down at her.

It startled her, but somehow she kept that to herself and didn't flinch.

"Well, aren't you quite the beach bum?" he said, his tone anything but teasing.

"Ethan," she said. "What are you doing here? And how did you find me?"

"You forgot to take the locations app off your phone."

The fact that she'd never enabled it crossed her mind, but she wouldn't accuse him. They had bigger things to talk about.

"This was really inconvenient, Quinn. All the hotels in Lahaina were booked, and I'm all the way over in Kihei. You need to come back with me so we can talk."

"I'm not going anywhere with you."

He ran his hand through his hair, releasing a long sigh. "Come on. Don't be ridiculous. I saw that tiny shed you're staying in, and it's not big enough for two. Not even to talk in."

Obviously he didn't know Maggie was there yet. That would really set him off. "It's not a shed. And no one invited you into it."

She could feel him simmering at that. He wasn't used to her being antagonistic, but it slipped out before she could guard her tongue. At least she hadn't told him to go find a room with Gina, which was what she wanted to say.

Logically, she knew starting a verbal war with him would get them nowhere. The emotional side of her wanted to jump up and kick his manly jewels for what he'd done, but that would also probably take things in the wrong direction.

"I can't say I'm surprised you came," she said, her tone less provoking. "But I'm definitely not happy about it."

He shrugged. "You wouldn't talk to me. What else was I supposed to do?"

"Let me have some space is what you were supposed to do," she said, feeling irritated. This was her place. And his arrival made it feel less so. He was ruining the day that had started on a good note. "Can you stop standing over me like that? Sit down if you insist on staying."

He gestured around him. "This isn't really a conducive location for discussing our relationship."

Everything in her wanted to run, but he had come all the way to Maui. She had to give him that. A part of her was glad he was finally there. That he cared enough to come find her. But he was going to have to work for it if he wanted her forgiveness.

"Well, you're the one who came out here. And you are the one who obviously has something to say. If you want me to listen, I'm here, in this spot, at this minute," she said.

His face was still shadowed, but she could tell he was frustrated. He grimaced like it was beneath him to sit on the sand but settled himself beside her anyway. "That Hawaiian woman directed me to the path. Said I'd find you down here."

"Maria? What did you say to her?" Quinn sat up straighter. She hoped he hadn't been a jerk.

"I just told her I'm your fiancé surprising you with a visit and asked where you were. What did you think I was going to say?"

"I never know with you," she replied, relieved that he hadn't just demanded they all get their stuff out of the house his fiancée owned. She could just see him having them all packed up and sitting at the curb within an hour, even with Pali laid up with broken bones. Ethan often showed no mercy and took pride in his ability to take on a challenge and succeed.

Now that she could see his face, she noted that he didn't appear to have had any sleepless nights or loss of appetite. If this was how he showed guilt and remorse, it looked good on him. He'd had a haircut, she saw, wondering if he'd gotten it for the trip or just because it was on his schedule.

"You made me come after you, and I'm here," he said. "But we've got to get back because I have to be in Phoenix by the end of the week, then Dallas after that. Both of our cars are scheduled for a tune-up, and you know my mom always comes to visit on the last week of this month."

Quinn felt exhausted just listening to him. Being in Maui had definitely opened her eyes to another way of living than what they were used to. Here, if there was a big swell coming or a day of sunshine after a week of rain, everyone dropped everything and headed to the beach. If someone had a small good thing happen to them, they gathered with family for food and celebration. No one lived on a tight schedule of must-dos and must-haves.

At first it had felt strange to her, even unsettling. But now she looked at Ethan and thought about how buttoned up their lives really were. How regulated. Boring, even.

"Do you ever get tired of outlining our life?"

"What are you talking about, Quinn?" He sounded irritated.

"I'm saying why aren't we ever just spontaneous?"

"In what way?" He sounded like she was asking him to solve the world's most difficult equation.

"Never mind, Ethan," she said. "Look, say what you need to say because I've got important things to tend to."

"Like the house fiasco?" he asked, grinning sarcastically. "Still working on that one, huh? You ready for some help?"

"Actually, no, I think I know just what to do. Things have taken an unexpected turn, and I've got a few ideas under my hat."

"Care to share them with me?"

"Not really," she said. "Next?"

"Quinn, forget about this damn house and this island. You need to come home where you belong," he said.

"Why would you even want me to come home when you obviously have the skinny, perfect Gina at your beck and call?" She hated the jealousy that escaped with her words. Betrayal tasted bitter.

"Gina meant nothing. It was just sex, and I didn't mean for it to happen."

At least he had the decency to lower his head as though he were ashamed. But that wasn't enough. She knew that Gina was everything that he always challenged her to be. Healthy. Slim. Driven.

The fact that Quinn wasn't enough for him hurt more than anything.

"It's never just sex," she said. "I want to know how many times you've slipped like this, and if you want even a chance of working things out, I need you to be completely honest and transparent. You've done a lot of travel. Sometimes I've had an uneasy feeling. A woman's intuition, if you will. But stupid me, I trusted you."

He sighed, his eyes still on the sand at his feet.

"Look, the past is the past. Talking over every little indiscretion won't help anything. I'm ready to move forward and forget all this if you are. You shouldn't have come here without me, and I told you not to buy that house."

"*You* are ready to move forward? And forget what? I've done nothing but be loyal and faithful to you for all these years. And just one time in my life I decide to do something impulsive and buy a house, and you think that gives you the right to sleep with someone else? What, out of spite?"

"No! Not out of spite. I was lonely, okay? You walked away and left me wondering what the hell was going on. You've no appreciation for all I've done for you. You were nothing when I met you, and look how far I took you. You've got options. A thriving career. The opportunity to marry a great catch who, you've got to admit, can pretty much pick and choose anyone he wants to."

"Stop talking about yourself in the third person," Quinn said. "It makes you sound like an idiot." Suddenly she saw Ethan in a new light. One less perfect than the one she'd held him to for so many years. Yes, he was handsome, athletic, and successful, but he could also be demeaning. Controlling, too, if she really wanted to be honest. And he was definitely not sorry for cheating on her.

She stood.

"Let's get something straight right here and now," she said. "I'm where I am in my life because I've worked for it. I studied harder than anyone, graduated school, and went out and found the career I wanted.

I've always done the right thing, even if it wasn't the thing I wanted to do. If anyone besides me should get credit for that, it's my mother."

She thought about her two mothers now and how she'd probably been shaped by them both in some way. She didn't even want to share her discovery about her family with Ethan. She wasn't ready for that yet.

"Your mother?" Ethan said, standing up to face her. "She practically begged me to stay with you so that her daughter would have a better life."

Quinn saw red. "That's bullshit. My mother wanted what's best for me, and you might be shocked to hear this, but she was never a fan of you, Ethan. And she's twice the person you will ever be. Say another word about my mom and see what I do."

It was ironic that she was defending the character of a woman who had basically stolen her from her birth mother, but she couldn't help it. She loved her. And she was ready to scratch Ethan's eyes out if he insulted her again.

A couple walking hand in hand strolled by, their faces curious as Quinn and Ethan stood glaring at each other.

"This is going nowhere," Quinn said, her voice barely audible through her gritted teeth.

Ethan nodded. He didn't even sound angry, which pissed her off even more. "You're right about that. Put some decent clothes on and do something with your face so we can go somewhere and have breakfast or a drink. I'm still on East Coast time."

Quinn couldn't believe his audacity. In two seconds he went from insulting her mother to telling her to do something with herself so they could go eat. As though he knew it would all be settled and he'd get his way like he always did. That she'd fall into his arms and thank him for choosing her.

"No," she said, feeling very decisive.

"No what?"

"No to everything. I said this is going nowhere, and I meant it. Our relationship is over. You need to go home, Ethan."

"Don't be stupid, Quinn."

She shrugged. She might be turning down the security of marriage and throwing away a lot of invested years, but the veil had been lifted, and now she saw what others saw in Ethan. What her mother and Maggie saw. What she knew deep in her own heart but didn't want to admit.

It was over. She'd never felt so sure about something. He might love her in his own shortsighted way, but it wasn't enough. In one tough moment, he'd gone off to find someone to help him lick his wounds. He didn't appreciate her, and he damn sure didn't respect her. That realization made her love him less. It also made it easier for her to do what she was about to do.

"I don't want to be with you anymore, Ethan. I don't want the life we built together, the ten-year plan, or the emotionless condominium with all the convenient perks that you like so much. I don't want us."

The surprising thing was that she wasn't crying over it.

He looked shocked. Quinn had no doubt that he'd expected to come to Maui, order her to behave, and have her back on a plane and home by the weekend. As he realized she was serious, his shocked expression turned angry.

"If I walk away right now, don't expect me to turn around," he said. "It will be over, and I won't change my mind."

She nodded.

"I know it will. Once you feel rejected, you don't forgive." She'd seen many friendships crumble under Ethan's impossible expectations.

"Don't do this, Quinn," he said. "Gina was nothing. It will never happen again, and we can go back to the way things were."

This was a first. His anger was morphing into pleading. He looked like a disappointed boy, ordered to take his toys and go home.

"Listen, Ethan, I don't want to hurt you like you hurt me," she said. "But I'm not the same person I was before I left. Being here in Maui has let me do some reflection. Some growing. I've finally had time to think about who I am, or who I want to be. I've still not totally figured it all out, but what I do know is being your wife isn't the dream anymore. We've grown apart, and it didn't just happen. You know as well as I do that the romance was over years ago."

"What do you want from me?" he said. "Do you want to set a wedding date? I'm ready now. We can do it before the year is out. Will that satisfy you?"

"That's just it, Ethan. I don't want anything from you. It's time for me to figure things out on my own. I'm not sure who I am right now, but I'm sure who I no longer want to be."

Quinn felt an ache deep inside. She'd spent so many years becoming what she thought Ethan wanted her to be that she'd lost herself. She knew that now.

She tugged at the ring on her finger, twisting it until it released her and came free. She put it in his hand and closed his fingers over it.

"You're making a huge mistake that you won't be able to undo," he said, giving her one last warning, his tone angry again.

She wanted to ask him to relax and let them be civil about the breakup, the division of their combined assets, and the removal of her things. But he gave her one more bewildered look and turned his back on her, walking away.

He expected her to follow him.

They'd played this game before. She always gave in.

But this time Quinn stayed where she was.

Sad. But no longer committed.

She thought of the man running on the beach with his dog and realized she might be feeling a sliver of what he felt, and she savored her first taste of freedom.

Chapter Twenty-Six

Nothing was easy anymore. Quinn wondered if it ever would be again. After Ethan left, she took a few days to recover from his sneak attack and the demise of a decade-long relationship. Then it was time to put it aside and think about how to proceed with her current predicament.

The thought of setting up a formal meeting with her birth family made her sick with anxiety.

It was Maggie who came up with a brilliant idea, and they were going to pull it off before she left. Unfortunately, her weeklong reunion with Quinn was about to come to an end.

Now Liam led the way, holding at least a half dozen new sleeping bags, while she and Maggie followed, carrying boxes of supplies. They'd spent the morning putting together gallon-size ziplock bags filled with shampoo, soap, and other hygienic items that the homeless sometimes didn't have access to. Maggie's contribution was pocket-size crossword puzzle books and pencils. She said they needed something to fire up their brains.

"I think they're already here," Liam said. "I see some people gathered around a portable table under the trees."

Quinn could see people, too, but couldn't make out anyone in detail. Her heart raced, but she told herself that she could get through it. She was grateful for the cap Maggie loaned her. She'd pulled it low over her face and added a pair of sunglasses in an attempt to disguise herself as much as possible.

It was brutally hot, and the sand was burning the sides of her feet where it touched, but Quinn was glad to be doing something to help the community her brother was a part of, even if she didn't identify herself. Quinn had thought about it all night and had come to the conclusion that Noah and Jules must've begun their work because of their son, as a way to reach him, or to at least let him know they still cared for his well-being. And who knows, maybe that was the only way they would ever get to see him.

They were fewer than thirty feet away now, and Quinn was afraid to look up. She took deep breaths in through her nose and out of her mouth. One foot in front of the other.

"I'll talk first. Noah will probably remember me," Liam said.

"Of course," Quinn said. She thought that was a given. She sure wasn't going to be the one to initiate a conversation.

Liam had asked around and found out that Noah and Jules had a fairly routine schedule. Ironically, today was the day they'd visit the people who camped out on the same beach where Carmen had found Quinn so many years before.

"It was meant to be," said Maggie.

Quinn agreed but she still felt light-headed. Her stomach fluttered with butterflies. Were they from anticipation? Dread? She really didn't know.

She also didn't know what she'd say to the man and woman who had given her life, who had loved her dearly and then lost her.

Hi, Mom. Hi, Dad . . . It's me, Nama. I'm back . . .

Yeah, that wasn't going to work.

So she might not say anything.

Both Liam and Maggie had agreed that first they'd help hand out the gifts. If she felt it wasn't the right time and wanted to leave, then she would shrink into the background, and they'd give out the donations so they could all leave quietly.

"Quinn," Maggie said softly. "Stop for a second."

They stopped and faced each other. Liam continued on.

"I bet there's panic behind those sunglasses," Maggie said.

Quinn nodded. Maggie knew her well.

"Listen," Maggie said, "I'm not going to put this heavy-ass box down to give you a hug, but I hope you can feel my support. You are stronger than you think. Damn, you stood up to Ethan for the first time in your life. So I know you can do this. *We* can do this."

"Okay." Quinn kept her eyes locked on Maggie's, taking every bit of bravery she could from them. She flashed back to when she and Maggie were about to enter the school gym for prom. The prom where no one had asked her out, and Maggie had dumped her date to go with Quinn. Behind those doors was every guy who had never given her a chance.

Quinn had felt the same sort of panic then, but Maggie had pushed her through it, and it had turned out well. They'd had the night of their lives, laughing and dancing, and by the end of it, several boys had asked her to dance.

Of course, this was much more monumental, but she would cling to that memory. With Maggie, she could do it.

And Liam was the icing on the cake of courage.

"Let's go," Maggie said, then turned back and led the way to where Liam now stood at a table, chatting with a man.

He looked their way and waved them over.

"These are my friends Maggie and Quinn," he said to the man as they approached.

Quinn forgot to look where she was walking and tripped over a huge tree root. Before she could recover, she catapulted forward, dropping the box and scattering everything in it in a wide radius around her.

"Oh no!" Maggie exclaimed. "Are you okay?"

A few guys rushed over. One gathered up the ziplock bags while the other held out a hand to help her to her feet. Quinn had lost her sunglasses, and she took the hand and looked straight up into the man's face.

He wore a baseball cap, and when she saw his face, a sense of familiarity washed over her. She'd seen him before.

She flashed back to the Sea House and remembered that he was the one she almost bulldozed over when she came out of the bathroom. The hat guy.

When she had her feet under her, she let go of him, and Maggie handed her the sunglasses. Quinn put them on quickly, but she was shaking when they finally approached the table. The other rescuer set her box on the table, so Quinn stood there, not knowing what to do. Maggie put her box down too.

"This is Noah," Liam said.

Noah held a hand out to Quinn, and though she was supposed to be the one holding back, somehow she was there and felt like she had to take it.

He was tall and looked quite athletic for his age. His hair was mostly gray, but she could tell it was once blond. He had thoughtful eyes, and he covered her hand with both of his, grasping it as he smiled at her. Quinn had thought she might feel something electric go through them when they touched, but all she felt was warmth.

"Thank you so much for your donations," he said. "The crew here on this beach can really use it. Many of them lost their belongings when they were run off from Baldwin Beach."

"You're welcome. I've been here a few weeks, and I felt like I should do something for the community."

"I see you've met my son, Jonah," he said, beckoning to the hat guy, who looked like he was more likely to be from the group of tent people than from Noah's family.

Quinn's breath caught in her throat. So Jonah was the connection who was supposed to meet with her. She'd practically run him over, and then he'd cowardly declined to show himself for who he was.

The same thing she was doing right now, she realized.

"I—yes, I suppose," she answered, pulling her hand free.

Jonah nodded, his face impassive.

Quinn thought of her mother. The one who had raised her and tried to teach her to be brave and always take pride in her actions. The one who used love and kindness laced with long talks to keep her from following other teens into drugs or alcohol. The one who had the courage to finally admit she'd lied, just before she took her last breath.

To Quinn, that meant something huge. That meant her mother had wanted her to be here, in this moment, seeking the truth. Even if it meant the truth would end up making Quinn hate her.

Then she pictured Ethan's face. He'd always treated her like she was too afraid to do things for herself. And she'd let him. After a while it had just gotten easier to slip right into the person that he wanted, his early hints and persuasions guiding her into his ideal partner. She honestly didn't even know what sort of person she would have been if left to her own choices. She'd allowed Ethan to take over her life and then walk all over her.

Was she really that person?

If she was, then she despised herself.

"And this is Maggie," Liam said, introducing her to Noah.

Quinn had a decision to make. They were all three here. She could take charge of her own life right here and now. Or shrink back and be the woman that Ethan had always expected her to be.

She locked eyes with Liam and felt like he knew she was struggling. He nodded, encouraging her to do whatever it was that made her the most comfortable.

But comfortable was overrated.

"Um . . . Noah, is your wife here?" she asked, her voice a little wobbly.

Maggie and Liam went totally silent, the smiles disappearing from their faces. Quinn could feel the nervousness coming off Maggie in waves.

"Why, yes, she's right over there," Noah said, pointing at a small gathering.

Quinn turned and saw a woman handing out sandwiches from a box at her feet. Each person also took a bottle of water from the cooler beside it. They thanked her and quietly moved on. She was lovely, the angles of her face pronounced, her cheekbones prominent. Her long hair was still a dark brown but glittered with gray as it settled around her shoulders in soft waves that mimicked Quinn's. She could see why Noah had fallen in love with her and had never left her side. The way she interacted with the people from the tents was something to see, her compassion etched in her movements and the gentle smile she gave each one. And they smiled back, some doing so in forced expressions that told of much sadness and regret but nevertheless thankful to be treated with respect.

Quinn wanted to know her. She needed to know her. There was a pull there that came completely unexpectedly.

"Can I talk to you both privately? And you, too, Jonah."

Noah looked confused, but he nodded. Jonah only stood there, watching her carefully.

"Of course. Let me just get Jules, and we'll meet you over there," he said, pointing to a bare picnic table farther down the beach. "Let us hand out the rest of the sandwiches real quick. These people are hungry."

Jonah studied her closely, trying to see beneath the reflection of her shades.

"I'll wait over there," Quinn said.

Then she turned to Maggie and Liam.

"Thank you both so much for doing this with me, but I think I need to finish it alone."

Liam nodded, and Maggie enveloped her in a huge bear hug, almost lifting her off the ground before letting her go. "I am so damn proud of you, Quinn Maguire. Or whoever the hell you are."

"You got this, Quinn," Liam said. "We'll hand out the supplies. You take all the time you need. I'll keep an eye out, and I can be over there in ten seconds if you need me."

Quinn felt their love and concern wash over her. She'd always thought she had only one good friend, but now Maui had given her another. She turned and headed to the table, psyching herself up to find the words to tell the Monroe family that they might need to add one more place to their holiday table.

~

Quinn sat at the picnic table facing the trees so that she could see Noah and Jules approach. She wanted to watch their body language. See if they acted like a couple. However, Jonah turned to follow her while they were emptying their last box.

He sat down in front of her, blocking her view of his parents.

"Can you take off the sunglasses?" he asked.

She took them off and laid them on the table.

"I know who you are," he said, his voice resigned.

Quinn wasn't surprised. It made sense that since he was the one who'd refused to believe she was lost at sea, he would be the one to submit to an ancestry site.

"Then why didn't you stay and talk to me at the Sea House?"

"At first I thought it wouldn't be true. *Couldn't* be true. I'd said since I was a kid that you weren't dead, but I don't know if I even really believed it. Then when I saw you and how much you look like my sisters, I was scared out of my mind. My suspicion that the Lineage site could be wrong was shattered. It was you. I knew it, and I needed time to process it. To find a way to tell them before you figured out who we were."

"So you've processed it now?" She hoped so, because she was about to blow his secret wide open.

He shrugged, but she could see his hands shaking.

"Looks like I don't have a choice," he said.

Quinn sighed. She felt sorrow. A deep, tender sorrow for the hurt she'd unknowingly and unwillingly caused him. And also a sorrow for whatever he'd endured in Iraq. She could see pain in his eyes that looked there to stay. How much of it was because of her?

"I've heard that it hit you the hardest. That you're still suffering over the loss of Nama," she said.

"Nama. You mean you?"

Now it was her turn to shrug. "I don't connect with her. I'm sorry."

He glared at her now, his voice turning angry. Or desperate. "Where were you? What happened? I was inches away from you when suddenly you were gone. I almost had you. Tell me what happened."

"I really don't know, Jonah. I don't remember. I can tell you that I washed up to shore, and then a new life began. But I'm not ready to give the details of that yet. Is it enough that now you know I survived? That you were right, and I wasn't dead?"

He hung his head. When he raised it again, his eyes were filled with tears.

"I told them I'd find you. I scoured the ocean for years for any sign of you. Until I just couldn't do it anymore. But your face, and the way you always looked up to me—trusting me to keep you safe—just wouldn't leave me alone. Then I thought a few tours of duty would get you out of my head. It didn't. And when I returned, I saw you every time I looked into my mom's sad eyes. I failed at erasing you from my memory and from theirs. I wanted to be the one to bring you home. Alive, of course, but if that wasn't to be, I at least wanted to find something to put you to rest. Put us all to rest." He placed his head in his hands, looking exhausted after his speech.

Quinn saw around him that his parents were on their way over. She slid her sunglasses back on.

"You were just a boy," she said, reaching across the table to put her hand on his arm. "It wasn't your fault."

He looked up, trying to pull himself together, but she could see that her words rang hollow. He'd carried the blame of her disappearance his entire life. But before he could respond again, Noah and Jules were there, and they sat down beside their son.

Jonah turned his head so they couldn't see the emotion on his face.

Noah put his arm around his wife's waist.

Quinn knew then that their bond was real, and that made her flush with quiet joy. She'd never seen her mother have that kind of love. Never seen anyone have it, actually.

"Hello," Jules said. "Noah said you and your friends brought some donations. I'd like to thank you for that. This time of year the support is slim to none, so we need all the help we can get. Liam was generous to point you in our direction."

Noah nodded, agreeing with Jules. "There're a few soup kitchens and mission centers around, but some of these guys don't like to go there, so we come to them. They're too private. Right, Jonah?"

His expression held nothing but kindness for his son.

Quinn was curious about the people who lived on the beaches. She'd always held a fascination for someone who could just leave a conventional life and take to nature for protection.

"How do you think most of them get to this place?" she asked.

"Many of them are just like you and me, but life threw them a curveball. See that woman over there in the flowery pink shirt?" Jules pointed to a woman squatting down next to the spigot outside the public bathrooms. She was wringing the water out of a shirt.

"She's smart as a whip. Before she came here, she worked for a big pharmaceutical company in Washington, blew the whistle on some of their unethical practices, was eventually fired, then blacklisted. After that she suffered from depression and then alcoholism. She got several drunk-driving arrests, then came here. She can't keep a job because of her anxiety, but she's been sober for more than a year. She gets disability, but it's not enough to afford a roof over her head and all that comes with it. It barely pays for her medication."

Quinn shook her head. Such a sad story. It seemed like anyone could be just a few setbacks from disaster.

Jonah pointed at an older man coming out of the restroom. "That's Paul. He's a vet too. When he came back, he opened a landscaping business in California. It was lucrative for a long time until times got hard, gas prices went up, and then he found out he got melanoma from so many years outside. He couldn't work for a while and lost everything. After battling with the VA hospital for too long, he decided to finish out his years here and just let the cancer take him. But Dad helped him get on with the top dermatologist on Maui, and now he's getting care and making payments. He still works at a golf course up in Napili but can't afford housing on top of his medical bills. He hops beaches because the police keep running us off. It's like musical chairs but with tents."

Quinn bit her tongue against the urge to ask Jonah why he didn't just go home to his family. It really wasn't her place to judge.

Noah nodded. "The point is that these people didn't just wake up one day and hit the streets. Most of them are from the mainland, and it took time for them to end up here. Usually a chain of events, piling up until they could no longer afford their mortgage or rent, sent them to the beach to live. They didn't want to be here—at least most of them didn't. You do have the occasional dreamer who has the ability to find work but only wants to move to Maui to surf and be one with nature. But for the most part, they want out of this situation. They'll work, but it's hard to get a job when you have no known address. And there's no housing assistance or rent control for low-income families here in Hawaii like there is on the mainland. Rent is outrageously high."

"Chris Pratt from *Guardians of the Galaxy* and the *Jurassic Park* movies was homeless here for a year," Jonah said. "But he found a way out."

"I'm starting to understand now," Quinn said. "Thank you for explaining."

She looked directly at Jonah, taking a deep breath. He got up and came around to Quinn's side, sliding in next to her where he could face his parents.

"Mom, Dad," he began, "she's got something really important to tell you, and I don't want you to be frightened."

Their expressions changed. Now there were worried faces all around.

Quinn slid her sunglasses off and then her baseball cap, letting her hair loose and free.

She could see the confusion in Jules's eyes. She looked like she wasn't sure what she was seeing. Or was supposed to be seeing.

"What's this all about?" Noah asked, for the first time losing the politeness in his voice. He was catching on that she wasn't just there to help the homeless.

"It's about me," Quinn said. She locked eyes with Jules, the mother who had probably suffered the most loss. Though she exuded grace and kindness, she also carried a certain sadness about her. Quinn had to admit, she'd hoped the woman would take one look and know who she was. But of course, this wasn't the movies; it was real life.

"You?" Jules asked.

"Yes, me. My name is Quinn Maguire, but once upon a time, I had another name." She directed her gaze at Jonah. "I was Nama, and your son found me," she said. "He was determined to bring me home to you, and now I'm here, thanks to modern technology and a vial of saliva."

Jonah looked surprised. Quinn thought briefly of Auntie Wang and hoped that she wouldn't mind not being acknowledged for putting the pieces together first. Quinn would have to have a talk with her, Helen, and Carmen later, but this was how she wanted it to go. It was the least she could do for a brother whose life she had ruined. And if he had stayed to meet with her that day at the restaurant, he would have been the first to tell her who she was.

Noah moved his arm higher around his wife, bringing her closer to him. Jules kept staring at her, taking in every inch of her face, hair, and hands. She still looked perplexed.

"What kind of sick joke is this?" Jules finally asked, her voice shaking.

"It's not a joke. It's true," Jonah said, reaching over to take his mother's hand. "The DNA proves it. Nama lived that day, and this is her. I swear it, Mom. This isn't one of my hallucinations."

Quinn turned her head and pulled back her hair, showing them the birthmark. But she knew even that could be manufactured with some ink and a good artist.

Noah was stone silent. Quinn wondered if he was going to call her a liar, a charlatan, and try to run her off his beach. But he did none of that. Instead, he spoke to Jules, though his eyes never left Quinn. His words were laced with tears.

"Jules, I think this is real. She looks just like the girls. And you. That's Nama's birthmark too. But listen, there are ways to make sure. Scientific stuff."

She ignored him, her eyes still locked on Quinn's, finally recognizing what her heart already had: she was looking at her child. One silent tear seeped out of her eye and ran down a line in her face, dropping onto the table. "Where were you?" she finally asked, her voice weak. "What happened? We looked and looked. You weren't out there. I swear, we looked for what felt like forever. Tell me. Where were you?"

Quinn gave her a sympathetic smile. "That's a really long story and one that will bring you both a lot of pain. It's going to stir up a lot of chaos that I'm not ready for, and I'd guess that you aren't either. I think we've had enough of that, don't you? Let's ease into this one step at a time."

"I need to know," Jules said, nodding. "But I'll give you time. You can tell us when you're ready."

Quinn smiled at her. "I'd like to get to know you a bit first."

Noah still looked shell-shocked, but Jules stood up and made her way around the table. Quinn met her halfway. They fell into each other's arms, and Quinn felt the tears begin to roll. But this time it was okay because they were happy tears, and they mingled with those of her first mother, a woman she didn't even know she'd missed until they were flesh upon flesh. Blood—it wasn't needed to be a family, but it sure had a strong magnetic draw when it was there.

Epilogue

Three weeks from the day that Quinn had stepped foot on Maui, she put the last box in the back of her brand-spanking-new white Jeep and then went up to the house. She'd spent the day packing and tying up loose ends. She was moving out of the cottage today, giving it back to Pali, who needed it now more than ever. The weeks he'd been nearly incapacitated had put him in the close company of his family for far too long, and though for the most part he'd kept his horns hidden, he needed his privacy.

Maggie was gone now, and Quinn missed her desperately. She was already working on getting her to come join them in Maui. She just wished Maggie could've been there today, but she knew Charlie needed her more.

Liam met her on the porch, and they sat down on the now-familiar steps.

"You look beautiful today," he said.

She laughed. He was making a point to compliment her now every time he saw her out and about without full makeup and the resort-style clothes she'd come with. Today, other than sunscreen, she was keeping it simple. Just a tad of mascara and a layer of lip gloss. Her recent tan gave her just the right amount of color. Not to mention, she'd finally become comfortable in her own skin. Comfortable with herself.

The self beneath the facade.

It started a week or so after she'd met Noah and Jules. Their family had accepted her wholeheartedly, and being with them—especially her somewhat overly demonstrative sisters—had finally given Quinn somewhere to belong without fighting for her place or pretending to be something she wasn't.

Maggie had been helpful too. Through back-and-forth phone calls, she'd encouraged Quinn to figure out who she was without someone telling her who she should be.

Quinn had to really think about it. Then she decided to take it one step at a time. First step: buy the Jeep she'd always wanted. The sense of empowerment she felt when she drove out of that dealership behind the wheel of her dream car would stay with her forever.

Then a few days later, she and her sisters went shopping, and Quinn bought her first bikini since she was in college. No more hiding the curves that God gave her. And for sure no more spin class and salads. From now on, she was going to be healthy but not fanatical. She was going to learn to love her body.

Life was short. She'd gone half of hers without knowing her people, her roots, or her land. Without knowing herself.

She was ready to make up for it now.

"You okay?" Liam asked, reaching out and taking a strand of her hair, then twirling it around his finger before letting it go. He didn't say he preferred it down, loose and free, but she knew he did.

"Yep. More than okay. I even told Ethan everything this morning."

"How did he take it?"

She chuckled. "As expected."

"What did he say about your new job?"

"That it wasn't a good career move to leave a big-brand hotel chain to renovate and manage an inn with only nine rooms."

Her grandmother was desperate for her to stay on Maui and had offered her the project of reopening the dilapidated inn they'd bought in Hana a year before. A project no one else in the family had wanted.

Quinn accepted. They set up terms, and if she pulled a profit after the second year, she'd be part owner. Helen was so grateful that Quinn had helped the family forgive her actions that she would've handed the entire property over free and clear, but Quinn wanted to earn it.

"You having second thoughts?"

"Not at all. I can't wait to get my hands on that place," she said. "Or should I say your hands? There's a lot of renovation to do, and this time you'd better not delay things just to keep me here longer like you did on Maria's house."

He laughed. "She's so happy with the maple butcher-block counters. You'd think they were inlaid with pure gold."

"I'm glad. She should have the house exactly as she wants it. We were just lucky the soapstone got delayed, and we could change it to Maria's preference."

Right on time, Maria stepped out of the house and walked out to them. She looked like she had something important to say.

"I'll go see what's left in the cottage to load," Liam said, then left them.

Tears welled up in Maria's eyes as she reached out and took both of Quinn's hands, holding them tightly.

"The new furniture came in yesterday," she said. "You're generous. The house is so beautiful now. It's everything I ever dreamed it could be. And it's ours again. How can I ever thank you?"

Quinn shook her head. "You don't need to, Maria. The Rochas caused your heartache, and they're making up for it. It was only fair to legally give the house back to you, this time with both of your names on it. Please don't thank me for that."

Maria's tears flowed freely now.

"But a pension too? How?"

Quinn wouldn't take credit for that either. She didn't want Maria thinking she owed anything to anyone. "Jaime worked for that pension. With the loyalty he had for that company, they should've had patience and given him more time to adjust. He's only getting what he's already worked for, what he would still have if he'd continued on there. Now he won't have to go out and get a job unless he wants to."

Maria pulled her into a tight embrace, and it felt so right to Quinn. It hadn't been long since they'd met, but it felt like what a real friendship should be. Warm. Accepting. Forgiving.

When she let go, she nodded forcefully. "Oh, he'll want to work. Jaime is not the type of man to let grass grow under his feet. Liam has talked to him. I just wish Jaime had gone to Liam before all this happened. His pride—that's something that has always gotten in the way."

"It's all going to work out," Quinn said.

"I think so too," Maria replied. "And Alani is thrilled she doesn't have to leave her best friend."

Liam joined them again, glancing from one to the other. "Did you hug it out?"

"Of course we did," Maria said, laughing. "Did you expect anything else? We're just talking about how, all at once, everything has changed."

"So fast it's making my head spin," he said. "I'm not complaining, though. I'm coming out ahead too. I guarantee I'll have the best site foreman on the island."

Maria turned and hugged him too.

Quinn loved seeing how affectionate they were with one another. Yes, they would be just fine. Maria was getting shortbread cookie orders faster than she could fill them and had hired Pali's girlfriend to help her. Of course, the girl wouldn't know the secret recipe, at least not until— or if—she became a permanent fixture of the family. For now, she was in charge of cutting out the dough and seeing the cookies through the packing process.

Even Pali had turned over a new leaf, actually becoming quite a nice kid. He'd simply needed his family back together. And Quinn was starting to understand just why that mattered so much.

"I'll see you two soon," Maria said, stepping away. "I'd better go corral the troops."

Liam turned to her. "There's a lot happening right now. People changing places, switching jobs, and building new relationships."

She nodded. "I just hope I don't screw anything up."

"You won't. But do you think your brother can handle the responsibilities you're giving him? Could it be too much too soon?"

She hesitated. Quinn's brother was a tender subject. She felt responsible for Jonah. For his troubles. She'd also found out that he was the lone survivor of an IED attack that had killed everyone else on his truck in Iraq. The trauma he carried had to be more than one man could bear. It had gnawed at her every day since she'd met him, especially after Jules had told her more of his story.

"I don't know. But I want to give him a chance. There's a small studio apartment off to itself on the property that'll give him the privacy he wants. He says he knows how to do maintenance, and as long as he doesn't have to deal with a lot of people, he can do it. The only rule I set was that he has to stay clean. But so far I don't think that's going to be a problem. He wants to prove to Noah that he can do something right."

"So, you ready to go?"

"I think so," Quinn said.

They were riding together. Quinn needed him by her side as she took care of this last thing before starting her new life.

"Let me tell Maria we'll meet them there." He went inside for a minute; then they walked out to the Jeep.

"This is a fine ride you got here," he said, buckling up. "Nice bumper sticker too."

"Thanks. It's been a long time coming." She pulled out of the driveway and took a left. Quinn had never put stickers on her car before. Ethan wouldn't allow it, saying it was tacky. The first day she got her Jeep, she bought one that said "Live Pono" and slapped that baby on.

She loved the sentiment that meant to do the right thing, and she planned to do just that from now on.

She'd already gotten a huge start too. Things were moving unbelievably fast, but, surprisingly, Quinn was doing okay with it. She'd found a small condo to rent until the hotel was livable, but eventually she'd move into a suite of rooms designed just for her. As for her belongings in Savannah, she didn't want them, except Ethan did say he'd send the rest of her photo albums and mementos.

Ethan was shocked when she told him all she wanted was her part of the equity in the condo and the money from selling her car. She instructed him to donate everything in her closet. She wouldn't be needing business clothes or high heels anymore. Here, she was embracing the casual, bohemian look, something she'd always admired but had been too afraid to experiment with in the corporate lifestyle she'd lived.

Today she wore a long tie-dyed skirt and a matching headband, her hair loose and free. Her feet were comfortable in sandals, her toes painted a bright pink that she never would've worn before coming to Maui. No more white-tipped fingers or toes for her—from now on it was going to be every color of the rainbow on her body. Unless she wanted to do something different.

Then she would.

They approached an intersection, and Quinn stopped for the red light. They didn't talk much. Liam didn't need to give her directions. She'd already broken her Jeep in by driving to every beach in Maui. She wanted to see them all before making a decision, but her heart brought her right back to the one where Carmen had found her, where she'd met Noah and Jules again.

Ten minutes later they arrived. There were already a lot of people there, more than Quinn imagined would come. Aunts, uncles, cousins, and grandparents stood together, unified in what was to come.

She and Liam got out, and he pulled the vase from the back seat, handing it to her. Quinn clutched it. She was feeling more somber by the moment, but she did want to introduce Liam to her sisters. They'd already spotted the Jeep and were walking over to meet her, both carrying colorful leis.

"You don't have to tell me who they are," Liam said. "You three could be triplets."

"Except I'm a lot older," Quinn replied. "But I know, I don't look like it."

He laughed.

"You made it!" the first sister said, throwing her arms around Quinn.

"I'm here, but, honestly, I'm feeling kind of shaky. I just hope this goes well," Quinn admitted. "Liam, this is Kira, and this one"—she put her hand on the other sister—"is Nalani, but we call her Lani."

"Nice to meet you," he said.

Quinn noticed the once-over and then the look of appreciation that Lani gave him, and it made her smile. Her sisters were some warm-blooded women. Thankfully, Kira was already married with small children, but Lani was free—and obviously wasn't afraid to show it.

"No, the pleasure is ours. My father said you've done a phenomenal job bringing these three families together for healing," Kira said.

"Most of it was because of Quinn," Liam said, his cheeks flushing. "I just helped some of the men walk through their feelings and come to accept this opportunity as a gift."

Auntie Wang joined them and threw her arms around Quinn.

"I'm so happy for you," she whispered into her ear.

"Thank you, Auntie Wang, for everything," Quinn said. They both knew that if Wang hadn't found Carmen, this possibly would never have happened, and Quinn would still be wondering who she was. But Auntie Wang didn't want to be the hero; she was just thrilled that she'd learned so much more about tracking lineage through helping Quinn. She'd also known that the match that had come up was a sibling, but she hadn't told Quinn that until it all came out. She was afraid to in case he didn't show up, and her gut had been right.

"Are the Makenas here?" Quinn asked, searching the crowd.

Auntie Wang nodded. "They are. Bless their grief-stricken souls. The Makena uncles are going to paddle out on their boards."

Quinn looked around and saw her brother, Jonah, perched on a log, alone as he stared out to sea. Then she saw Noah and Jules sitting together in fold-up chairs, and she waved. They knew that today was more about Quinn and the Makenas. They would let her set the pace and come to them when she was ready.

"There's Maria's car," Liam said, leaving Quinn with her sisters. He went to the car to help Kupuna out and over to a chair. Jaime and Maria followed closely behind.

Alani burst out next and ran over, throwing her arms around Quinn's waist.

"I'm going to miss you, Quinn!" she said. "You promise you'll visit?"

"Of course, Alani. I can't just forget about my little mermaid, can I? Now run over and help your mom while I get things going."

Alani gave her one more squeeze, then took off. Quinn was really going to miss her. She took a deep breath, then sighed loudly.

"I can't believe everyone showed up," she said.

Her sisters both leaned in and put their leis over Quinn's head before enveloping her in their arms.

"*You* made this happen," Kira said.

It felt so good to have sisters, though Jonah had already warned her that not too much time would go by before she got pulled into a sisterly spat. It was human nature, he kidded her, then warned her that his sisters had sharp tongues and even sharper claws when they needed to use them. Quinn had all but memorized a dozen or more stories about her siblings when they were growing up. She wanted to know everything, even if sometimes it hurt her deeply that she'd missed it.

Kira was the youngest of them all at twenty-four, and also the most spiritual. She was soft and thoughtful and very concerned about how Quinn's sudden reunion would affect her psyche or upset her recovering aura. She was a natural caretaker, always fluttering around her family to see where she was needed. It amazed Quinn that she had married so young and immediately produced a family, but everything told her that her sister was a good mother.

Lani was the energetic, fun-loving one with a wicked sense of humor and a streak of orneriness. According to Kira and Jonah, it was always Lani who got them into trouble growing up. She was daring and full of mischief, dragging them in when she could. And Noah said nothing had changed just because she was older now, other than that her drama had far greater consequences than when she was a child.

Quinn hadn't met their significant others yet. She was glad because she already knew she had a lot to learn about how she would fit into the pack. Adding more personalities to it was going to make it that much harder.

"See how many people's lives you've touched? You've brought nothing but good luck to Maui," Lani said. "I might have to take you to Vegas with me."

"Stop, Lani," Kira said. "This is not the time to joke around."

Lani's smile turned into a scowl, and Quinn could see how they might go at each other if given a chance. It was going to be tricky to suddenly figure out how to have sisters and not side with one or the other when spats popped up.

"It's fine," Quinn replied. "But excuse me. I need to go talk to the Makenas."

She searched the crowd until she found them, then headed their way. They stood side by side looking out at the ocean, not touching but close enough to do so if they wanted.

Quinn had gone to them less than a week ago, and finally they knew where their daughter had gone. Sadly, if her mother had only checked in with them, she would've found out that less than five years after she ran away, her parents divorced, then both found their sobriety on their own. Once they'd battled their demons, they came back together for companionship. And probably to share their sorrow that the only good thing they ever had together was gone. They'd waited for their daughter to come home, waiting with hope up to the very minute that Quinn knocked on their door and introduced herself.

It was a hard meeting but one that was necessary. There was no Elizabeth Senna. Not officially, anyway. Instead, Quinn now had to reconcile the memory of the woman who'd raised her with that of Beth Makena, the long-lost daughter of a heartbroken couple who needed closure.

Quinn had brought her box of photos when she met the couple, and sorting through the pictures gave them relief that their daughter had lived a decent life and had been happy in her role as Quinn's mother. They admitted that the crime she'd committed against the Monroes weighed heavily on their minds but said that it appeared their daughter was projecting onto Quinn what she herself had lacked as a child: a devoted parent and a childhood free of trauma.

"It wasn't right what she did," Mr. Makena said, "but we understand *why* she did it." Mrs. Makena agreed and said she knew her daughter probably thought she was saving Quinn from the ongoing battle between the Rochas and Crowes—and probably the curse as well.

As Quinn left them that day, they asked her if they could keep in touch, as she was their only connection to their daughter. That meant now Quinn had even more family, as, eventually, once they'd gotten over the awkwardness, she planned to treat the Makenas as the grandparents they wanted to be.

"Of course," she said.

And Quinn believed that. Her mother—Elizabeth—was a forgiving person. As she matured, she wouldn't have wanted to cause her parents pain, but her fear of losing Quinn had probably kept her from reaching out.

Quinn felt so sorry for them. They'd lost so much. But at least today they'd have closure. They stood there so silently. So many years of hope had come to this for them.

"Good morning," she said.

They both turned, and Mrs. Makena smiled. "Quinn, thank you so much for arranging this. It's going to be beautiful."

Her husband nodded in agreement. "I think Beth would love the gesture. Maui was in her heart, even if she did have to leave. I don't think she ever stopped feeling Hawaiian."

"You're welcome. I'm glad we could all come together to make this happen," Quinn said.

Liam crossed the sandy stretch between them. He'd brought the wreath, and he handed it to Mr. Makena.

"It's time," he said.

He led them to an outrigger canoe that waited at the edge of the water. Someone had draped it with flowers of every kind. The sweet aroma that carried on the winds over the ocean came to Quinn, bringing her comfort.

"Beth never had a favorite," Mrs. Makena said. "She loved them all, so we brought a variety."

Somehow knowing that they had decorated the canoe themselves made Quinn happy, because her mother would've liked that.

Quinn took her hand and helped her into the canoe, then climbed in front of her and set the vase between her knees. Mr. Makena took the front seat. Two family members she hadn't met yet sat in each end and began paddling them out to sea.

On either side of them, the rest of the burial party came out on surfboards, their leis bobbing colorfully around their necks as they paddled out, their timing perfect with the gradual setting of the sun.

Quinn turned to look at the shore again. Kupuna had gotten up from his chair and stood solemnly in the shallow waves, his pants rolled up and the water lapping at his ankles as his gaze appeared to settle on her. She could see his mouth moving and knew he was quietly chanting, his heart and voice melding together as he called out to Beth's ancestors to bring her home. It felt reverent with him there, and Quinn was so grateful for his presence that she nearly cried. This wasn't his family. And she'd tried to take his home. Still, he came.

For her.

They were yet another family she'd gained in Maui.

The canoe moved smooth and silent through the water, and no one spoke. At first it felt strangely awkward, but then the sounds of Liam playing his ukulele floated over the sea, finding its way to Quinn and calming her nerves.

He played the same thing he'd played that night on the beach when she'd been so taken with the emotional words he sang. Mentally, she'd titled it "Liam's Love Song," and that was how she always thought of it.

When Quinn turned back to look, they were too far to make out his face, but it was mesmerizing the way everyone on the beach swayed back and forth, quietly paying their respects.

Once they were out far enough, the lead paddler lay his paddle over his lap and lifted his face to the sky. He balled up a fist and brought it over his chest, then loudly chanted a prayer in the soothing old Hawaiian language.

On either side of them, the surfers sent up their own whistles and chants, then, almost perfectly synchronized, they raised clasped hands and then lowered them to make a huge splash.

Quinn said her own prayer, then picked up the urn.

She held it to her heart, not sure if she was ready to let go. Her mother—and, yes, Quinn would always give Elizabeth the honor of thinking of her that way—was all she'd had in the world for half of her life. Saying goodbye permanently was going to hurt.

She felt a hand on her back and turned to find Mrs. Makena watching her, tears streaming down her face. "Let me help you," she said.

Quinn unscrewed the top and handed her the vase, feeling as though she were handing over a part of her soul.

Mrs. Makena took a handful of ashes and threw them out over the ocean. "We love you, Beth." She sobbed quietly as she handed the vase to her husband. He poured some ashes into his hand and let them trickle through his fingers on the other side of the canoe, slowly, as though he didn't want them to float away.

"Forgive us," he said, his voice thick with unshed tears. "Rest soundly, daughter."

They passed the vase back to Quinn, and she held it once again. There was only a little of her mother left. She considered putting the lid back on and taking the rest of her back to her bedside table.

But her mother wouldn't want that.

As much as she had tried to deny it, Quinn knew now that her mother loved Hawaii: the people, the land, and, yes, even the sea. It was where she needed to be set free. It was where she'd asked to be returned to.

No more hiding. No more fear.

As the last ashes poured from the vase, Quinn cried from the depths of her being, tears streaming down her face like a river, nearly blinding her with their ferocity. Along with the ashes went the small bit of anger that she held toward her mother. Forgiveness flooded through her.

When the vase was empty, the container no longer felt symbolic. Quinn set it down and picked up the white flowered wreath, then dropped it over the side and gave it a nudge. She'd tied a note to it:

Thank you for sending me to Maui, Mama. This journey has taught me that I need to be true to me first. And I forgive you.

Your daughter, Quinn

She liked to think her mother had wanted her to find her birth parents and embrace them, even if it meant Quinn's love for her would be marred.

While the wreath floated away, Quinn watched it, praying that her mother was there in spirit, and then knowing she was.

The Makenas gently tossed out the leis and the other flowers that draped the canoe. Once that was complete, the surfers maneuvered their boards to point up toward the sky in salute, then turned and headed back to shore.

Quinn wasn't ready to leave yet. As the last beams of the setting sun bounced off the sparkling water, she watched the petals bobbing up and down.

To the Makenas, her mother was a wayward daughter they'd pushed away with their own selfish actions. To Quinn, she represented the only family in her childhood and young adult life. Her mother had showed her unquestionable loyalty and love. And Quinn wouldn't remember her as anything but the best human she'd ever known.

The reflections of the petals on the surface of the soft waves were beautiful. The song flowing over it was even more so.

When she was ready, the paddlers turned the canoe around, and as their strokes hit the water in a gentle rhythm, she watched the shore approach. She marveled that for the first time ever, the Crowes and the Rochas were together in one place and at peace, their grudge over for good.

Carmen stood in the middle of them, her face stoic. She'd made her deepest and heartfelt apologies to the Monroes, but she still hadn't forgiven herself. Quinn had encouraged her to let it go, but she could see that it would take a long time for her to release the guilt.

Helen Rocha—it was still hard for Quinn to think of her as her grandmother—stood beside Carmen, their unusual friendship solid. Helen was feeling better these days now that her poisonous secret was laid bare and no longer flowing through her veins. Quinn could swear she stood taller than she had before.

Forgiveness wasn't complete for everyone yet. It would take Noah and Jules some time to completely absolve Helen, but Quinn had talked them into working on it. There was far too much sorrow to put behind them without continuing the blame. Helen was just relieved no one was knocking on her door with an arrest warrant, though Quinn could see through her tough facade that she longed to be a bigger part of the family. That would hopefully come in time, along with healing for everyone.

Quinn finally felt her life had meaning, for she was the catalyst in monumental changes in the history of three families. She still had questions, though. Like had her coming back to Maui really ended the long feud? Perhaps even dissolved the supposed curse? She didn't really believe in magic, but she couldn't deny something extraordinary had happened in her story.

Of course, she was also the cause of much sorrow, but she chose not to dwell on that. And as they moved closer to shore, she was excited to start her new chapter surrounded and supported by the big family she'd always dreamed of.

She also couldn't help but look for Liam, and as she drew closer, he continued to play, his fingers strumming the strings of the ukulele, his eyes locked on hers. He looked so proud of her. She saw promise there—even a trace of commitment, if she wanted it.

Quinn needed time to heal from all that had transpired, and she knew that Liam was just the kind of man who would give her that time. Her experience in Maui had taught her that she could stand on her own if she wanted. There was no need to rush into another relationship.

She also wanted to concentrate on building new bonds with her family. Then, when that season was over, she planned wholeheartedly to explore just what those silent promises meant.

The canoe finally skimmed the sand and came to a stop just beside Liam. One of the men hopped over the side and held it steady, beckoning for Quinn.

She climbed out and stood in front of Liam, locking her gaze on his.

He stopped playing and took her hand, then leaned in and put his forehead to hers softly, comforting her in his own tender way. She responded, drawing closer to him, her eyes closed until their shoulders touched too. The electricity that flowed between them was unnerving and, admittedly, intoxicating.

For now, it was enough.

When they broke apart, he still held her hand, and they turned to face the water. Looking out to sea, Quinn felt truly at peace for the first time in her life. She realized that with her journey, she'd won a difficult but important battle. She'd pursued her truth, and because of that, she'd finally found her place in life, down by the sea.

Acknowledgments

To my dedicated readers, thank you for continuing to read my work and recommending it to others. If you enjoyed *True to Me*, I would be very grateful if you could post an honest review on Amazon and/or Goodreads to help the book gain visibility and new readers.

My gratitude also goes out to the people of Maui. Your land is beautiful; thank you for sharing it with the world. To Amanda, this book wouldn't have been written if not for you. The premise was conceived and the first chapter written while you slept next to me in our Maui hotel room. I needed something to keep my mind off leaving you behind to live your life five thousand miles away, and I can honestly say that some of your adventures and discoveries have made it into Quinn's journey as she navigates such a special island. To my Ben, thank you for helping me get through the first year without our baby girl and for encouraging me to write this book.

Virtual hugs of thankfulness to my first reader, Karen McQuestion. Your insight and suggestions made this a better story. Friends, if you haven't yet started your McQuestion Collection, I suggest you seek her out because her books are loved by many. To Alicia, Gabe, and the rest of the team at Lake Union Publishing, thank you for all your help getting this story ready for everyone else. Your hard work is appreciated. Lastly, to Holly Ingraham, your keen eye on character development was instrumental as we dug down to see what Quinn's true self was meant to be.

From the Author:
The Story Behind the Story

According to yourgenome.com, DNA, or deoxyribonucleic acid, is a long molecule that contains our unique genetic code. Like a recipe book, it holds the instructions for making all the proteins in our bodies. Unlike the social conditions we live under or the effect that those around us have on forming parts of our identity, our DNA is regarded as unchangeable. It carries the characteristics and qualities of each of us, making every human a unique person on this earth. It can also link us to our biological heritage in a way that is indisputable. In 2017 there was a revolution of sorts within the field of genealogy due to an advancement in the use of DNA. Easy-to-use kits and databases, along with television shows that depict the search for long-lost relatives, have made it easy for the public to embrace this new frontier of science.

If you are as infatuated with true crime as I am, you'll know that these days, DNA is also making it possible to solve more crimes. Detectives can now track career criminals from previous arrests in which they mandatorily submitted their DNA to the worldwide database. I'm so thankful to scientists and their research because this amazing tool is bringing a new meaning to "guilty beyond a reasonable doubt."

On the personal side, there are thousands of stories of people using DNA to find relatives, clear up adoption mysteries, or dig up family secrets that for many years have been buried. In *True to Me*, I wanted to create a story in which the use of Quinn's DNA could help her find her family, as well as accidentally unearth the serious travesty that was perpetrated upon her in childhood. Ultimately, circumstances made it possible for her to find the truth without the DNA, but it could've happened with it as well.

Now that public DNA testing has hit an explosive growth spurt, it is evident that no genealogy project will be complete unless the paper trail is accompanied by the scientific results of DNA matching. We will see more emotional reunions, and there will be more family secrets that may be better left untouched.

I hope you've enjoyed Quinn's journey, as she not only discovered who she is biologically but also who she is as a person with her own strength. Lastly, please stay in touch by subscribing to my newsletter on my website, because next up is Maggie's story, and in it, you'll be seeing more of Quinn, Liam, and all the characters you've gotten to know in *True to Me*.

With gratitude,
Kay

READERS DISCUSSION GUIDE

1. According to the National Center for Missing and Exploited Children (citing US Department of Justice reports), nearly eight hundred thousand children are reported missing each year. That's more than two thousand a day. With the new ease of genetic testing available to the public, do you foresee more news stories of reunited families in the coming years?

2. Quinn was raised without any other family nearby in order to keep her true identity a secret. How do you think that sort of isolation formed her personality and affects her as an adult?

3. The older Rochas believe the family is cursed because of the original wrongdoing perpetrated by the Charles Rocha in regard to their fortune. Do you believe in karma, that the sum of one person's actions can affect their future lives and possibly that of their descendants?

4. Buying a property unseen and traveling alone to Maui is completely out of character for Quinn, yet she determinedly does both. Have you ever felt an unexplainable inner pull to a specific place that holds meaning for you? Do you think that's possible?

5. When Quinn returns to Maui, she is able to overcome her fear of water because of her experience with the sea turtle. Native Hawaiians believe that sea turtles (*honu*) can show up as a person's guardian spirit, known as an *aumakua*. Do you think that this turtle was with Quinn when, as a child, she fell into the ocean and went missing? Do you or someone you know have a fear of water? If so, where do you think that fear stems from?

6. As Quinn spends more time in Maui, she realizes that she's been living for other people and not herself. Her epiphany allows her to find the courage to start a new life, one that she can build on her own with her own choices. Have you ever felt you are living life for others instead of yourself? If you could choose one thing to begin doing for yourself, what would it be?

7. Helen Rocha harbored her horrible secret for more than three decades. Do you think that secrets can affect your health and well-being, and if the secrets are laid bare and forgiveness is granted, do you believe that someone's health can be restored?

8. What do you think the future holds for Quinn? Do you see her and Liam together? Do you feel that she will easily slip into the life of her first family, or do you see upcoming difficulties?

About the Author

Photo © 2013 Eclipse Photography

Kay Bratt learned to lean on writing while she navigated a tumultuous childhood and then a decade of domestic abuse in adulthood. After working her way through the hard years to come out a survivor and a pursuer of peace, she finally found the courage to use her experiences throughout her novels, most recently *Wish Me Home* and *Dancing with the Sun*. She lives with the love of her life and a pack of rescue dogs on forty acres of rolling hills called Windy Hill in South Carolina. For more information, visit www.kaybratt.com.

Made in the USA
San Bernardino, CA
14 May 2020

71732437R00166